RAGE OF THE DEAD

Book Three in the Realm of the Dead Series

Jeremy Dyson

Dartmoor Publishing

CONTENTS

For Eliza

CHAPTER ONE

I never signed up to be a hero. It wasn't because I wanted to defend my country either. As far back as I can remember, my father wanted me to follow in his footsteps and join the Air Force. So, as soon as I was old enough, I joined the Marines instead just to piss the old bastard off. He's a real pain in the ass. The funny thing about it was my grandfather was a Marine, and my father joined the Air Force just to piss him off. That's probably where I get it from. Being a stubborn asshole just runs in the family.

Joining up doesn't seem like the best idea now that I'm freezing my ass off up on this godforsaken mountain in Pickel Meadows, California. Hell on a hill— that's what the old guys at base camp called it. It's cold enough to make me miss being back at Camp Pendleton. Hell, I'd rather be back in The Stan.

Even though we already went to that godforsaken goat country, our company commander still sent our platoon up here for more mountain combat and survival training before redeploying us back to Afghanistan.

Of course, it snowed the whole goddamn time we've been here. Command probably just wants to piss us off so we're ready to kill some goatfuckers when we get the chance. It is what they would call boosting our morale. That's their logic. They want to be sure every man in this recon unit is more than ready to kill.

Some guys of Nightmare Company are happy to be back stateside, but I have been counting the days before I ship out again. I just can't take all the bullshit here. First world problems. All that trivial crap. If people here had any idea what the fuck the world was really like for everyone else, they would probably have a hard time sitting through their fake ass reality television shows. Not like that will ever happen. The media keeps everyone in a brainwashed bubble so they can go about their meaningless lives. At least until the shit hits the fan.

"Just a few more hours," Rodriguez consoles us.

"I can't feel my toes," gripes Harding.

"Suck it the fuck up, Marine," Rodriguez tells him. He gives the kid a hard look to make sure he stops complaining.

It isn't easy around here when you're the Fucking New Guy. PFC Corey Harding just happens to be the FNG, which means everyone gives his ass a hard time. But Sarge isn't just doing it to be a dick. Sergeant Pedro Rodriguez is probably the best team leader in the whole battalion because he expects a lot from everyone on his squad. He knows he can count on us to make sure he gets home to his wife so he can make some more kids.

That's a joke.

See, Pedro has like six little motherfuckers running around his house already. After he found out about the last one, I told him to use a damn condom already, but he said he is trying to have a lot of kids to properly live up to his Mexican stereotype.

"Pedro. You married a white girl," I reminded him.

Pedro just laughed. When we are in combat situations, he is all business, but he is also my close friend. We screw around on a daily basis.

"She makes good tamales, though," he said. "That makes her like half-Mexican, at least."

"Her name is Melissa," I told him. "That's like the whitest white girl name there is. Besides, aren't you in the wrong line of work then? You should be fucking mowing lawns or something."

That cracked him up pretty good. Some people would probably get all offended by our conversations, but there is a reason those kind of people don't serve in the Marines.

"Seriously," Harding slips off his boot and lifts his leg up so we can see his foot. "Does this look like frostbite?"

"Hardcore," says Mac. "If you keep whining like a little pussy these guys are going to start calling you Softcore instead."

Everyone gets a good laugh at that one, except Corporal Gibson. He has his headphones in his ears, and I can faintly hear the hip hop pumping through the speakers. Can't blame Gibby for needing to block out the stupidity now and then. Normally, Deshaun is singing or joking along with the rest of us, but he has been quiet all morning. The battery in his phone is running low and he is probably dreading the possibility that he will be stuck up in the mountains without his music and have to listen to Arnes the rest of the day.

"Maybe we should get Doc Noonan to shove a thermometer up his ass," Arnes suggests. "See if he is really as cold as he says."

"Fuck you, Arnes," Harding laughs.

"Just looking out for you, kid," Arnes smirks.

I blow into my hands to warm them and watch the cloud my hot breath makes in the cold air. I'm not used to weather like this, being from Texas and all. It doesn't agree with me in the slightest. I don't get paid to like it, I just have to do it.

"Going to be eating steaks tonight, gentleman," Rodriguez says. "Just hang in there."

"And head back to Camp Margaritaville tomorrow," says Arnes.

"Got that right, brother," Rodriguez agrees.

"We should hit up Wildcats," Arnes suggests.

"The chicks at that other joint are hotter," Mac says.

"What place?" says Arnes.

Corporal Mackenzie looks at me because he can't think of the name. Mac is smart as hell but he suffers from CRS. That stands for can't remember shit, which can be a good or bad thing, depending on your perspective.

Mac knows I will remember because I, on the other hand, have been cursed with a photographic memory. I never forget anything, even the things that I want to forget.

"He means Dollhouse," I say.

"You don't know what you're talking about," Arnes says. "They don't even take all their clothes off there."

"Just stating a fact," Mac says.

"Better watch it, Mac," I say. "Arnes won't tolerate any unflattering remarks about Georgette."

"Damn straight," smirks Arnes. "That's my gal."

"I thought Sally was your gal," Harding says.

"She is," says Arnes. "Back at home."

"Banging every willing Whiskey Tango Jody back in the trailer park," adds Mac.

"As long as they ain't liberal shitbags like you, Mac," Arnes grumbles.

"Is she hot?" Harding asks.

Arnes pulls the infamous prom picture of him and his high school girlfriend from his chest pocket. She broke it off with the dumb bastard during our last deployment, but he still keeps the lame-ass photo on him at all times.

"Put that damn thing away, dawg" Gibby says. He pulls off his headphones when he sees Arnes holding the photo. "You'll scare the kid."

"Don't pay no attention to them, baby," Arnes says to the photo. "They just jealous they ain't never had someone as good looking as you."

Arnes smiles as he holds out the picture for Harding to see.

"Ain't she something?" Arnes asks.

Harding flinches at the sight of her. Might be the most terrifying thing he will see for the rest of his life. Lucky for him, Arnes is too busy staring at the photo to notice the horrified expression on the kid's face.

"Yeah," Harding stammers. "She looks... nice."

The guys quiet down for a moment and salivate at the thought of a hot meal, or maybe getting a lap dance. It's been a long, cold couple of weeks up here. Digging out trenches in the snow. Practicing casevac operations on sled gurneys. God knows how many miles we hiked up and down the mountain trails on snowshoes. Then they stick us up here with some tents and rations in the freezing mountain temps. They know we will manage. Marines make do.

"You hear that?" Rodriguez says.

We all turn to look at him as we listen. I hear the distant rumble of the diesel truck engines as they accelerate up the steep dirt roads.

"Thought they weren't picking us up until this afternoon?" says Mac. He barely glances up from the copy of *For Whom The Bell Tolls* that he is reading. I tried asking him about it yesterday, but it sounded boring as shit, so I just stuck to reading *Penthouse*.

"You complaining?" Arnes asks.

"Start packing up your shit, Marines," Sergeant Rodriguez orders us. "Sounds like we might be getting out of here early."

I resume breaking down my white tent. It blends in well with the snow but reeks so badly of feet, ass, and nuts that it would probably draw every hostile for miles if this was an actual combat zone. Then I grab my pack and begin stuffing my few personal items inside as I watch the team of old LMTV's rumble into the camp. Our company commander, Captain Cal Kellogg, hops out of the passenger seat of the lead vehicle.

"Shit," grumbles Mac. "Special K is here."

Trying to figure out how anyone ever saw Captain "Special K" as fit for command is a total mindfuck. The guy is just too stupid. Probably got hit too much when he was playing football in college. Maybe I resent the fact that he didn't do anything to earn this command, but I also have zero confidence he will not get us killed if we see any actual combat when we ship back out.

"You believe this shit?" Gibby says. "Motherfucker comes rolling up here in full battle rattle."

"Somebody better tell the captain we're not in Afghanistan yet," I joke.

The captain surveys Nightmare platoon as he talks with our platoon commander, Lieutenant Will Reasoner. Luckily, we didn't get stuck with a complete dumbass as our Lieutenant.

Will was smart enough to get into any Ivy League college. Probably could have had any career he wanted but decided he would rather do something with his life other than sitting behind a desk all day. It takes balls to do that. If I had the opportunities he had in life, I doubt I'd still choose to be here in The Suck.

The two officers are joined by Gunnery Sergeant Lewis Rocco. Everyone in the squad just calls him Gunny. He is the oldest member of Nightmare One and has been in the Marines since before the War on Terror had even started. The guy has seen everything, unlike the rest of us, and Will relies heavily on his combat experience.

Rodriguez joins Sergeants Colin Lowe and Micah Strong, the leaders of the other fire teams of Nightmare One, and they make their way to the conference near the vehicles. Colin is the platoon scout sniper, and everyone calls him Hollywood because he will probably star in his own action movies someday. Micah always sports a shaved head and a serious expression. After two tours in Iraq and one in Afghanistan, he came to the disheartening conclusion that he is fighting for the oppressors instead of against them. I'm the first to admit he probably has a valid point there.

Even though I could easily believe the captain might just have showed up here ready for battle because he is an imbecile, the sight of him makes me uneasy. I can't leave this place fast enough, but I have to wonder what could be going on. The military doesn't just decide to pick you up early for no reason. Something must be up. It's not my business to ask questions, I just do what they tell me. With my pack and rifle slung over my shoulders, I wait with the rest of the team while Rodriguez gets our orders.

"What do you think is going on?" Harding asks me.

"Somebody probably fucked up," Arnes says, even though nobody asked him. That's typical Arnes for you. Always running his mouth.

"If somebody fucked up it was probably you," Gibby jokes as he ties the laces of his boots.

Arnes gives him a hard look but just shakes his head and picks up his pack.

"It's probably nothing," I tell Harding. "At least we're getting out of here."

Sarge leaves the conference near the trucks and shuffles back toward us, his boots crunching through the snow. Judging by the creases in his brow, it seems like he is leaving the meeting with more questions than answers.

"What's the word, Sarge?" Mac asks.

"There's been some kind of attack or something," Sarge says.

"Probably the fucking North Koreans," Arnes concludes.

"Where?" Mac asks.

"Here," Sarge says. He stares blankly at the empty space a few inches in front of his face.

"Where'd they hit?" I ask him.

"Everywhere," he says.

"What do you mean everywhere?" Gibby asks.

Sarge continues to look lost. I've never even seen him like this. The fact that he is hitting a wall tells me something really big has gone down.

"Sarge?" I actually have to wave a hand in front of his face. It takes a few seconds before he snaps out of it.

"I don't know anything more than that," Sarge shakes his head as he scoops up his pack. "We'll get our orders when we get back to base camp. Pack the rest of this shit up. We're Oscar Mike in five."

CHAPTER TWO

We squeeze into the troop hold of the LMTV along with Sergeant Strong and the rest of team three. The truck rumbles down the rocky path as we start the anxious drive down the mountain. The hairpin turns and steep drops unsettle my empty stomach and make me glad that I had nothing for breakfast this morning.

Gibby tries checking his cell phone for news, but the mountain is a huge dead zone. The other guys left their phones back at base, figuring they'd have no use for them out here without a signal.

"Must have been the fucking Taliban," says Corporal Lester Pittman. Les holds the battalion record for most insurgent goat kills during our last deployment. He always runs point for team three. Usually, teams will rotate who runs point because you're most likely to get your ass shot, but that's exactly why Sergeant Strong keeps Pittman there all the time. Dumbass Les still thinks it's some kind of honor, though.

"Nah, man," Arnes says. "They don't have the resources. Had to be the Nips, man. We should have nuked their goddamn asses when we had the chance."

"Shut the fuck up, Arnes," Sarge says.

Arnes takes a look at the tense face of Sergeant Rodriguez and leans back in his seat.

"Just want to find out who we get to go fuck up," Arnes mutters.

Most of these guys have not seen much actual combat. By the time we went through training, the operations in Iraq and Afghanistan were winding down. We mostly acted as a security force or trained hajjis not to death blossom when bullets start flying. It was like finally getting put into the football game during garbage time. But that might all change now.

At the same time, a lot of these guys are just worried about their families. They want to know that their loved ones are okay. That's one of the good things about not having a lot of people to care about. I can't say I would really care too much if my old man eats it, but I know the bastard is too hard and mean to be killed.

We climb off the trucks at base camp and the platoon files into a classroom. While we wait to be briefed, I collapse into a chair behind a desk like the kind I used to carve swear words on in high school. The guys begin speculating what kind of attack could have happened. Some of them say nukes. Some suspect it's some kind of biological attack. It's all just noise to me. I realize none of them know anything yet. A few minutes later the door swings open and Captain Kellogg walks in with a stack of file folders in his hands. We all stand and salute.

"At ease," Kellogg says.

He situates himself behind the desk and seems to think for a moment how he should begin. The platoon is unusually quiet as they anxiously wait for the company commander to proceed.

"This morning the President declared a nationwide state of emergency," he finally tells us.

We listen as he tries to explain what is happening, even though it sounds like nobody knows what the fuck is happening. There is some kind of outbreak all over the country. There are large-scale riots happening in every major city. State and local police have been largely unsuccessful in maintaining order anywhere. It's a widespread clusterfuck.

"Listen," he finally says as he tosses the reports down on the desk. "I'm going to drop the official bullshit for a minute and lay it all out for you. Before dawn we got reports of vagrants outside the main gates at Camp Pendleton. An MP was attacked and suffered bite wounds so severe that it killed him. Several minutes later, that MP got back up and bit the first responders on the scene. Within an hour, there were six more reports of similar activity from personnel on base."

Everyone listens in stunned silence.

"We scrambled everyone on the base. By then it was already starting to hit the news networks. It was happening in London, New York, Atlanta,

Chicago... everywhere. People were starting to panic. Cars flooded the highway from Oceanside, trying to get to the base for protection and medical assistance. We set up an armed blockade at the entrance to try and maintain control of the situation. But it was too late for some of the people outside. A number of them must have been sick or something. They turned into those things. Then they started attacking each other in the streets. We tried to evac as many civilians as we could on boats in the harbor, but within an hour we lost control over the perimeter. It was a goddamn bloodbath after that."

Captain Kellogg leans back on the desk and swipes a hand down his face.

"I watched a lot of people die today," he says. "Those things just ripped them apart. When we knew we couldn't hold the base, we fell back to Camp Pendleton North. We managed to hang on to the airfield for a while, but it wasn't easy. Nightmare Two and Nightmare Three both took heavy casualties."

As much as the guy always seemed like a cocky motard, now he just seems... scared. I think I liked him better the way he was before.

"I wanted to stay with our other platoons and defend the base, but I received orders straight from Washington. Right now, the top priority is to extract key personnel and evac them to a secure facility in the hope that they can figure out how we stop whatever this is," the captain explains. "It might be our last best chance to keep the human race from being wiped off the fucking map."

Figures that the congressman would find some sort of excuse to get his kid out of the shit. Probably going to pin a bunch of medals on him after all this blows over, too.

"You guys are probably one of the last full platoons we've got left, so you're it," says Kellogg. "A Super Stallion will airlift you to Las Vegas. The drop point will be the rooftop of The Palace Hotel. Your objective is to locate the targets and get them the hell out of there. To the best of our knowledge, they are still alive. They secured themselves in a conference room on the first floor of the facility, but they cannot hold up there forever. Time is of the essence, gentleman. To speed up our operational tempo, the fire teams will split up to cover each of the three stairwells and work your way down to the last known locations of the targets."

He pauses for a moment to glance around the room. Maybe he feels guilty for the orders he is giving us. It could be that he doesn't think we have a chance in hell at making it out alive. Something about the look on his face gives me a very bad feeling about all of this.

"Satellites show a lot of unrest in the area. There will probably be a lot of civilians looking for help. Do what you can. However, our primary objective is to extract the key personnel," he lifts the small stack of folders off the desk and opens them up. "We're spread too thin already to take anyone else."

Captain Kellogg leaves the floor to Will and passes the files over to Gunny. Will looks around the room at the faces of the men in his platoon.

"This is it, guys," Will says. "I know you're the best damn team in the military, but now it is your chance to show everyone. The world will be watching us, gentleman. This is real hero shit. Let's make sure we don't fuck it up."

Will nods to Gunny who closes the files and comes to the middle of the room to address our team. Gunny plans most of our ops. He is a real hard ass, but the man knows his stuff.

"Listen up, Marines," Gunny says. "As the Captain said, it's a real shit hole out there right now. The nation is currently under martial law, so you're cleared hot to engage anyone that impedes the mission."

Gunny flips open the file and retrieves a photo from the folder.

"We have three civilians that we need to locate and extract." He pauses and holds up a photo of a woman with red hair and glasses.

Mac whistles softly.

Gunny pauses and gives Mac a stern look.

"What?" Mac says. "She's hot."

"Quit fucking around," Sarge tells him.

"Dr. Claire Davies," Gunny says. "She was checked in to room 946."

"Dr. Ahmed Shah," he holds up another photo of an older dark-skinned guy with thick, black-rimmed glasses. "Room 1231."

"And Benjamin Winters." He holds up the last picture of a dark-haired guy that could pass for a fashion model with his expensive looking haircut. "Room 2268."

None of them look like they could be worth all this effort. That's the job, though. We risk our asses to protect people that mostly don't deserve it.

"Our intel tells us that the last known location of the targets was in a conference room on the ground floor," Gunny continues. "That was several hours ago. Since the cell towers went down, we have had no further contact. There is no way to know if they are still inside or if they are even still alive. I don't care if we have to clear every room in The Palace. We will find them."

Gunny pauses to pull out another paper with the layout of the hotel. I can barely make it out from my seat, but it wasn't like they had a lot of time and resources to plan this operation. We will likely have to adapt and improvise our way through this shit show as usual, so it probably doesn't matter much if we know where we're going or not.

"After we insert through the rooftop and secure the top floor. Will and I will set up shop in this maintenance room with the roof access. Each team will proceed down one of the three fire stairwells and head to the last known location of the targets," Gunny says. "When we hit the ground floor, you will have to work your way across the casino floor to this walkway into the mall. You'll find the door to the conference room there. Once you make a positive ID on any of the targets, move them immediately to the maintenance room for extraction. The Super Stallion will be on standby at Nellis Air Force Base to get us out as soon as we complete our objective."

He pauses again to look around the room to make sure everyone looks to be paying attention.

"Get in and out as quickly and quietly as possible," Gunny reminds us. "Speed and stealth, gentleman. Keep a low profile. No fucking around... and I want suppressors on those rifles."

"Just one more thing," Kellogg says. "Any sound you make will just draw more of those motherfuckers, so I suggest you do not engage them unless you have to. They may seem like they aren't much of a threat alone, but you draw a crowd of them, and shit can get out of hand real goddamn quick."

Captain Kellogg paces across the front row of the desks.

"I know some of you will have a hard time engaging unarmed civilians," Kellogg says. "Do not hesitate. These things, whatever they are, they aren't people anymore. You can empty a mag into one of the motherfuckers and it will just keep coming. Headshots are the only way to drop them."

He pauses to let all of the information sink in. The room is completely silent. It doesn't concern me too much. The reality is we try for headshots much of the time now anyway since our enemies often wear similar body armor as us, and we always have to worry about somebody with a bomb strapped to their chest. I'm pretty sure we will be able to handle whatever the hell these dead things are just fine.

"Any questions?" Kellogg asks.

"How do we know if they're hostile or not?" asks Mac.

"If they try to bite you, shoot 'em," says Gunny. "If they appear disoriented, shoot 'em. If they do not respond to verbal communication, shoot 'em. And if you're still not sure, just shoot 'em anyway. We can't afford to take any chances out there."

The captain looks around the room at the faces of the men once more.

"I just want to say, I have full confidence that you will complete this mission," says Kellogg. "When the General told me he needed some volunteers, I said I know that my guys would volunteer to be the ones to do it because nobody is tougher, more determined, or better prepared to do this job."

Nothing like being "voluntold" to do a mission. Only in The Suck. Nobody complains, though. These guys might seem like a bunch of cocky assholes to some people, but every single one of them will stick together through anything.

"Let's gear up then," the captain says. "We step off in fifteen mikes."

After he dismisses us, a murmur fills the air as the platoon files out of the room into the hallway.

"I better call home," Sarge says. He eyes the phones on the wall where a few guys are dialing anxiously. "I need to see if Melissa is okay."

"Something is wrong with the phones," says Sergeant Lowe.

"I can't get through either," complains Corporal Eddie Carrasco. He makes up the other half of our platoon sniper team as the spotter for Sergeant Lowe.

"Fuck," says Pittman. He slams the receiver down. "The fucking phone lines are all fucked."

"Gibby," Sarge says. "You got a signal on that thing yet?"

Corporal Gibson checks his phone, then looks back at Sarge and shakes his head.

Sarge collapses onto a bench in the hallway. He props his elbows on his knees, clasps his hands together and hangs his head. For a long moment, he just stares at the floor. The thought that he can't get in touch with his wife must be killing him.

"I'm sure she is fine," I try to assure Sarge. "We'll go handle this shit and get you home in time for tamales."

Sarge exhales a loud, angry breath and shakes his head.

"If something happens to them..." Sarge trails off.

In the years I've known Sarge, I've never seen him afraid. Nothing ever phased him. No matter what might happen to him, he always knew his family was safe back home. But now he knows they are in danger, and he is away, so there is nothing he can do. In spite of all that, I need him to get his head right. If he isn't thinking straight out there it could be bad fucking news for me, too.

"Come on," I say. "They'll be fine. It can't be as bad as they're saying."

"I sure hope you're right," he says.

"I'm always right," I smirk. "Come on. Let's get this shit done."

CHAPTER THREE

The rotating blades of the Super Stallion kick clouds of grey dirt into the sky as we crowd into the troop hold. As I strap in between Sarge and Arnes, my eyes scan the rest of the men of Nightmare One. Each one of them has their game face on. There is no shit talking or screwing around while we wait for the helicopter crew to prep for the flight. Everyone just looks calm to the point of being bored. That's how we act when we're all focused and ready. No one shows any indication of tension, but we all feel it.

I check my weapons and ammo again. Arnes rests his head against the wall and closes his eyes. Gibby puts his headphones in his ears and bobs his head in time with the music. Mac scrawls some notes in one of his journals. Harding munches on a protein bar, crumbs sticking to the corners of his mouth.

We all have our own ways to avoid thinking too much.

Sarge just stares at his hands, though. He has this tattoo of a wedding band on his finger that says his wife's name in fancy lettering. I try to think of something to say to distract him, but I know it isn't likely to work, so I just put on my sunglasses and stare out the loading door as we leave the ground.

The mountains below us disappear over the horizon, and as we cross the desert, the temperature inside the helicopter steadily increases during the flight. From the air, there is no evidence of chaos. The small highways surrounding Death Valley are mostly empty and quiet. Then again, there aren't ever that many people out here. This forsaken desert is probably always this quiet.

It seems like the flight takes an eternity. Even traveling at top speed, we spend two restless hours cramped in the troop hold. Finally, as a helicopter crewman preps the ropes, a smell drifts into the cabin. Towering black columns of smoke reach for the sky, blotting out the afternoon sunlight as we descend toward the streets of downtown Las Vegas.

We get ready for insertion as the pilot steadies the helicopter. Sarge leads the way and fast ropes down to the rooftop of The Palace. I grab the rope next and wrap my leg and step off as soon as he is clear. The gusting desert wind pummels me as I descend to the roof, thirty-five stories above the ground. From up here, I immediately realize the situation is even worse than we could have ever imagined.

The streets of Vegas are teeming with people covered in blood. Flames engulf several of the buildings surrounding the casino. The toxic fumes burn my nostrils and make my eyes water almost immediately. My boots hit the rooftop and I run over to regroup with Sarge near a red access hatch on the surface of the roof. He stares out at the city, his gloved hand covering his nose and mouth to shield it from the smell.

"It won't be as bad as they said, huh?" Sarge leans in close to yell in my ear.

"Could be worse!" I yell back.

A general rule of thumb is that the situation can always get worse, but this time I am not sure how much that rule applies.

After the rest of the platoon ropes down, the helicopter peels away from the building and climbs back to the safety of the skies. As the pilot banks around to fly toward the setting sun, the sound of small arms fire erupts on the streets below. I've been in some chaotic situations but nothing like this.

"Team one," Lieutenant Reasoner says. "Take point."

"Arnes," Sarge gestures at the hatch. "Pop that bitch open."

We stack up on the door. Arnes twists the handle and yanks the hatch open with a grunt. He steps aside and leaves Harding staring at a staircase that descends into a darkened room. A strobe light flashes and a fire alarm blares inside. The kid hesitates. I put a hand on his shoulder to urge him forward and I descend the stairs behind him. He checks to the left and I scan the shapes in the darkness to my right. The room is cluttered with all sorts of tools, ladders, and shelves full of paint and cleaning supplies.

"Clear," Harding says.

"Clear," I call out as I lower my rifle.

I walk over to the closed door across the room and flip the light switch as the rest of the platoon files down the staircase. The lights flicker on. At least we won't be searching through darkened hallways.

"We'll set up shop here," says Will. He pauses while the alarm blares again.

An automated female voice informs us there has been an emergency and that we should remain calm and head for the exit while the cause is determined.

"Jesus," says Arnes. "That's gonna get annoying real fast."

"Clear this floor," Will orders us. "Let's locate those civilians and get the fuck out of here."

The platoon seems to settle into our cocky ass-kicking groove after our successful rooftop insertion, until something slams into the opposite side of the door behind me.

I pivot around and raise my rifle. Harding opens fire and peppers the door with a burst, punching holes through the solid wood. He pauses until he hears a groan on the other side of the door, then he pulls the trigger again. Fucking new guy.

"Cease fire!" Sarge yells.

There is another groan from the hallway. The doorknob rattles, but it's locked by a card reader. I look down and notice blood trickling beneath the frame of the door. There is no way whatever is on the other side should still be standing, but it bangs on the door again.

We stack up and I give Harding a nod to open the door. As soon as he turns the handle this guy crashes into the room. I open fire and manage to hit him a couple times, striking his arm and shoulder as he falls to the floor. There are several exit wounds on his arms and legs and a couple on the back of his blue polo shirt, which is turning purple as it soaks up his blood. Still, the guy groans and pushes his body off the floor. Sarge fires a couple rounds into his back to finish him off.

"Help," the guy gasps just as Sarge pulls the trigger. The man collapses back onto the linoleum.

"Target down," I say.

"Did that guy just say something?" Will asks.

We all heard it. Harding looks at me, not sure what to say. I exchange a glance with Sarge. We both know that guy was still alive when we shot him, but admitting it won't do anything to change what happened.

"Negative, sir," Sarge says. "We didn't hear anything." He claps Harding on the shoulder to tell him to forget about the fuck up. Harding keeps his eyes on the body on the floor.

Shit happens.

The fact that we might have just killed an innocent civilian is pushed aside when we hear another moan from the hallway. I raise my rifle and crouch down in the doorway, keeping most of my body behind the wall for cover. Using cover probably is not necessary, but I'm most comfortable sticking with the tactics that have been drilled into my mind for years. Gibby takes up a position at my six to cover the opposite end of the hall.

"Contact," I call out.

"Don't engage," Sarge says.

Sarge steps out into the hall and spots the man in a tropical shirt trudging toward us.

"Show me your hands," Sarge orders.

We might have fucked up already, so I'm sure Sarge wants to be sure this person is actually unresponsive.

The man moans and raises his arms as he staggers toward us. Streaks of blood trickle down his pale face. There is no doubt in my mind that there is something wrong with this guy.

"Drop him," Sarge says.

I pull the trigger and the shot shears off a chunk of his bald head, and he crumbles against the wall and slumps to the floor. Farther down the hallway several more figures shamble toward us. The sound of gunfire rings out behind me as Gibby opens fire in the opposite direction. Sarge raises his rifle as well and takes aim at a woman in a short red dress staggering toward us. Her gaudy hair and makeup are all fucked up.

"Ma'am," he says. "Ma'am."

She just snaps her jaws and keeps coming at us, so we open fire. Our first few rounds hit her center mass, but she only staggers back a step before rushing forward again. I adjust my aim and open fire again, this time the chick hits the floor. Sarge takes aim at a maid about halfway down the long hallway and squeezes the trigger again. One of the bullets hits her in the face and she crashes back into the cart behind her and topples it to the floor.

"Clear," Sarge yells out.

"Clear," Gibby calls back.

"Let's move up," Sarge says, and our team pushes ahead to the elevators in the center of the hotel where the three wings of the building intersect. More figures emerge from the other hallways. Sarge holds up a fist and we pause our advance. I drop to my knee and shoulder my M4.

"Engage," Sarge orders.

Bullets tear through the hallway, shredding the bodies to pieces and splattering the elevator doors with flecks of blood.

"Tangos down," Sarge confirms.

We resume our advance down the hall. As we step over the bodies on the floor, I keep expecting one of them to reach out and grab me for some reason, but they're all dead as hell. I'm probably only nervous about it because this shit just feels like some kind of horror movie. We check the other hallways, but they are empty now except for one guy way at the end of the west wing growling at a door.

"I got him," Colin Lowe says, raising his M110 SASS to his shoulder. He takes a few seconds to aim and then fires a single shot from the sniper rifle. The 7.62 mm round blows half the head off the poor bastard.

"Damn!" says Pittman.

"Fucking showoff," snorts Arnes.

"Watch it, Corporal," Colin winks at him. "Sassy don't like that."

"Nightmare One Actual, this is Nightmare One-One Romeo," Gibby hails the lieutenant on our comms. "Hallways on the top floor are clear. Over."

"Copy that, Nightmare One-One Romeo," says the Lieutenant. "Tango Mike."

"What about the rooms, Sarge?" Gibby asks. "Should we check them?"

"Fuck that," Sarge shakes his head. "We don't have that kind of time. Besides those things don't seem to have much luck opening doors."

Just then a handle clicks in the quiet hallway and a door squeaks open. I raise my rifle as I see a face emerge from the doorway.

"Marines!" I yell.

"Show me your hands," yells Sarge.

The woman screams and ducks back inside the room as soon as she sees a dozen assault rifles pointed in her direction. The door slams shut, but a moment later, it opens a crack and the old woman peers out.

"I'm not sick!" she cries. "Don't shoot me."

"It's okay, ma'am," Sarge says. "We're United States Marines. We're not here to hurt you."

The old woman steps out into the hallway, her fingers cover her mouth when she spots the carnage on the floor. Farther down the corridor another door slowly opens, and a little boy and a teenage girl emerge into the hallway. Sarge holds up a hand and the little boy waves back at him.

Lieutenant Reasoner steps over the body in the doorway of the maintenance room after hearing the commotion in the hall.

"What's happening out here, Sergeant?" he asks. "I thought this hallway was clear."

Sarge starts to answer but then the old woman howls. She collapses on the floor next to the body of the first guy we shot. The one that wasn't dead.

"No, no, no," she wails, and she clings to the dead man in the bloody polo shirt.

Sarge clears his throat to speak, but the woman howls again. The lieutenant leans down to try and say something but before he does, he notices something that makes him take a step back. He reaches for his sidearm, but before he can do anything the dead man on the floor lurches up and bites the woman on the face. She screams in pain as he tears off a chunk of her face with his teeth.

The lieutenant doesn't hesitate to open fire. He hits the man and the woman, pulling the trigger as he backpedals into the room. Will keeps shooting the guy repeatedly until the magazine is empty.

"Motherfucker," he yells. "Doc!"

Doc Noonan rushes out in the hall to attend to the old woman. She is slumped face down on the floor. Doc rolls her limp body over and checks for a pulse. Then he looks at Will and shakes his head.

The lieutenant holsters his sidearm and takes his rifle off his shoulder. He brings it up and fires a round into the silvery-haired head of the dead woman on the floor. Then he lowers the M4 and turns to look at Sarge.

"Sergeant, we can't afford any more fuck ups like that," the lieutenant says.

"Yes sir," says Sarge.

"I mean it," the lieutenant moves closer. "That could have been my face that got ripped off. I don't feel like getting killed today, copy?"

"Won't happen again, sir," Sarge assures him.

The lieutenant gives me a stern look as well and then turns to leave.

"Sir," Sarge stops him. He gestures at the kids standing in the hallway. "What should we do about those two?"

"Get them back in the rooms, Sergeant. We don't need more problems."

"We're going to take them with us, though, right sir?" Sarge says.

Will leans to the side a few inches and looks at the kids. The older girl looks to be maybe thirteen and she stands behind the younger boy with her hands on his shoulders. He can't be more than ten or eleven.

"You know that's not our mission," Will says.

"But sir," Sarge says. "They're just kids."

"Do what you can for them," Will says. "I'll put in a request with command."

The lieutenant turns and steps through the doorway to the maintenance room. Sarge mumbles to himself as he turns and heads down the hall towards the two kids, but I don't catch what he says as I follow along beside him.

"Hey," Sarge says as he crouches down next to the boy and the girl. "It's not safe out here. You need to go back inside your room and lock the door."

The little girl nods.

"You guys have some food in there?" Sarge asks. "Water?"

The kid shakes her head.

Sarge takes out a pair of MRE's from his pack.

"Give me a couple cans of Rip It," Sarge says.

"Shit, man," I say.

"Come on," Sarge urges me.

I open my pack, grab the cans, and hand them over.

"Stay inside until someone comes back for you," Sarge tells them, even though he knows we probably won't be coming back.

The kids disappear back inside the room and close the door. As Sarge and I walk down the hall, I hear the locks tumble into place on the door.

"No way command is going to approve that request," I tell Sarge. "You know that, right?"

"I don't like it," Sarge says. "We're supposed to leave these kids here to die? It's not right, man."

"We don't get paid to like it," I remind him.

"Yeah," Sarge sighs. I can tell the old saying doesn't make him feel better.

"Didn't have to give them the last of my Rip It," I say.

"Those kids are going to die in there," Sarge says. "And all you can think about is your fucking Rip It."

"Right," I tell him. "They're already fucked. It would have done more for me than it will do for them."

"Damn, that's ice cold, Chase," he says. "Makes me wonder what kind of shit your parents did to make a messed up motherfucker like you."

"You don't want to know," I tell him.

CHAPTER FOUR

Since the emergency alarm shut down the elevators and returned them to the ground floor, we hit the fire stairs. When we open the door, motion sensors detect our presence, and the lights click on and illuminate the top floors of a concrete stairwell that reeks of stale cigarette smoke. I peer over the railing at the darkened floors below. If there were any of those things down there, the sensors would have tracked their movement and engaged the lights.

I take up my usual position as the slack man behind Harding and follow him silently down to the next floor. Although the rest of the hotel is probably swarming with these things, it feels relatively safe in this stairwell. Knowing the lights are there to warn us means that nothing will sneak up on us.

The alarms are the only thing that make me edgy. The monotonous blare, the flashing lights, and the droning voice of the woman, repeating the same warning over and over again is unsettling.

"Those alarms are getting on my fucking nerves already," Arnes complains.

"At least it covers the babbling stream of nonsense flowing steadily from your mouth," Mac says.

"Very poetic," Gibby compliments Mac.

"Thank you," Mac laughs.

That just pisses Arnes off even more. In his eyes, he is always the victim even when his mouth is getting him in trouble.

"Kiss my ass, mister fucking William Hemingay," Arnes growls.

"It's Ernest," Mac corrects him. "Ernest Hemingway."

"He can kiss my ass, too," Arnes says. No matter what, Arnes always has to get the last word. His ego never allows him to let it go.

I look back and urge them to shut the fuck up with my eyes. Mac just gives me a shrug as we keep descending the stairs. We still have a couple dozen flights left to go before we reach the ground floor.

As we pass by some of the flimsy stairwell doors, I think I hear some of those things in the hallways on the other side. It could just be my imagination, though. With all the noise from the alarms, I can't be sure. In any event, none of us are about to open them to find out.

Finally, we reach the ground floor. Going down the thirty-five flights of stairs was not too bad, but I'm already dreading the climb back up to the top floor. We stack up on the door and pause a moment to make sure everyone is ready to rock and roll. Gibby radios to let the rest of the squads know that we are in position, then listens to the radio as we wait for the other teams.

"Solid copy," Gibby says into the radio. He looks at Sarge and gives him a thumbs up.

Sarge gives a nod and then I follow Harding as he rushes through the door. We find ourselves in a hallway off the main casino floor. Several corpses wander around outside the bathrooms, and I open fire at a mutilated cocktail waitress on the right, while Harding takes out a dead security guard and another fresh corpse in a bowling shirt with flames printed on it.

We move forward toward the casino floor, and I hear the other squads opening fire as they engage the dead. The room is a noisy nightmare of flashing lights, jingling bells, and moaning corpses. There are napkins, broken glass, poker chips and puddles of blood on the floor. Hundreds of those things wander around between the slot machines and blackjack tables.

I crouch at the end of the hallway and start laying hate on the closest targets, trying to suppress their advance as they close in on our position. As soon as I drop one, another emerges from between the machines. They all have bloody flesh dangling from their mouths. Their arms, legs, and faces have been partially devoured. Some of them already have multiple bullet wounds that should keep them from walking around at all, but these things really do shrug off anything but a bullet to the head.

The tracers come out as I fire on a bartender coming at me from behind the bar at my three o'clock. Several rounds miss and shatter the mirror and bottles on the racks behind the bar before I drop him. A fat guy in a suit stumbles at me from behind the bartender, but I have enough time to pause and change to a fresh mag.

I reload and fire on the guy in the suit. As soon as he falls, I shift my rifle and take out a black woman with a shaved head in a fancy evening gown. After blowing half her head off, I engage an old man in a shirt that reads "VIVA LAS VEGAS." After he hits the floor, I take aim at a gangly white guy in baggy shorts and a wife beater. Half of his tattooed arm is gone and the goatee around his mouth is caked with crimson blood.

Tracer rounds take him out, so I grab another mag.

"Conserve your ammo," Sarge reminds us.

These things wobble around so awkwardly that it sometimes makes headshots too difficult. I start double-firing for center mass, counting on the recoil pattern of the M4 to get the second shot hit the things in the head.

One after another, the corpses rush at us. It gets unnerving when they show no hesitation about walking into the line of fire. Even as they stumble over the fallen bodies, they keep pushing toward us.

They are relentless, I'll give them that. No fear whatsoever. But with all of us laying down heavy fire from the hallway, they never even get close to us.

Tracers.

I change mags again and rejoin the bloody siege. Dozens of bodies are piled between the slot machines and the hall. Here and there lies an arm or leg that was shot completely off. A couple of corpses continue to reach for us from the ground, but their bodies are so fucked up they can't do more than drag themselves across the patterns on the carpet.

Finally, the steady flow of the dead turns to a trickle. I fire a round at the last one, a casino worker in a red vest and white shirt, and his brains splatter all over the screen of a video poker machine.

We hold our positions for several seconds as the firing at the other end of the casino floor tapers off. I scan across the rows of machines, most of them shot to shit now. Some of the lights still flash and a few of them make garbled noises.

"Clear!" one of our guys calls out across the casino floor.

"Clear!" Harding calls back.

"That's how we get shit done, boys," Sarge says. "Good job."

We advance into the casino, stepping around the bodies on the floor. One of them reaches for me as I get close, so I finish it off with a round to the head. It slumps over on top of several corpses stacked up beneath it as his brain spills out from the entry wound in his skull.

It's hard to tell with all the noisy machines if more of them still lurk in the dimly lit casino. We move ahead cautiously along the rows of slots, checking each aisle as we work our way across the room.

Out of the corner of my eye, I detect movement. I pivot around and center my rifle on Pittman checking the opposite side of the room with his back to me. I lower my rifle and start to say something, but he pivots around and fires. Dumbass had his finger on the trigger again. I try to move but I'm too late. The bullet hits me, and I fall back on the ground.

"Fuck!" I yell. "I'm hit."

I glance down to see how bad it is, expecting the worst. A giant fucking hole below my body armor from the 5.56 mm round. But there isn't anything there.

Then I feel the pain coming from my hand as I try to grip the rifle.

I look over at the bloody mess where all my fingers used to be. The two middle fingers are completely gone. My pinky dangles by a thread of muscle and skin.

"Shit," Pittman curses. He knows he fucked up bad.

"Doc," Sarge yells. "Graves is hit!"

"What the fuck is wrong with you?" Mac grabs Pittman by the collar of his uniform and shoves him back.

"I'm sorry, man" Pittman says. "Fuck!"

"Get the fuck out of here," Mac tells him.

"I'm sorry, Chase," Pittman says again.

He might be an idiot, but at least he didn't kill me. Right now, I'm just glad I still have my trigger finger.

Doc rushes over and tries to keep me from getting back to my feet.

"Stay down," he tells me.

"I'm alright," I tell him.

"Let me look at it," Doc insists.

I let him take my hand and inspect the wound. The last thing I want is to be out of commission while the rest of my team risk their lives. I'd never forgive myself if something happened.

"Just patch me up," I tell him. "I'm good to go."

I hold out my hand trying my best not to look at it. I'm not too squeamish usually, but my hand looks like I shoved it in a meat grinder right now.

Doc sterilizes it and pours some kind of stuff to stop the bleeding. Then he sprays some numbing shit on me before he wraps it up in layers of gauze. The rest of the teams resume clearing the casino floor, but Sarge and our squad hang around while Doc tends to me.

The pain is bad, but the misery that I feel is almost unbearable. I don't want to let my fucked up hand jeopardize the lives of my team. Now I'm more of a liability than anything else.

"Fucking Pittman," I curse.

"Must have thought he saw a goat," Mac says. "Goddamn moron."

In spite of the pain I'm in, I find myself laughing. Mac has a way of doing that. Nothing ever seems as bad as it is when he is around.

"It ain't too bad," Arnes says, eyeing my hand. "You're one lucky son of a bitch, Graves."

"You know," I say. "I always thought you would be the one to fuck up and shoot me, Arnes."

"I still might," Arnes shrugs then he leans to the side and spits tobacco juice on the floor.

"Good to go," Doc says as he tapes the wrap around my hand.

I take a second to inspect the barrel of my rifle. I wipe the blood off it, but it appears to be only cosmetically damaged on the vertical grip below the barrel where my hand was. Might have been more pissed about being stuck down here with a disabled rifle than a disabled hand. At least I am still in business.

Time to suck it up. I turn and follow the rest of our squad. Gunshots on the far side of the casino, get me moving again. I know there isn't time to sit around. We still have a mission to finish.

CHAPTER FIVE

At the opposite end of the casino floor, corpses pour in from the long hallway that connects to the mall. Team two and team three are laying down heavy fire, pushing toward the conference room steadily as they drop the dead. By the time we reach them, they are just outside the closed double doors.

Sarge pauses next to Sergeant Lowe and points up to the doorway and barks something in his ear. Colin nods and then moves his men up to set up a defensive position just passed the conference room entrance. Sarge gestures for us to follow him and then leads us to the doorway. He tries the handle, but it is locked, so he gestures to Arnes who lifts his leg and kicks the door off the hinges with one of his massive boots.

We rush inside, sweeping our rifles around the room. Several corpses with name badges pinned to their shirts wander amongst the rows of chairs. I don't see any survivors. I square my rifle on one of the dead and fire. My first burst misses hitting the thing in the head.

Fucking hand.

It hurts like hell to hold the grip and my aim is shit because of it. I cringe in anticipation of the pain as I squeeze the trigger again. My second attempt punches through the forehead of the corpse and it slams into several folding chairs as it topples to the floor.

We quickly clear the remaining threats in the room and then look around at the carnage. Blood splatters the walls and pools of dark crimson soak into the maroon carpet on the floor. Chairs are toppled sideways. A slideshow flickers through images of white cells or some shit on the blood-splattered screen.

"Start checking bodies," Sarge orders us as he grabs the radio on his jacket.

We begin checking the corpses around the room to see if any of our targets are among them. I don't spot anyone that might possibly match the pictures we were shown. The rattle of automatic fire continues in the hallway as team two and team three hold back the dead.

"Nightmare One Actual," Sarge says into the radio. "This is Nightmare One-One, how copy?"

"Copy, Nightmare One-One," says Will. "What is your status? Over."

"We just reached the conference room," Sarge says. He pauses for a moment to look at me and I look up from the body and shake my head. "No sign of the targets. How should we proceed? Over."

I glance back down at the dead body on the floor. It seems wrong for some reason. The guy with the thick glasses falling off his face and receding hairline looks dead as hell. There is a massive bite wound in his neck.

Then I realize what bothers me.

His head seems fine. No sign of trauma.

As soon as I come to that realization, his eyes open. I swing the rifle around and pull the trigger several times as the dead guy opens his jaws and tries to sit up. His face fragments, sending chunks of flesh and bone flying before he falls to the ground again.

Will transmits something on the radio, but I can't hear it over the report of the rifle.

"Negative copy," says Sarge. He covers his ear to hear better. "Say again."

I glance around the room and wonder how many more of the bodies could get up at any moment.

"I repeat, split into teams and check out the rooms," Will says loudly. "Do you copy?"

"Solid copy," Sarge says.

He waves a finger around in a circle.

"Let's go," he tells us.

We follow him back out of the bloodbath in the conference room. Scores of dead bodies line the hallway now, but more and more stiffs are still emerging from the mall entrance. Sarge gestures to Lowe and Strong and they pull their teams back behind us, though dozens of corpses pursue us back to the casino.

That's when it really hits me how fucked we are.

Even though we have remained in complete control of the situation at all times, it is just a matter of time before something goes wrong. No matter how many of these things we drop, there will always be more of them coming for us. We will run out of bullets before we could possibly kill them all. The only way it will end is when we're dead. We need to hurry up and get the fuck out of here before that happens.

I turn around as we enter the casino again. We walk back through the endless flashing lights of slot machines.

"We'll take the ninth floor," Sarge says to the other team leaders.

"We got twelve," Lowe says.

"I guess we'll take twenty-two then," Strong says.

"Let's head back up the same stairwells," Lowe suggests. "Make sure they all stay clear so none of these things get back upstairs."

"Good call, Lowe. See you boys up top," Sarge says, but then he stops walking.

His eyes focus on the front doors of the casino where a massive mob of the dead pounds at the glass. The things outside must have heard all the gunshots and swarmed to the entrance. There must be thousands of them out there now.

"Mother of God," gasps Sergeant Lowe as he turns to look.

"Those doors won't hold them forever," says Sergeant Strong.

"We better get moving," Sarge says.

As soon as we start walking again, we hear glass shattering. A loud roar from the moaning corpses outside fills the casino floor as the first of the things stumbles into the lobby.

Staying to try and fight the entire city is not an option, so we break into a sprint for the stairwells.

"Nightmare One Actual," Sarge radios to Will. "This is Nightmare One-One. We have heavy contact at the front entrance. Please advise."

"Roger, Nightmare One-One," says Will. "Do not engage. Charlie Mike. Fall back to upper floors. Copy?"

"Solid copy," says Sarge as we reach the hallway.

We race up the stairs. Within a few flights of climbing the steps two at a time, I feel the burn in my leg muscles. Sarge pauses at the door on the ninth floor.

"Hardcore," he says. "Post up out here. The second anyone comes up those stairs I want to know about it."

Harding nods. We stack up on the door. After Sarge glances around to make sure we are ready, he nods to Arnes to tell him to open the door to the hallway. Arnes twists the handle and shoves the door.

The corpse of a guy wearing a heavy metal t-shirt with long blonde hair, stained red with blood, stands just a few feet from the door. About a half-dozen more walking dead stumble around the hallway just behind him.

We open fire.

Errant bullets zip down the hallway, shattering sconces and tearing holes in the drywall. High-caliber rounds shred the dead bodies at close range, and within a few seconds all of them are down.

I check the numbers on the doors as we advance.

"What room was it, Chase?" Sarge asks. He knows I will remember.

"Nine forty-six," I tell him.

Several other corpses stagger around the corner near the elevators as we work our way down the hall. We have to pause again and drop the last of the dead. Then we push forward until we reach the room that Miss Davies was checked into.

Sarge knocks softly on the door and listens for a moment but hears nothing inside. He looks at Arnes and jerks his head toward the door and then moves out of the way.

Arnes shotguns the door. A woman screams inside as he kicks the door open. We rush in to find the redhead clutching a lamp in a threatening manner.

"Miss Davies," Sarge says her name right away.

The woman scans our uniforms and our faces but does not respond. She stands there in her Stanford t-shirt and pajama pants that are filthy and bloodstained. Her fingers clench the base of the lamp tightly and she takes a step back toward the cracked window.

"We're here to help," Sarge says. "It's okay."

I lower my rifle and take a couple steps toward her.

"You can put the lamp down now, lady," I tell her.

She retreats another step but lets me take the lamp from her. She wraps her arms around me and lets out a sob into my chest. I drop the lamp and it hits the floor with a thud. The lightbulb pops when it shatters.

"You're okay, now," I assure her. "We're going to bring you someplace safe."

I pry her off me and sit her down in a chair beside the window. Her fingers find the armrests and squeeze the padding.

"Nightmare One Actual, this is Nightmare One-One," Sarge radios to the lieutenant. "We've located Miss Davies. She's alive."

"Copy that, Nightmare One-One. Good work, Sergeant," says Will. "Find out if she has any idea as to the whereabouts of Shah or Winters, copy?"

"Solid copy," says Sarge. He looks over at me and tells me with his eyes to question Miss Davies, but I have my doubts that we will be able to get much information from her.

The chick is a mess.

"Miss Davies," I say as I take a knee beside her in the chair.

She stares at her trembling hands, and then clutches them together in her lap, so I put a hand on them to steady her.

"I need to know if you know where we can find Dr. Shah and Mr. Winters. Do you know who I am talking about?" I ask.

"Ben," she whimpers. "He's dead."

"You're sure about that?" I ask.

She nods her head.

"I was having drinks with him late last night. That's when this all started," she explains. "I saw it. I watched him die right in front of me."

I can tell she is about to lose it as she replays the incident in her mind.

"What about Dr. Shah?" I say. "Ahmed Shah?"

She looks at me with a puzzled expression.

"I don't know," she says. "The last time I saw him was downstairs at the conference yesterday."

"Are you sure?" I question her.

"No, wait," she thinks about it. "I saw him with a woman in the casino last night. He was there when it started, but I don't know what might have happened to him."

I look back at Sarge and he grabs the mic on his jacket.

"Nightmare One-Three, this is Nightmare One-One," Sarge radios to reach Sergeant Strong and let his team know that Winters is gone. "Be advised Miss Davies has confirmed Winters is down. How copy?"

There is a long pause on the other end. The sound of small arms fire coming from the other end of the building echoes through the halls along with the incessant blaring of the fire alarm.

"Nightmare One-Three, this is Nightmare One-One," Sarge repeats. "Do you copy?"

"You should grab your things, ma'am," I tell Miss Davies. "We need to get moving."

She nods and gets up from the chair to grab her bag and her laptop. Then she moves over to the dresser and scoops out her clothes.

"Nightmare One, this is One-Three" Sergeant Strong yells. Gunshots cut off his voice. "We have heavy contact on twenty-two. Requesting support. Over."

"We need to get the fuck out of here," someone yells in the background.

"Copy, One-Three," Sergeant Lowe responds. "One-Two is en route to your position."

"Hurry the fuck up," Strong yells.

The sound of gunfire picks up briefly and then tapers off again.

"One-Three, how copy?" transmits Lowe.

The comms fall silent. Claire puts her duffel bag over her shoulder and nods to let Sarge know she is ready to go.

"Come in, One-Three," Lowe repeats.

The comms go quiet for a long moment, finally a mic clicks on, but no one speaks. We just hear the sound of those things snarling and chewing followed by muffled screams in the background. Then the comms go quiet again.

"Hang on, One-Three. Almost there," Sergeant Lowe pants into the microphone. "Shit!"

More gunfire crackles before the transmission ends again.

"Nightmare One-Two, come in," radios the lieutenant.

Nothing but dead air. I look at Sarge and can see the concern on his face as we lose contact with the other squads.

"What is your status, One-Two?" Will repeats.

"Sarge, are we going to get our asses down there and help them or what?" Arnes says.

Sarge holds up a hand to tell him to shut up as the comms come to life again. A fierce firefight rages in the background as Sergeant Lowe barks orders at his men.

"Fall back!" Lowe yells. "There's too fucking many of them."

"Lowe, give me a fucking sitrep," orders Lieutenant Reasoner.

"Strong is down," pants Lowe. "Reeves, Mack, and Riddle all down. Break."

"Copy that. What is your position One-Two?" Reasoner asks.

"Twenty-second floor, west stairwell. Fuck... lay down some fucking fire on those things, Javi!"

Someone screams in the background as more gunfire erupts over the comms.

"Fuck this," Arnes grunts as he turns and starts back down the hall. "We need to get in this fight."

"Hold up," says Sarge.

"Pull your men out of there, Lowe," the lieutenant orders him. "Haul ass back to the extraction point, copy?"

We hear the gunfire pick up on the floors above us. Sergeant Lowe either can't respond or he is being torn to shreds right now.

"Nightmare One Actual, this is One-One," says Sarge. "Request permission to provide additional support for One-Three. Over."

"Negative, One-One," Will says. "Miss Davies remains the priority. Get her up top to prep for evac. How copy?"

"This is bullshit," Arnes gripes.

"I don't like it either," Sarge says. He scans the faces of our team. None of us wants to go back upstairs and leave our guys to die. Then he clicks the mic on again.

"Negative copy," radios Sarge. "Picking up a lot of static, sir. Say again. Over."

"Charlie Mike, One-One," the lieutenant says. "Proceed to the evac point immediately. Do you copy?"

Sarge doesn't bother responding. There is no way we are leaving our guys.

"Mac, take Harding and get Miss Davies upstairs," Sarge says. "We'll be right behind you."

Mac nods and then he leads the redhead out to the hallway to pick up Harding and head upstairs.

"Nightmare One-One, do you copy?" the lieutenant demands over the radio, but Sarge makes no move to respond.

"You guys with me?" Sarge asks the rest of us.

"We got your back," says Gibby.

Arnes grunts and racks the shotgun.

"Ready," I nod.

"Let's go bring our fucking guys back then," Sarge says.

CHAPTER SIX

We haul ass down the hallway and hustle up the west staircase to the twenty-second floor. The closer we get, the more we can clearly hear the fierce battle and the mob that awaits us. Arnes grabs the handle and pushes the stairwell door, and we spot Sergeant Lowe halfway down the hall dragging Corporal Pittman by the collar of his uniform.

Behind him, Corporal Dakota Hurst and Doc Noonan help a bloody Corporal Sykes by draping his arms across their shoulders and pulling him along between them. Zamora and Carrasco take up firing positions behind them to hold off the advancing horde long enough to cover their retreat.

Picking the dead off one or two at a time had been pretty easy, but now hundreds of them surge down the hallway all at once. There is no way we can stop all of them. All we can do is slow them down enough to give Lowe and his squad a chance to get the hell out of here.

"Last mag," Carrasco calls as he retreats behind Zamora and reloads his rifle. Zamora picks off the closest targets until his mag runs dry, then he turns and falls back as Carrasco resumes firing.

Sarge waves an arm to signal them to keep moving as we open fire on the oncoming wall of bloody meat bags several doors down.

As much as I try to be accurate, these things don't make it easy. They hunch over, jerk to the side, stumble, and knock each other around awkwardly as they move. The unnatural movements mean it often takes several bursts of fire before I hit one in the skull and drop it.

No matter how many rounds we send their way, it does little to slow the advance of the horde. They just trample the fallen bodies into the floor as they relentlessly surge toward us.

"Come get some, motherfuckers!" Arnes yells out in between blasts from the shotgun. The rest of us fall back but he keeps firing as they close in on him.

"Arnes, maintain your distance!" Sarge barks.

Arnes ignores him, sticks the barrel of the shotgun into the mouth of a chick as she lunges for him and pulls the trigger. Her brains splatter all over the stiffs behind her, but they don't even seem to notice. Arnes turns, grinning like a madman, his eyes wild with adrenaline as he races down the hall to catch up with us.

"Did you see that shit?" he laughs.

I ignore him and focus fire from my M4 on the swarm of humanity. I drop several more of the dead before retreating further down the hall, but it all feels so futile. At least we bought enough time for Sergeant Lowe and his team to make it to the stairs. I crouch next to the door of another room, put in a fresh mag, and take aim again. I keep firing and drop half a dozen bodies before the tracer rounds come out. My mag is almost empty. Sarge yells at me to run for the stairs, so I start moving as fast as I can. Zamora stands beside him with the M32 grenade launcher pointed in my general direction. As I move through the doorway, I hear the bloop of the grenade being fired. Sarge and Zamora duck into the hall behind me and slam the door just before the explosion rattles the building.

"That won't slow them down for long," Sarge says. "Let's go."

We scramble up the stairs, grabbing at the rails to haul our bodies up flight after flight. Before we even climb five levels, the things are pounding at the door to the stairwell. Somehow, they get the door open as we round the landing at the thirtieth floor and the sound of the things snarling and moaning fills the stairwell.

I'm already gasping for air. Only five more flights to go. I glance down over the railing and see the motion sensor lights several floors below us. Those things are slow, but they never need to stop and catch a breath.

"Nightmare One, this is One-One," Sarge says into the comms. "We are Oscar Mike to your position with two critical wounded and multiple hostiles on our six. How copy?"

"Copy One-One," says Will.

"Nightmare One, interrogative," says Sarge. "What is the ETA on that inbound dust off?"

"One-One, we have a situation developing up here," says Will. "Be advised, we lost contact with Nightmare Actual. Nellis may be compromised. Over."

"Shit," says Sarge.

"We're fucked now," Gibby says as he rounds the corner and continues up the stairs.

"They got to send somebody to get us out of here," I pant.

"I wouldn't count on it," Sarge says. "I think we're on our own now."

By the time we reach the top floor, my muscles burn and I'm sucking air through my mouth. I look down and see the things are maybe ten flights down and still coming. We move into the hallway and close the door.

Doc rushes over to take a look at Sykes and Pittman. Sykes has a wound on his arm and a big gash on his head, but he does not seem critical. Pittman looks like shit though. He had a chunk of his face ripped off and his leg was chewed up so bad that I can see the exposed bone in the pool of gushing blood.

"Is it bad, Doc?" Pittman asks.

"You'll be alright," Doc lies. He injects Pittman with a healthy dose of morphine and the Marine immediately goes limp on the floor.

"Hang in there," Doc tells him.

"Fucking North Koreans," Pittman laments as his eyes close.

"Let's move him," Doc says.

Lowe and his squad help carry Pittman into the maintenance room.

"We need to block that door," Sarge says.

He is down on one knee, sucking wind from our sprint up the stairs. Sarge pauses to take in some air before he manages to finish his thought.

"Those things will bust right through it," he says.

As usual, Sarge is on point. Barricading the door is all we can do to buy us enough time to regroup, refill our magazines, treat our wounded, and try to figure out some way out of this mess. Still, it takes a moment until we have caught our breath enough to get moving again. When Mac and Harding return to the hallway, Sarge gets back to his feet.

"Let's get everything we can out here and pile it up to block the door," Sarge says and gestures toward the nearest hotel room.

Arnes raises the Mossberg and shotguns the door and kicks it open. We move in to clear any threats, but the room is vacant. All of us work together to haul out the dresser, tables, and mattresses and pile them in front of the door.

"Think that's enough?" Mac asks me as he tosses a chair on top of the pile.

Before I can answer the mob in the stairwell reaches the door and starts clawing and pounding. The door opens a crack and the pile of furniture shifts but keeps them from pushing through for now.

"We better get some more shit," I say.

Arnes breaches another room across the hall. We rush in with our rifles ready to fire but find nothing inside the empty room except for the furniture, clothes, suitcases, and a bottle of champagne in a bucket of melted ice. Arnes grabs the bottle of bubbly and chugs it down. He cringes and looks at the bottle.

"Who the fuck is Dom... Per-eeg-non?" he wonders.

"That's Dom Perignon, you illiterate fucking bumpkin," Mac says as he takes the bottle from Arnes. "This shit costs like two hundred bucks a bottle."

"Tastes like ass," Arnes says.

"Quit fucking around," I remind them and gesture to the dresser. "Help me move this thing."

Mac puts the bottle down and grabs the other end after Arnes waves a dismissive hand in my direction.

"You worry too much, Graves," Arnes tells me as he picks up a chair. "We got this."

"We just lost nearly half our platoon, asshole," I remind him. "We don't have anything under control."

"He's losing his shit, man," Gibby warns me as he carries out a large round table.

The best advantage you can give the enemy is a lack of respect. Our team has held our own, but these things have shown that they can be deadly if we get cocky and put ourselves in a bad position.

Arnes has never seemed all that stable, but we can't afford him going off the rails right now.

"Get it together, Arnes," Sarge urges him as he picks up a nightstand and hauls it toward the door.

After we clear out the second room and barricade the hallway with the furnishings, we head back to the maintenance room. Sarge and Colin Lowe are having a powwow with Lieutenant Reasoner, while Corporal Collins tries to contact anyone on the radio. Doc continues to work on stabilizing Pittman, while the rest of us stand around waiting for the word. I find myself staring at the redhead, sitting alone on the stairs to the roof.

"Can you believe it?" I ask Mac.

"What?" he says.

"All this for one chick," I say.

"Don't seem like saving her ass is worth more than everyone we lost," Gibby agrees.

"At least she's kind of cute," says Mac.

"Not that cute," I complain. She lifts her eyes and sees us watching her, so we turn around and pretend to be interested in something else.

"Ain't got no ass," Gibby says.

"Solid seven," Mac says.

"Four, tops."

"Nah," he says.

"I'm not into redheads," I confess.

"I'm not into white girls," Gibby says. "Too much drama."

Maybe we're assholes for even having this conversation right now, but it's better than dwelling on everything that just happened.

"Alright, listen up," Lieutenant Reasoner announces. "I realize this op did not go down as smooth as it should have—"

"We got our fucking asses kicked, sir," interrupts Gibby. He isn't usually one to get out of line, but we're all a little high strung right now.

"Some of that... a lot of that is on me," admits Will. "But we have to put that behind us."

"Bullshit," says Arnes. "Captain knew he was dropping us into a clusterfuck. This is on him. I'm going to kick his fucking teeth in."

"Shut up, Arnes," says Sarge.

"The point is," Will continues. "We can't change what happened. We can only control what happens next. I remain confident that we will make contact with command and that the extraction will be coming. Until then we need to make do. Copy?"

There is a murmur of agreement.

"I'm not hearing the level of intensity I'd expect from the best damn recon platoon in the business," the lieutenant says.

"Oohrah!" the men bark.

"That's more like it," he says. "See your team leaders for your assignments. Everyone stay fucking frosty. Be ready to bug out if the situation goes sideways again. We can't afford any more fuck ups."

The lieutenant pauses to look around the room, assessing our morale and readiness by the expressions on our faces.

"Let's get moving, gentleman," Will says. "The world won't save itself."

I got to admit, the guy knows how to talk to people. In spite of everything that just happened, the fight and the attitude swiftly returns to every man in the room again. All of us still respect his command. If we're going to get through this, it will be because Will kept his head right when the shit hit the fan.

Our team huddles up around Sarge and he relays our responsibilities.

"Okay listen up," says Sarge. "Gibby, you and I will post up by the east stairwell. Arnes and Harding, take the SAW and set up outside the west stairwell. Mac and Chase, we need eyes up on the rooftop. Even if we can't reach Nellis on the radio, there might still be some birds up in the sky that made it out of there. Bring some extra flares. Maybe you can hitch us a ride out of here."

"Copy that," I say.

"See Gunny on your way out and load up on ammo," Sarge says.

"What happens if the helo doesn't come, Sarge?" Gibby asks.

"I don't exactly have a lot of faith in the captain," I agree.

"Will is working on it," says Sarge.

"Those motherfuckers are eventually going to get inside here," Gibby says. "It's just a matter of time."

"East stairwell was still clear," Arnes says.

"We should get out while we still can," Harding agrees.

"Enough," Sarge says. "I know we got our backs against the wall, but we still have our orders. Do your jobs and we'll get out of here. And if those things do get inside before we bug out, then we won't go down without a fight."

Sarge waits to see if anyone has more concerns, but no one has anything else to say.

"Time to punch in," Sarge says. "Get to it."

CHAPTER SEVEN

Gunnery Sergeant Rocco Lewis and PFC Jackson Carver crouch on the floor next to a black bag filled with additional supplies and ammunition. The two men load rounds into some of the expended mags. Beside the two of them, Corporal Dom Collins and the Lieutenant continue to try and make contact on the long-range radio.

Mac and I walk over, and we each grab a couple boxes of 5.56 mm rounds from the bag. Since this was supposed to be a brief op, we left the bulk of our equipment back on the helicopter, opting for a pair of emergency caches of extra ammunition. Given how quickly we have had to burn through magazines, it seems like Gunny made the right call there. But if we can't get an extraction soon, we might live to regret it.

"How's the hand?" Gunny asks me.

"I'll live," I tell him.

"Is that the hand you use to pet the snake?" he asks. He jerks his hand up and down.

"No," I tell him.

"Then you'll probably live," Gunny tells me.

"Got any extra flares, Jax?" I ask PFC Carver.

Jax reaches into the bag beside him and pulls out several smoke flares and hands them to me.

Mac and I turn, walk across the maintenance room, and head for the roof access where the redhead is sitting on the steps, watching Doc work on stabilizing Pittman.

"Excuse us, Miss," Mac says as we approach the stairs.

The redhead stands up and moves to the side to let us pass.

"You doing okay?" Mac asks.

"I'm okay, I guess," she says.

Mac puts a hand on her shoulder.

"Hang in there," he says.

She tries to smile, but it seems like she might cry instead.

We move up the stairs and out onto the scorching rooftop in the middle of the desert. The sun is just starting to set, and hot gusts of dry air rush at us from the west. I follow Mac to the edge of the building and look out over the city, what is left of it anyway.

"Those things really know how to fuck shit up," I say. "I'll give them that."

"You ain't kidding," Mac agrees.

"Kind of hard to believe," I admit.

"What?" he asks.

"This," I say, gesturing a hand at the city. "That shit could get this bad."

"Nah, man," Mac shakes his head. He pulls his Wayfarer shades out of his pack and slips them over his eyes. "We had this coming for a long time. This kind of thing is inevitable. Part of nature. You should feel lucky."

"Lucky?" I ask.

"Yeah, Chase," he says. "Look around. You're lucky to be alive to see it. I mean, think about it. All those generations of people before us. All those civilizations. All the disasters, all the wars. None of that compares to being here for this. Probably the most important event in human history. You should feel fucking honored to be here. I do."

Mac drops his gear and takes his notebook out searches around his pockets until he pulls out a pen.

"You're fucking crazy, Mac," I shake my head.

He unbuttons his jacket, slips it off and drops it on the ground before he climbs on the edge of the building and sit down. He dangles his feet over the abyss.

"You might be right about that," he says as he flips to a blank page and scrawls words on the paper.

I get the feeling someone is watching us, and I turn around to find the redhead standing beside the access door. After I raise my hand to say hello, she begins walking toward us across the hot roof.

"Red queen coming up on our six," I mumble to Mac.

"She looking at me?" he asks.

"You're hanging halfway off a thirty-story building," I tell him. "Of course, she is fucking looking at you."

Mac smirks but just keeps scrawling away on the page.

"That looks kind of dangerous," Claire says.

"I like to live dangerously, baby," Mac purrs.

Claire scoffs as she crosses her arms and turns away.

"Don't mind him," I tell her. "He watches too many movies."

"It's fine," she says as she turns back around. "I wanted to say thank you. I am sorry about your friends—"

"Brothers," I correct her.

"Right," she says. "I'm sorry."

"Maybe you can tell us what all this was for," I say. "You must know something about everything that is happening. What are these fucking things?"

"I don't know," she sighs. "I have an idea what they are from a biological aspect, but I have no idea what may be causing it to happen."

"So, let's start with what you do know," Mac says.

"It's a long, complicated explanation," she says.

"I think she is saying we're too stupid, Chase," Mac says.

"That does sound like what she is saying," I agree.

"That's not what I meant," Claire sighs.

"Maybe you can dumb it down for us," he tells her.

"The company I used to work for has been researching genetic bioweapons for over a decade. These are weapons that can target a population based on specific factors of their DNA like their race or their gender."

"Like releasing a bubonic plague that only affects hajjis," Mac says.

"Something like that," Claire says.

"Sounds like a noble profession you got there," I say.

"I said I used to work for them. I don't work for them anymore," she says. "Along the way we made a discovery. In the scientific community they were being called, zombie genes."

"Zombie genes?" Mac says. "That is the stupidest thing I ever heard."

"It does sound pretty stupid," I agree.

"It was just a name people could attach to the concept," Claire explains. "We discovered that after death the human body continues to create enzymes; mRNA that transcribes certain DNA into proteins. Essentially, the dead body still tries to repair itself after death. To bring the dead body back to life."

"That doesn't happen," Mac says.

"Of course," she says. "These proteins are never produced in sufficient enough amounts to restart the mechanisms needed to keep the body alive, but if someone or something helps them along... then." She gestures at the things wandering around in the streets.

"How?" I ask her.

"That's the part I'm not sure about," she says. "A few years back, I was part of a team in South America. We tried a number of... experiments. We tried to trigger a similar response using chemical supplements prior to death, but never achieved any measurable success. The closest we came was Dr. Schoenheim, who used high doses of a very specific band of low-frequency microwave radiation to temporarily stimulate reanimation of lab rats. But there were too many complications.

"What kind of complications?" I say.

The subjects were unstable and never fully regained all their functions. So, Winters scraped the project once it proved to be unprofitable, although I truly believe he realized the potential for harm was too significant. I did, too, but I still believed it was better to try and understand everything that we could before the knowledge could potentially be used against us in the future. I was relieved when the company decided to focus the discoveries of our research to help better preserve organ donor tissues. It literally saved thousands of lives."

"Until now," Mac reminds her.

"I don't know for a fact that what we're seeing here is related to my work at all," she says. "This is all just speculation. The only reason I believe it's related is because you're here. Someone must have thought my work was somehow relevant."

"They said you might be able to help stop all this," I say. "Is that true?"

"I don't know," she says. "I mean, I will do everything I can, but I am just one piece of a very large puzzle. You wanted to know what your brothers died for here, and I'm telling you this so that you realize it hopefully won't be for nothing. I felt like I owed you that much for saving my life."

"You did," I tell her.

She presses her lips together and tilts her head back as she turns and heads back toward the access door. Maybe I'm an asshole, but I don't really feel good about losing our guys to save someone that may have had a hand in causing this, even if she had good intentions.

"You're welcome," I say as she gets to the door.

She glances back at me and gives me a half-assed salute.

"Fucking bitch," I grumble.

"Still say she's a seven," Mac says. He returns to scrawling in his note-book.

"Three," I say back.

"You said four," Mac reminds me.

"She's a three now," I tell him.

"Fucking hell," Mac says.

"What?" I ask him.

"My pen is out of ink," he says. He turns around and starts searching through his stuff for another pen.

"Some people just don't realize how evil they are," I say.

"Damn it," Mac says. "Do you got a pen?"

I shake my head and then he curses and walks back toward the access door.

"We're on watch up here," I remind him.

"I need a pen!" he calls back as he disappears down the stairs to the maintenance room.

Through the clouds of smoke, I watch the red sun sink into the gold mountain range along the western horizon. In the streets below I see those things wandering around in the dwindling light.

"Zombies," I mutter to myself. "Un-fucking-believable."

For years, I thought the world cannot possibly get any more fucked up, but then something like this happens. I'm not all philosophical like Mac or anything, but part of me thinks maybe we did have this coming. Most human beings pretend to be civilized. We like to think we have some higher purpose. But take that purpose away and we really are just animals. We will kill each other for no reason at all.

As night falls, the dwindling lights of Las Vegas still glow but the burning fires illuminate the city in a sinister glow. Mac returns, whistling some tune as he crosses the roof. If any of this is bothering him, he is doing a pretty good job of keeping it in.

"What's the word?" I ask him. "We getting out of here any time soon?"

"Nellis is still dark," he says. "Dom was able to reach Pendleton, but it sounds like shit is out of control there. No one has the resources available. Guess we're running low on helicopter pilots."

"Sounds like we're going to have to get ourselves out of here," I say.

"Probably," Mac agrees. "Lieutenant is on top of it. He'll figure something out."

"I hope so," I say. "We can't hold out up here forever."

Gunfire erupts inside the building. Shouts of alarm inside the maintenance room.

"Graves! Mackenzie!" Sarge barks over the comms. "Get your asses down here!"

CHAPTER EIGHT

I follow Mac down the stairs and we hurry through the maintenance room. Everyone is scrambling around, trying to mobilize our injured men and gather up the radio equipment and supplies.

"They're pushing through the west stairwell," Arnes yells over the comms.

The gunfire picks up as we make our way into the hall and head for the stairs in the west wing.

"We need to move now, Will," Sarge barks over the comms.

"Hold them off!" yells the lieutenant.

No one is bothering with standard radio protocols now. A sure sign that shit is getting bad real quick.

We hustle down the hall. Gibby, Sarge, Harding and Arnes lay down suppressive fire on the mob of the dead pushing through the barricade. The things just keep coming forward, one after another, climbing over the lifeless bodies as we shoot them down.

We must have drawn every walking stiff in town after that firefight in the casino.

"We're Oscar Mike," Will says on comms to let us know they are moving out.

The remnants of our platoon have to haul all our gear and Pittman. They won't be moving very fast and it will be up to us to keep the horde at bay.

"Hold them off us as long as you can, Sergeant," Will says. "Then head for the east stairwell and get down to the parking garage."

"Copy that," says Sarge. "We're right behind you."

The dead topple the pile of furniture and force the door open halfway. Several of them push through at a time now. Within a few minutes, they will come pouring through, but it won't matter because we don't have the ammunition to hold them off forever.

I pull the trigger and spot a few tracers marking the last rounds of my mag. I swap in a fresh mag and fire again.

Only five mags left before I'm out.

I space my shots a little more, trying to focus my fire and conserve my 150 remaining bullets.

Meanwhile, Arnes is tearing up the hallway with the SAW. Bullets splinter the furniture, sending chunks of wood and stuffing from the mattress flying in every direction. Arnes keeps his finger on the trigger of the light machine gun and sprays bullets at the dead with impunity.

"Focus your fire, Arnes," Sarge barks, but Arnes just holds the trigger down, the discipline from his years of training is gone.

"These fucks just keep coming," Arnes growls.

The dead crawl over the destroyed furniture. One of them completely clears the barricade before I put a round into the cranium of the fuck, and it collapses on the ground. There are at least a dozen more in the hallway behind it, and still more pushing through the door, which is flung wide open now.

"I'm out!" Arnes yells as he scoops up the SAW in his arms.

"Let's move!" Sarge calls back.

I keep firing as the guys retreat down the hall. After shredding the faces off a few of the corpses that get within twenty feet of me, the tracer rounds come out and tell me it's time to move. I turn and sprint down the hall to catch up with my team.

We bolt by the elevators and head for the stairs at the far side of the building, putting some distance between ourselves and the dead. I have no idea what the plan might be for now, other than running for our fucking lives. The only thing I know for sure is that we won't be sticking around here and waiting for a helicopter to rescue us.

Before we reach the stairwell, the entire building goes black. Without any windows, the hall is as dark as the inside of a coffin.

I try to slow myself down, but I bump into someone in the darkness. A fresh surge of pain hits me as my hand makes contact with something.

"Damn it," I curse as I double over in agony.

I flip down my night vision goggles to find Sarge fumbling with his rifle in the darkness.

"Fuck man, fuck, I'm sorry," Sarge pants. "You got to keep moving, Chase. They're coming."

We hit the door and begin taking the stairs two at a time. I grab the handrail to guide me in the darkness, but the sudden pain reminds me that isn't an option.

As we round the landing on the twenty-fourth floor, the door above us slams open and the sound of those things moaning fills the stairwell. The horde stumbles down the stairs after us, tipping over the railings and crashing onto the floors above us.

Getting down the stairs without stumbling is becoming increasingly difficult. I have to watch my feet through the unsteady goggles to make sure I don't miss a step, so I start to lag behind the rest of the squad. When I dare to look back up I discover the stairwell is empty in front of me. I glance back down at my feet, but it's already too late. My foot misses a step and I tumble forward. Unable to grab the railing and steady myself, I crash down the steps.

"Sarge!" I yell out. I cradle my mangled hand to my chest and reach down to grab my rifle off the ground with the other. I struggle to get to my knees and get moving again.

"Don't quit on me," Sarge yells. He yanks me up by my arm and hauls me onto my feet.

With Sarge pushing me to move faster, I limp down the stairs. We finally reach the main floor. My knee will probably hurt like hell later, if I live long enough for it to swell up.

We keep going down to the sub-level and follow a long hallway that leads to an underground parking garage. Muzzle flashes flicker in the darkness as the guys up front engage the dead inside the garage.

"Clear!" someone yells.

"We only have minutes," says Will. "Let's get some vehicles and get our asses out of here."

"On it," says Jax. He holds up a pair of car keys he pulled out of the pocket of a corpse and clicks the button. Headlights flash on the other end of the garage, and Jax dashes off to retrieve the vehicle.

"Gibby!" Arnes yells as he jabs out the window of an old electrical repair van with the butt of the shotgun. "I got this one. Get that truck over there."

"I don't know how to hot wire a truck!" Gibby yells.

"I thought you were from the ghetto?" Arnes shakes his head before he ducks inside the van.

"I got it," says Mac. He opens the door of the truck and climbs in to the driver seat.

"Hurry it up," Sarge reminds them.

"Just start getting in," Arnes tells the rest of us as he reaches below the steering wheel.

Sarge helps me over to the back of the van and I crowd in with Doc, Sykes, what is left of Pittman, and the redhead. There is hardly room for all of us with all the electrical supplies in the back. The engine of the van turns over and the headlights illuminate the inside of the garage.

"Here they come!" someone yells.

Sarge leaves me in the van and moves to engage the corpses. The door to the access tunnel smashes into the concrete wall and the things start moaning as they rush into the garage. They are greeted with a barrage of 5.56 mm rounds. A moment later, the truck engine fires up as well.

"Let's go, go, go!" yells the lieutenant before he hops into the Hummer that Jax acquired.

Arnes slams on the gas and pulls the truck out of the parking space. I notice Claire losing her balance and toppling over, so I hold out my arm to steady her. All I end up doing is causing myself a ton of pain.

"Fuck!" I growl as I retract my hand and clutch it to my chest.

The van crashes through the thin metal door to the garage and out into the night. Tires screech as Arnes swerves around the road.

"Will. Where the fuck are we going?" he yells into the comms.

"Take a right up here, Arnes," responds the lieutenant.

Arnes tells us to hold on and cranks the wheel to the right. The force of the turn causes Doc to lose his balance and fall forward. He places a hand on the floor beside Pittman to steady himself.

Then he seems to notice something.

Doc turns his head to the side and leans down close to Pittman.

"Damn it!" yells Doc.

"What is it?" I ask him.

"Pittman stopped breathing," Doc says.

"When?" I ask him.

"I don't know," Doc says as he reaches a hand behind him to grab his medical supplies. "I need to start CPR."

I glance up at Pittman and notice that his eyes are open.

"Shit," I say and fumble with my rifle, but I remember the mag is empty. "Doc!"

Doc jerks away as Pittman sits up and grabs onto him. He sinks his teeth into Doc's jugular and rips out a chunk of meat. Blood sprays all over. It even splatters the front windshield of the van.

"I can't see!" Arnes yells right before we slam into something in the road.

The van lifts off the ground and tosses us around as the vehicle flips over. Tools, ladders, spools of electric wire and bodies fly around the rear compartment. I hear Claire screaming and Pittman snarling, and then the van crashes down on its side and skids to a stop in the middle of the road.

CHAPTER NINE

After we come to a stop, I open my eyes. Through the hole in the windshield, I spot Arnes lying in the middle of the road. Hunks of the windshield are embedded in his face and blood trickles down to the pavement.

I hear someone moan inside the van.

It could be Pittman. It could be Doc. Hell, it could be anybody.

I feel around for my rifle, but I can't locate it in the dark, so I pull out my sidearm. As soon as I have it out of the holster, Pittman lunges at me out of the darkness. I fire off two rounds from the nine-mil into his face at point-blank range. His body collapses on top of me and goes limp.

"Claire," I call out into the dark as I shove Pittman off me.

"Here," she moans back. Claire sits up and crawls over the copper wiring and tools to get to me.

"Come on," I urge her.

The back door of the van pops open and a trio of flashlights illuminates the interior.

"Damn," Gibby mumbles when he sees the chaos.

"Come on," Sarge urges us. They help Claire out while I take a look back inside the van.

Sykes is doubled over against the front seats with his neck at an awkward angle. His eyes are open and pupils fixed. I lean to the side and see Harding in the front passenger seat but his face is smashed, his brains spilling out onto the dashboard. I finally locate my rifle and climb out of the chaos.

The rest of my team covers me while I limp toward the overloaded pickup truck. Sergeant Lowe and Corporal Hurst have to reach down and haul me up into the truck bed as the remaining members of my squad hold off the dead closing in around us. Sarge bangs on the fender of the truck as he hops on and then Zamora peels out and speeds into the night.

"What the fuck happened back there?" Sarge asks me.

"Pittman," I say. "He turned into one of those things and attacked Doc. I couldn't stop him. Then Arnes lost control."

"Listen, it's not your fault, man," Sarge says. "Nothing you could have done."

Maybe if I had two hands I could have done something.

"We ain't out of this shit yet," Sarge says. "I need you back in this fight, Marine. You copy?"

Hurst, Lowe, Gibby, and Mac call out different targets and open fire as Zamora follows the Humvee down the side streets. I look down at my hand, feeling useless.

"Hey," Sarge says. "Don't you fucking quit on me, Corporal."

"Yes, sir," I manage to say.

Sarge grabs my helmet off the bed of the truck and places it on my head. Then he bangs the top of it down with his fist.

"You're a badass motherfucking Marine," he reminds me, then he turns and covers his ear so he can hear the lieutenant on the comms.

"We need to get out of this city," says Will. "Then we can find a place to hole up until dawn."

"Will," says Zamora. "I sure hope you know where the fuck we're going, homie."

"We got navigation," says the lieutenant. "Garmin is leading the way."

"The world's greatest fighting force in the world and we're relying on commercial-grade GPS in a stolen Hummer," says Mac.

"Sir," says Sarge. "We're nearly black on ammo back here."

"Then Corporal Zamora better make sure he keeps up," Will says.

"Copy that, sir," Zamora says.

As the vehicles speed up, I twist my body around and get to a kneeling position in the back with my M4 propped on the wall of the truck. I manage to swap in a fresh mag and flip down my NVGs and scan the street for targets. The rifle still feels all wrong, and I keep adjusting my grip on the hand stop to try to compensate for my missing digits. I finally pull the trigger and fire a burst at one of the green figures about twenty meters out. Every bullet misses.

"Fuck," I curse myself.

I pull the trigger again and this time the bullets hit home. The body collapses on the street.

"Goddamn Graves," says Gibby. "You're a better shot with one hand than Mac is with two."

"Normally, I'd take exception to that," Mac says. "But Graves is a cold-blooded killer."

The guys are just trying to help, and it does, a little. But I know I'm just not as effective as I could be. I glance up at Sarge and notice he is staring at my injured hand. I grin to let him know I'm still in this fight.

"Enough fucking around," Sarge chimes in. "I'm getting tired of getting our shit pushed in, so stay fucking frosty."

We pass by a gentleman's club with half-devoured strippers on the sidewalk. The dimmed neon sign in the window that says "LIVE NUDE GIRLS" is clearly outdated now. Abandoned vehicles, debris, broken glass, and bodies fill the streets. Some of them are already starting to smell from being out in the desert heat all day.

I mentally count the rounds left in my mags until I am completely out. One hundred fourteen bullets. The scary thing is, I probably have the most rounds left out of all of us.

The Hummer hooks a left turn and the pickup follows cautiously down a narrow residential street. Parked cars line the curbs on either side of our vehicles.

"Help!" a young girl slides open a second-story window on one of the houses and sticks her head out. "Help me! Please!"

Her yelling draws moans from the dead all around us. They emerge from alleys and doorways, swarming toward the street in droves. The line of parked vehicles prevents the dead from reaching us. Even if we tried we couldn't possibly help that woman. We would all just end up dead.

"Shut up lady," Gibby grumbles.

She curses and screams at us as we roll away. The horde surrounds her building. Even after she closes the window, the dead remain outside. They moan and pound away at the front door.

"We should have helped her," Sarge says.

"That's not our mission," I remind him.

"Would have been the right thing to do," Sarge says.

"I'm starting to feel like shooting her would have been the right thing to do there," says Gibby.

We reach Nellis Boulevard and take a left turn to head north toward the airfield. In the distance, a massive fire burns, and a huge cloud of smoke drifts up to the sky.

"Is that the basc?" I ask Sarge.

"Has to be," Sarge says.

"Looks like the party is already over," says Mac.

"Listen up," Will says on the comms. "We need to recon Nellis. Stay frosty and maintain dispersal, copy?"

Sarge hesitates as he looks at the fiery military installation in the distance.

"Do you copy, Sergeants?" Will repeats.

"Copy," answers Sergeant Lowe.

"Sir," says Sarge. "Not to question your orders, but that base looks pretty wasted."

"Unless you guys feel like rolling around in civilian vehicles with no ammo, we have to recon the base and salvage some supplies," says the lieutenant. "If you have another option Sergeant, I'm listening."

"Negative, sir," says Sarge. "Solid copy. Over."

The convoy rolls on.

"This is a bad idea," says Mac.

I get a bad feeling I can't shake either, but I keep my mouth shut. As much as I don't like it, I know the lieutenant is right. If we don't figure out a way to improve our situation we will not last very long out here. Complaining about it won't make anything better.

"Our first priority is to hit up the armory," the lieutenant says. "Then we will head for the motor pool."

We pull up to the roundabout at the entrance, with corpses wandering around the burning guard posts. The Hummer rams through bodies, sending them skidding down the grass embankments beside the road.

The inside of the base is worse than a fucking war zone. Hundreds of the dead shamble around the grounds. As soon as they hear the engines of our vehicles, those things swarm toward our position.

"Don't shoot unless they grab onto the truck," Sarge says. "Conserve ammo."

We pass by the BX and the officers club, both of which are also on fire.

"Left on Range Road," the lieutenant says over the comms.

We make the turn and drive down a road lined with vast rows of solar panels. About half a mile down we turn into a parking lot for the gun range and the armory. We climb out of the truck and scan the area. Several of the recently departed wander through the solar panels, but we seem to be far enough away from the other facilities that there are not too many immediate threats.

"Let's move," says the lieutenant. "Five minutes. Graves, wait out here with Miss Davies. You radio at the first sign of trouble, copy?"

"Copy, sir," I tell him and I move over to the Hummer to post up outside the vehicle as the rest of the guys run inside.

A few gunshots ring out before the guys call out clear on the comms. I glance at Claire and notice her eyes on the building.

"Don't worry," I tell her. "They got it under control in there."

Claire glances down at my injured hand. I turn to the side casually to prevent her from staring at it.

"I'm trying..." she begins, but then seems to lose the thought. I notice how tired she looks. She probably hasn't slept in nearly two days by now.

"Pardon ma'am?" I say.

"I'm not sure I can get used to living like this," she says. "I don't know how you guys do it."

"No choice," I tell her.

"I guess you're right about that," Claire says. She tilts her head back and rests her head on the back of the seat and closes her eyes. She seems to doze off so I continue to scan the area through my NVGs. A little snore sneaks out of her nostrils and then her eyes jerk open again and she lifts her head. She glances around.

"What was that?" she asks.

"I believe you woke yourself up when you started snoring, ma'am," I inform her.

She raises a hand up and shields her eyes.

"I'm sorry," she mumbles.

"It's okay," I tell her. "You should try to sleep if you can, ma'am."

"Please, stop calling me ma'am," she says.

"Shh," I tell her.

Something scuffles over the sands nearby, but I can't locate the source. I listen as I scan the darkened shapes surrounding us for movement. I raise my rifle to a firing position and keep scanning the area near the corner of the building where the sounds are coming from.

"Nightmare One," I whisper into the comms. "I'm hearing some activity out here, but I don't have a visual."

"Hold tight, Graves," says the Lieutenant. "We will be out in two Mikes. Over."

Something moans and I hear glass shattering.

"Stay in the car," I tell Claire as I advance toward the building. I shoulder the rifle and pull out my sidearm. I know I need to keep the brainiac in the Hummer safe, but I don't want those things getting inside and taking the squad by surprise. I catch a glimpse of the stiff, moving slowly out of the shadow of the building and I pull the trigger.

The first shot hits it in the neck and it gurgles. I fire again and hit it in the skull. It groans and drops to its knees, and then the stiff topples over and lands face first in the sand. I start to lower the pistol until I hear another moan.

I take a few steps to the left to see around the side of the building and more shapes begin to emerge. There are dozens of the things coming at us from a trailer park a couple of hundred meters behind the armory.

"We need to go now," I call into the comms as I make a run for the Hummer.

Several seconds later, the doors to the armory swing open, and Mac and Sarge hustle out carrying a bag between them. Gibby hauls out as many weapons as he can carry. I holster the nine-mil to switch back to my M4 and begin firing at the dead as they round the corner of the building. The recoil makes it difficult to focus my fire with much accuracy so I run through a mag in a matter of seconds trying to slow the damn things down. My team loads the munitions into the back of the truck and then they begin firing

on the dead. Tracer rounds streak through the darkness, so I pull the trigger

once more and swap in a fresh mag.

The lieutenant bursts through the door, followed by Corporal Collins.

Each holds one end of another heavy bag. Corpses focus on the closer prey

and start trudging toward the entrance, ignoring the vehicles.

"Get ready to move!" the lieutenant yells as he waves his free arm to urge

us to get back in the trucks.

Gunny and Sergeant Lowe push through the doors with another bag as

the dead close in on the entrance. The first of the dead bastards reach their

position and Gunny reaches back and slugs it in the face as the thing lunges

for him.

"Shit stain!" Gunny barks.

The two men have no choice but to drop the bag and raise up their

weapons to open fire on the corpses that surround them. More and more

of the dead emerge from the darkness. Some of the population from the

base is approaching through the solar farm.

We are running out of time.

"Get ready to move, Corporal!" the lieutenant says to me as he reaches

the Hummer.

We still have people inside the building. Zamora, Carrasco, Hurst, and

Carver have yet to return. Reluctantly, I open the door and squeeze in the

backseat of the vehicle beside Claire, then I prop my rifle and lay down some more fire through the window. From this distance, in the dark, with dozens of moving targets, we hardly even slow them down.

"Javi! Eddie! Get the fuck out of there!" Sergeant Lowe yells over the comms.

The things encircle the building, cutting off the rest of our platoon. Gunny and Lowe keep firing as they backpedal to the Hummer, even though the lieutenant is yelling for them to get inside the vehicles.

"My guys are still in there!" Lowe screams. "I'm not fucking bailing on them!"

"We are leaving, Sergeant!" yells Will.

Gunny climbs in behind the wheel as Will hops in the passenger seat. Sergeant Lowe keeps firing at the corpses as they pour into the front door of the armory. A segment of the mob splits off from the crowded entrance and focuses on the vehicles. Colin keeps firing until his mag runs dry, then he swaps to a new mag.

"Get in this truck right now, Sergeant!" the lieutenant barks, but Lowe just keeps shooting at the dead.

Rifles rattle inside the building.

"Hurst is down!" yells Eddie on comms.

"Fuck, we got to go back in there!" Colin yells.

The lieutenant doesn't answer right away. He looks at Gunny who shakes his head. He knows we can't go back even if we want to.

"We're boxed in," Zamora comes through on the comms. "I'll keep them busy as long as I can, sir."

"No!" insists Sergeant Lowe. "Get your ass back out here, Javi!"

"Go get him," the lieutenant says to Gunny.

Gunny gets out and opens the back door. He grabs Lowe by the collar and yanks him toward the truck. I scoot over as Gunny tosses him into the backseat and slams the door. Lowe loses his shit and curses at Gunny as he accelerates away from the armory. A frag grenade explodes inside the building as we pull out of the parking lot, then there are three more explosions in short succession.

I can't think of anything to say. Colin just lost his whole squad. Nothing will make that any easier. I just put a hand on his shoulder as we flee the endless throngs of the dead.

CHAPTER TEN

My hand throbs as I stare at the blood-soaked bandage. I try to put the pain out of my mind as the convoy speeds down the road toward the airfield. The lieutenant assures us that we will be able to requisition more adequate vehicles.

"I sure hope you're right. We're running on fumes here, sir," Sarge informs him.

"What the fuck is that?" Gunny blurts as he stares through the window at something along the right side of the road. A tall fence topped with barbed wire separates the street from a huge field. In the distance, the shape of a large building looms. Several raging bonfires burn out front. I hear the faint pop of small arms firing in the distance and spot figures moving around in the firelight.

The lieutenant consults the onboard navigation and then looks back out the window.

"That's a correctional facility," Will says.

"Looks like somebody let the inmates out," Gunny says.

"Fuck," says the lieutenant. "Get us out of here Gunny. We don't need more problems right now."

Gunny pushes the gas down as bullets ping off the side of the vehicle. The prisoners have definitely spotted us on the road.

"Nightmare One," Sarge says. "We're taking fire back here."

"Copy that, Rodriguez," says Will. "That is a prison to our nine o'clock. We're going to push passed it. Keep your heads down. Over."

More shots zip passed the Hummer and I turn my body to shield Claire from any bullets. We lost too many of our guys to let something happen to this woman now.

A round ruptures one of our tires with a loud pop a second before the Hummer swerves to the side of the road. Gunny curses as he maneuvers the wheel to steady the speeding vehicle, but the damage is done. The rims grind against the pavement as the tire runs flat.

"Don't slow down!" the lieutenant orders him.

Gunny keeps the pedal to the metal, even as the tire shreds away and sparks fly up into the night. I can see the airfield ahead in the dim glow of dawn on the horizon. We just have to make it another half a mile and hope to god the whole damn motor pool isn't overrun with the dead.

As we near the intersection, the gunfire from the prison tapers off. I glance over and notice pairs of headlights outside the massive buildings.

"Looks like they're coming after us," I tell the lieutenant.

He glances back over his shoulder.

"I've had about enough of this shit," the lieutenant growls. "Stop the truck, Gunny."

Gunny brings the Hummer to a stop in the intersection. The brakes on the pickup squeal behind us. The pair of vehicles form a blockade across the intersection.

"You sure you want to do this, sir?" Gunny asks.

"I'm done fucking around," the lieutenant says.

He opens the door and steps out of the truck. Will positions himself behind the hood with his rifle pointed at the vehicles and men approaching us on the road. Sergeant Lowe takes up a shooting position behind the trunk of the Hummer and I scoot closer to the window and prop my gun in the opening.

A mob of men marches up the road alongside a pair of pickup trucks. Some of the prisoners appear to have shotguns and pistols, but most of them carry makeshift weapons. They notice our vehicles stopped in the road and charge toward us.

"Those men aren't dead," Claire says.

"They will be soon," I inform her.

"Stop this," she begs me.

I ignore her so she sticks her head out the window and pleads with Lieutenant Reasoner.

"They can always turn around instead of dying," he tells her.

"This is insane," she complains.

"They're criminals," Sergeant Lowe reminds her. "The less of them there are now the better."

"That's not the point," she says.

Will fires a warning burst from his rifle. The men in prison jumpsuits duck in the road as the bullets fly over their heads.

"Stay the fuck back!" Will yells.

The prisoners seem to pause for a moment, then begin sprinting toward us, yelling and screaming like a bunch of fucking savages.

"Engage!" Will orders and we unleash hell.

The hail of bullets stops their advance in an instant. The unfortunate ones in the front of the pack get chewed up and drop to the ground. Their bodies trip up the men behind them.

Bullets punch holes in the windshields of the pickup trucks. One rolls off the road into the ditch. The horn blares as the dead driver slumps against the steering wheel. The other truck wheels around, plowing over several prisoners as it speeds away.

As the mob turns to run the other way, we keep firing. Bullets tear through the backs of the men. By the time Will tells us to cease fire, there are only a handful of prisoners still fleeing. The rest are either dead or writhing on the ground in pain.

The whole thing only lasts about a minute.

It wasn't a fight. It was a slaughter.

"Mount up," the lieutenant says and the men of Nightmare Platoon return to the vehicles.

"What the hell is wrong with all of you?" Claire asks.

"We're doing our jobs," says Will. "We're keeping you safe. Let's go, Gunny."

Gunny accelerates the broke-ass Hummer and we grind along the road.

"You murdered them," Claire insists.

The lieutenant doesn't answer but turns to look out the passenger window at the horde of the dead headed for us. All our gunfire out on the perimeter road drew them away from the fires near the BX and the private military industrial buildings. There are so many of those things that it looks like a massive audience for a concert as they wander through the sandy desert.

"Did the world a fucking favor," Sergeant Lowe mumbles.

"It was wrong," Claire pushes back.

"Wrong?" The lieutenant spins around. "You think that was wrong? Look around, lady. I lost seventeen men to save your sorry ass, and you don't see anything wrong with that fucking picture?"

The lieutenant swivels back around in his seat.

"How about you just show a little goddamn appreciation for the sacrifice those guys made and shut the fuck up?" Will says.

Silence fills the vehicle.

Maybe I should feel bad about what just happened, but that doesn't mean I do. I lost some of my brothers in all this.

Hell, I lost half my fucking hand.

If it comes down to it, I'm willing to kill anybody that gets in the way before I accept losing any more than I already have.

We grind to a stop in front of a row of long storage buildings alongside the airfield. We scan the columns of parked fighter jets and drones on the tarmac.

"There's the motor pool," says Sergeant Lowe. "Ten o'clock."

Gunny turns the wheel and steers between the hangars. This area of the base is eerily empty, but with the dead on the way that won't last long. We pull to a stop beside a fleet of Humvees and get out.

"Let's load this shit up quick," says the lieutenant before he opens the door.

After Claire exits the truck, I follow her out and escort her to one of the Humvees.

"Out of one Hummer and into another," she sighs and climbs in the rear passenger seat.

"This is a Humvee," I tell her. "It's got armor and shit."

"I liked the leather seats better," she says.

"Suck it up," I tell her. I close the door and try not to let her complaints get to me, but I'm tired and she is the last person I want to listen to right now. The rest of the guys are grabbing the bags of supplies and ammunition out of the truck, so I go over to give them a hand instead.

"We got this," Sarge tells me as I reach for a bag.

I give him an annoyed look.

"Just because my hand is fucked up—" I start to say but Sarge interrupts me.

"That's not what I meant, Chase," Sarge says. "Chill out, bro."

I take a deep breath and watch as Sarge and Mac remove the bag from the truck bed. I walk alongside them as they carry it over to the Humvee.

"Hold up," Sarge tells Mac before they load it up. He pats me on the chest with the back of his hand. "I got you something, man."

He unzips the bag and pulls out a rifle and hands it to me.

"What's this?" I ask. I turn it to inspect it and my mouth drops open. "Is this a fucking Honey Badger?"

"Told you he'd like that shit," he says to Mac.

Mac bends down and zips the bag back up, then he stands up and smiles when he sees me checking out the gun.

"Holy fuck," I smile, in spite of all the shit that has happened. This assault rifle costs like three grand. It has a telescopic stock, signature suppression, and chambers .300 Blackout rounds. The shorter seven-inch barrel makes it only slightly bulkier than a submachine gun, but with all the firepower of an assault rifle. It is an efficient dealer of death.

"Spoils of war," Sarge says.

"It's fucking light," I say assessing its weight.

"You be careful with that," Mac teases me. "Don't shoot your eye out."

I know these guys only grabbed this for me because I fucked up my hand. This rifle should be easier to handle than the M4. Maybe they did it out of pity, but I don't care. It still means a lot to me to know they got my back.

"Thanks, Sarge," I say.

"What about me?" Mac says. "I helped carry it."

"You didn't do shit," Sarge says.

"Hurry the fuck up!" the lieutenant yells. "I don't feel like dying today."

"Come on," Sarge says. "You got the wheel, Graves."

I climb in and start the engine as the dead round the corner of the hangar behind us. They hear the rumble of the Humvees and start moaning and hobbling as fast as their fucked up bodies will carry them.

We roll onto the highway and leave Las Vegas behind us. The throbbing pain in my hand returns once again. Maybe it was there the whole time. I was just too riled up to notice it.

Once the adrenaline is gone, that's when the real battle begins. When you have to deal with the pain and the loss. I'd heard that from guys who had really been in the shit before, and now I understand it.

CHAPTER ELEVEN

"We're going to pull over at that gas station up ahead," the lieutenant informs us over the comms.

We are just a half hour outside of Vegas. The 24-hour travel stop appears desolate in the middle of the desert. Several cars, semi trucks, and a taco truck are stationed in the parking lot.

But the place seems empty.

After everything we've been through, I still pull the Humvee into the service station cautiously and keep my eyes peeled for any movement.

The interior lights are on in the shop, but there are no signs of activity inside. Blood streaks the glass of the doorway, and the interior lights reveal rows of empty shelves inside.

"Looks like somebody cleaned this place out already," says Gibby.

"Probably got out of the city, loaded up, and headed for the mountains," says Mac. "That's what anyone with a lick of common sense would have done."

We climb out of the truck, and I keep my head on a swivel as we approach the store. Sarge, Gunny, and the lieutenant trail along behind us, covering our backs. I push the door open and the bell jingles over my head. I wait to see if the sound attracts any attention, but the inside of the store stays quiet so I proceed inside.

Several empty rows of shelf fixtures occupy the right half of the storefront. Cleaned-out beverage coolers line the rear wall. To the left, a couple of aisles of maroon booths lead back to a sandwich counter.

"Looks clear," I call out.

The remnants of Nightmare Company move inside, glancing around at the barren interior. Claire sighs when she steps through the door and looks around. She moves over to one of the booths and sits down, laying her arms across the table and using them like a pillow to rest her head.

"They took everything," I say as I stare at the empty store. I spin an empty rotating display rack on the counter. "Even the fucking keychains."

"That's not accurate," says Mac as he walks out from behind the counter. "They left the attendant. Most of him anyway."

I peer over the counter and see a man in a gas station uniform slumped on the floor. Close-range shotgun blasts left a blossom of wounds to his chest and a gaping hole where his face used to be.

"Corporal Collins?" the lieutenant hollers.

Collins leaves the truck and jogs over to the building.

"Yes, sir," says Collins.

"See if you can get anyone on the radio," says Will. "Hopefully we can figure out what the fuck we're supposed to do with Miss Davies now."

"Copy, sir," Collins says and he jogs back to the truck to grab the long-range radio.

"I don't want to stay here any longer than we have to, so take a break but don't get too comfortable," the lieutenant tells the rest of us.

I follow the rest of the guys over to the closest booth and set my rifle down on the table. The throbbing pain in my fingers is so intense that it seems to resonate throughout my body. I even have a splitting headache, but maybe that's from clenching my teeth as I endured the pain for so long.

"I have to take a piss," I tell the guys before I head to the bathroom. Even though I have had to go for a while now, I also just need a minute alone.

The bathroom smells of urinal pucks and mold. I stand in front of the sink for a minute and unravel the bloody bandage around my hand. The painful sting as I pry the crusted material off my skin causes my vision to momentarily blur.

My hand is crusted in dried blood. Bone fragments stick out from the partial segments of my fingers. A sickly opaque puss oozes from the tissue.

I lean in to sniff the wound, but can't detect anything.

With my other hand, I attempt to touch it out of some morbid curiosity to see how bad it will hurt. The instant I touch the remains of my middle finger, I flinch from the searing pain. The top half of my pinky which was hanging by a thread of skin falls off from my sudden movement. It lands in the stained porcelain sink and slides down toward the drain.

"Fuck," I curse.

I pick it up, but can't figure out what I should do with it. So I wrap it in several paper towels and shove it into my pocket. Then I put down my pack and take out a bandage. I rewrap my fingers in the clean dressing and step over to the urinal. I tilt my head back and stare at the ceiling tiles while I piss.

In spite of everything, at least I'm still alive, but I feel like I don't deserve to be. My eyes close, but then I feel lightheaded and nearly lose my balance. I step back and zip up and leave the bathroom.

I come back out and walk back over to the booths. Mac glances up from his notebook and gives me a strange look.

"You all right?" Mac asks me.

I avoid his stare and look out the window where Gunny, Sarge, and Gibby are keeping an eye on the perimeter.

"Just tired, I think," I tell him.

"You look like hell," he says.

"I'll be fine," I insist.

Near the front register, the lieutenant and Collins send out calls over the radio.

"They make contact with anyone yet?" I ask Mac.

Mac shrugs as he continues writing in his notebook. Even as the world is going to hell his writing is still more urgent. Seems crazy to me. If we don't figure out some way to resolve this clusterfuck, there won't be anyone around to even read that stupid shit.

I leave Mac to his writing and make my way to the booths at the end of the row and listen in as Will transmits on the radio. Beside him, Collins fiddles with the antenna, while Claire sits on top of a table across the aisle.

"Any luck, sir?" I ask them.

The lieutenant pulls off his kevlar helmet and combs a finger through his short brown hair.

"Camp Pendleton is gone," Will informs me. "Miramar. All of it."

Although it doesn't come as a total shock after everything that has happened today, it still hits home to hear it from Will.

"So what is the plan?" I ask him.

"Hang on," says the Lieutenant. He reaches over and raps his knuckle against the window and waves the guys inside. Gunny puts out his cigarette and then he follows Sarge and Gibby around to the entrance.

"I made contact with a secure facility about 130 klicks northeast of our position," says Will. "As far as I can tell, that's our best option right now."

"130 klicks northeast?" Sarge says. "That's..."

"Area 51," Claire says.

"Apparently, she's been there before," says Will. "Once we escort her up there, we can pack it in. Head home. So let's get moving."

We grab our shit and drag our tired asses back out to the Humvees. Once we're out in the hot sun, I start to feel woozy again. Maybe it's from the amount of blood that I lost, or because we haven't had much to eat since all this started. As I climb behind the wheel, everything starts to go black. I hang on to the door to keep from falling over. I squint my eyes and shake my head to fight the sensation off.

"Shit," Mac says as he hurries to my side to help support me. "Sarge, we got a problem here."

"I'm fine," I insist, even though I feel pretty fucking far from fine.

"I'm not a doctor," Claire tells Sarge from the backseat of the Humvee. "But if I had to guess I'd say he probably has an infection."

"What can I do to help him?" Sarge asks.

"Get him to a doctor," she says. "And fast."

"You better drive, Mac," Sarge says.

"Yes, sir," Mac says as he helps me into the backseat beside Claire.

Sarge moves around the truck and climbs in the passenger seat. He looks back at me and I can see the concern on his face.

"Hang in there, Graves," Sarge says.

"I'm too fucking tough to die, sir," I smirk.

I don't want him worrying about me.

"Damn straight, devil dog," Sarge grins.

The engine rumbles to life and we get back on the deserted highway through the vast and unforgiving desert. I lay my head back and stare out at the blinding sun that hangs above the distant mountains in the clear blue sky. After a couple of miles, my eyes start to burn, so I turn my head the other way and find Claire staring at me, her fingers wrapped around the barrel of a nine-mil. I wonder briefly where and when she got it.

"Don't worry," I tell her. "I meant it. I'm too tough to die."

"I probably couldn't hit a damn thing with it anyway," Claire smiles and she hands the gun back to me.

"Keep it," I tell her. "Just in case I'm wrong. I've been wrong before. Once or twice."

"That's very thoughtful of you," she smiles.

"You just got to promise me one thing," I say.

"What's that?" she asks.

"You have to swear that you will shoot Mac if he starts singing," I say.

"I hear every word you're saying back there, Chase," Mac chimes in.

"Promise me," I insist.

"Is it really that bad?" she asks.

I nod my head.

"He's just jealous of my incredible talent," Mac says. He starts belting out a song, one of his driving favorites by REO Speedwagon.

"Shoot him," I whisper loudly.

"Shut up, Mac," Sarge says.

"Come on, Sarge," Mac says. "I need to defend my honor here."

"Your honor?" Claire laughs.

"Hell yeah, I have honor. You see, I am a man of knowledge and culture, not just some neanderthal killing machine like my jarhead colleague back there." Mac continues.

"Shut up, Mac!" Sarge repeats.

After thirty hours of no sleep, we're all starting to reach our limits and losing our focus. But for just a minute there, everything felt normal again. Just four people riding along in a car, getting on each other's nerves.

"So what were you up there for before?" I ask Claire. "In Area 51. You must have been involved in some super secret squirrel shit."

"I'm not really supposed to talk about that," she tells me.

"I thought you'd say that," I say.

"Don't worry, I never saw any aliens there or anything like that," she says.

"Thank god," says Mac. "I honestly do not think I could handle seeing a zombie and an alien on the same fucking day."

"Mac," says Sarge. "Shut the fuck up and watch the road."

"The truth is actually rather dull," she says. "They only let me examine samples of alien DNA."

"What?" Sarge says.

The Humvee is silent for a long moment. She gives me a sneaky smile then turns to look at the desert out the window.

"She was joking, right?" Mac says.

I'm not sure whether this gal is messing with us or not, but it helps keep our minds off the bad shit we've been through out here. I've got to admit,

I feel bad for giving her a hard time before. Maybe this chick isn't so bad after all.

CHAPTER TWELVE

"Hold up," says the Lieutenant when we reach the outskirts of a small town.

Mac brings the Humvee to a stop behind the lead vehicle in the middle of Great Basin Highway. Sarge gets out to join the lieutenant and Gunny while they scope out a pair of vehicles a couple hundred yards up the road.

I feed some subsonic .300 Blackout ammo into empty mags for the Honey Badger. Focusing on something else distracts me from the nauseous feeling I have been battling during our drive through the desert. I'm not the type to get motion sickness. I take it as another sign that something is not right. I'm getting sick.

"The pickups are shot to shit," Gunny says. "Looks like the work of a fitty cal."

"You think somebody cleared the town out for us already?" says Sarge.

"It's possible," the lieutenant says. "I'm not seeing any movement."

He lowers the binoculars.

"We could play it safe," Gunny says. "Backtrack to that dirt road a few miles back and try to cut through the mountains."

"If we get lost on some of these backroads and run out of gas in the middle of the desert we may never get there," says Will. "Let's punch through."

"I'm with you, sir," Sarge says. "We don't have time to fuck around. Graves needs to get some medical attention soon."

"Be ready to rock and roll in case we run into trouble," says Will before he and Gunny return to the lead vehicle.

As we approach the bullet-riddled wrecks, Mac follows the other Humvee off the road. I situate my rifle in the window so I am ready to fire at anything that moves.

The door of one of the trucks creaks open and a body flops out on the ground. The thing is so shot up it can only move one arm, but I engage it anyway. I kind of just want to test out the new rifle. The Honey Badger spits out a bullet that rips through the skull of the corpse. It collapses and splatters gore across the pavement.

Sarge looks back at me from the front seat.

"I fucking love this thing already, Sarge" I tell him.

He smiles and turns back to look at the town. The rifle is compact and lighter than my M4, but still tears through bodies with ease. The Trash Panda silencer makes it incredibly quiet in comparison, too.

"You look like you need a minute alone with that thing," Claire says. "Should I close my eyes?"

"Very funny," I shake my head as I turn back and position the rifle in the window as we pull into town.

Bodies lie in the dirt along the street in front of shot up buildings and mobile homes. A number of other structures are nothing more than smoldering heaps. The tires nudge aside spent bullet casings that ring like faint chimes as they roll along the pavement.

"Keep your eyes peeled," Sarge reminds us.

"Whoever came through here and wiped out this town was pretty thorough," I say.

"This wasn't a bunch of trigger happy locals," says Mac. "This was military. They even killed the dogs."

I look over and notice the lifeless body of a big Rottweiler in the grass.

"Like someone is trying to sterilize the place by wiping out anything that's alive," says Sarge.

"Probably the Air Force," says Mac, gesturing at an impact crater. "They bombed the hell out this place."

We roll out of town and proceed up the highway. About ten miles down the road we reach another smaller town that was also wiped out. The buildings are mostly reduced to ashes or rubble. We drive around another giant impact crater in the center of town and take a left on to Extra Terrestrial Highway.

When we reach Groom Lake Road, a sign warns against trespassing on Air Force grounds. We proceed up the gravel pass that climbs the mountains.

Sarge pokes his head out the window and looks up at the sky.

"What's wrong?" asks Mac.

"I think we got a drone watching us," Sarge says.

"What the fuck?" I say as I lean my head to the side and peer up at the sky. With my blurry vision I can't make out much of anything.

"Maybe they just want to make sure we get there safe," Mac says.

"I don't like it," Sarge says.

We reach the top of the bluff and I see a sprawling complex and airstrip beside a dry lake bed. It is more than just an installation. This place is nearly the size of Nellis.

"There she is," says Mac.

The road to Area 51 descends the mountain and skirts around the edge of the lake bed. From across the expanse, it's difficult to see what we might be heading into. All of the buildings appear intact, but there doesn't seem to be a lot of activity.

"Looks too quiet," I say. "Doesn't make sense."

"Stay frosty," says Sarge.

Gunny slows down the vehicle in front of us as we cautiously approach the entrance. No guards are posted outside the gates. This is definitely not standard procedure for one of the most secretive installations in the nation.

"Are those bodies?" Mac asks as he gestures at a hangar off to the left.

Several corpses in maintenance uniforms are sprawled on the tarmac beneath the scorching desert sun.

"I doubt they're just getting a tan," I say.

We pull up to the runway and bring the trucks to a stop. I look up and down the strip, but the place seems deserted.

"I don't get it," I say. "This place is like a ghost town. There's no one around."

"Not up here," Claire says. "The real stuff happens underground."

A pair of vehicles appear at the far end of the runway.

Ambulances. They turn and speed toward us.

"Here comes the welcome wagons," Mac says.

The trucks skid to a stop and a squad of men wearing CBRN suits and carrying submachine guns burst out of the back doors and approach our vehicles.

"Get out," one of the men demands.

"Who the fuck are these guys?" I ask Sarge.

"I don't know," he says. "But we don't take orders from them."

The lieutenant opens his door and steps out of the other Humvee. One of the guys in the CBRN suits moves around the vehicle and has a word with Will, then Will looks back and gestures for all of us to get out, too.

I open the door and follow Mac and Sarge toward the emergency vehicles, but I can barely walk. My equilibrium is all fucked up. Claire takes hold of my elbow and helps steady me as I focus on putting one foot in front of the other.

"Sergeant," she says.

Sarge looks back and sees me struggling and pauses to drape my arm over his shoulder to help me along.

"Hold up," one of the MOPP suits puts a gloved hand up to prevent Sarge from passing.

"What's wrong?" Sarge asks.

"Is that a bite?" the guy gestures at my hand.

"No," says Sarge. "Friendly fire. He needs a doctor right away."

The MOPP suit looks at me for a long moment before he waves us into the truck.

They close the doors and drive us across the facility. The men let us out into a hanger where a huge ramp leads down to a massive blast door. The head CBRN guy talks to someone on comms and then the huge doors slide open and reveal a lobby with several elevators.

The CBRN squad leader pushes the button to call the elevator and we stand around waiting.

"What is this?" I ask Claire.

"With all kinds of satellites watching the surface, everything of any importance is kept underground."

The elevator dings and then the doors retract and we all step inside.

There are buttons for a dozen floors. One of the MOPP suits hits a button and the doors close before the elevator descends for about ten seconds. When we step out the guards escort us into a small holding room.

"Take off your clothes," the guard says.

"You got to be kidding me," says Mac.

The lieutenant looks annoyed but he takes off his helmet and begins unbuttoning his jacket.

"Just do what he says, Mac," says Sarge.

We strip down and move into another room where they put us through this whole decontamination procedure. Spraying us with some harsh chemicals and scrubbing us with brushes. The stuff burns the shit out of my wounded hand and eventually I collapse on the ground in agony.

When the water shuts off they open a door to a dressing room. A pair of nurses with a wheelchair hurry over and help me into a gown and then they wheel me out of the room. They bring me into an exam room and begin asking me about my hand while they remove the bandage.

The skin looks even more inflamed now. Puss oozes from the tissue, but when the nurses touch the wound it doesn't seem to hurt as much now as it did when I messed with it in the bathroom.

Maybe that's not a good thing.

Maybe my nerves are so fucked up that my body isn't registering the pain. Or it could be the local anesthetic they injected is kicking in already.

"Shit," I say. "I left my finger in my pants."

The nurses look at each other and then one leaves the room. The doctor comes in and examines my hand while he asks me some more questions.

"Did you touch anyone that was infected?"

"No."

"Did you have any contact with infected blood?"

"No," I say. "I don't think so, at least."

The nurses get me on an IV and inject me with antibiotics and then I stare at the ceiling while the doctor works on my hand. The doctor tells me they won't be able to reattach my finger. While he can treat my hand, they just aren't equipped to handle a surgical transplant of that nature.

"That's fine, Doc," I say. It's just a fucking pinky anyway.

After about an hour, the doctor finishes up and leaves the nurse to bandage me up. As soon as she is done, they move me to an observation room down the hall where Mac, Sarge and Gibby are waiting for me.

After some fist bumping with my good hand, they wait around while the doctor comes back in and tells me I was very lucky.

"A few more hours out there and you might have gone septic," he says. He tells me I should be on bed rest a couple days and take antibiotics for the next ten days. Instead of complaining about being told to stay in bed, I nod and wait for the doctor to leave the room.

"What's the word?" I ask the guys.

"I regret to inform you that we have not seen any aliens yet," Mac says.

"They got this place locked down pretty tight," says Sarge. "We've been in a holding room since we got here."

"Where's the LT?" I ask.

"He went with Miss Davies," Sarge says. "Talk with whoever the fuck is in charge around here, I suppose."

"The rest of us just hurry up and wait," says Gibby. "Same old shit."

"I just want to get the fuck out of here," I say.

"I hear you, brother," says Sarge. "The whole time we were out there, I didn't think about getting back home once. Just staying alive, you know? Now I can't stop thinking about it."

"We'll get you home, Sarge," Gibby says. "That's a promise."

"I ain't got nothing better to do this week," Mac adds.

"Soon as they cut us loose, Sarge," I tell him. "I'm with you guys."

"Thanks," Sarge says. "You better get some rest while you can then. Come on, guys."

The guys take off and leave me alone again, though Mac hangs just outside the door, keeping an eye on me as he chats up a nurse in the hall. Even though I am wiped out, I still feel edgy. The images of everything that happened replay over and over again in my mind. I'd rather get back out there again than have to sit here and think about it. I close my eyes and eventually the exhaustion wins out and I fall asleep.

CHAPTER THIRTEEN

When I open my eyes, I find Claire sitting in a chair beside the bed. Her eyes are closed and she snores slightly. My aching hand causes me to wince in pain and I raise it up and inspect the bandages and my lack of fingers. It takes a moment for me to recall everything that happened.

"Fuck," I whisper.

My stomach growls. It's been way too long since I had something to eat. Being out there, it was the last thing on my mind, but now I am hungry as hell.

Eventually, I start getting impatient so I sit up in the bed. I look around for something to wear besides the hospital gown, but I don't see anything. I don't feel like waiting around for help, so I start unhooking the monitors.

"Where you running off to?" Claire says.

"I'm hungry," I tell her. "Can't stand to just sit around in here either."

"You should take it easy," she tells me.

"I'm fine," I insist. "Can you tell me where the rest of the guys are?"

"They're asleep," she says. "Just relax."

Reluctantly, I settle back into the bed. The nurse comes rushing in the room and when she sees I'm fine and just removed the monitors she folds her arms across her chest and scowls at me.

"Mr. Graves, you need to stay in your bed," she says.

"I'm fine," I tell her. "Really. I don't want to be hooked up to all this shit."

"But—" she complains.

"Please, can I just get something to eat?" I beg the nurse. "I'm starving."

The nurse realizes she isn't going to get me to cooperate so she leaves the room.

"What time is it?" I ask Claire.

She looks at the watch on her wrist.

"Close to three in the morning," she tells me. "The guys just went to bed a couple hours ago. They didn't want you to wake up to an empty room. I had to promise them I'd stay with you to get them to get some rest. It will be a few hours before they start getting ready to go."

"Go where?" I ask. My guess would be to head home with Sarge and help him find his family.

"New Mexico," she tells me.

"What?" I ask her.

The nurse returns to the room with some food and places it down on the tray table and swivels it around so I can reach it from the bed. Soup, crackers, applesauce and a banana. None of it looks particularly appetizing, but I'm so hungry that I dive in. I even forget what Claire had said until she starts speaking again.

"There is this CIA agent here," Claire explains. "Some guy named Logan. He is in contact with the Pentagon."

"What the fuck does that have to do with us?" I say as I peel back the skin of a banana.

"Apparently that doctor I told you about... Dr. Schoenheim..." she says.

With my mouth full, I nod to let her know I remember.

"Well, everyone thought that he died, but apparently he is still alive," she explains.

"He's going against the trend then," I say.

She looks at me and furrows her brow. Then she gets my point and presses her lips together.

"Very funny," she says. "I mean it. Two years ago was his funeral, but apparently he's been off the grid this whole time."

"Why?" I ask her.

"I don't know," she says. "I guess I will find out soon enough. We are supposed to meet them at a secure facility in New Mexico."

"Why don't they just fly him out here?" I ask her.

"This facility is primarily for testing experimental aircraft. It isn't equipped for that kind of research," she says. "Los Alamos has some of the most brilliant scientists and advanced technology of any research facility in the country."

I groan as I push the tray of food out of my way and begin to get up off the bed.

"What are you doing?" she asks.

"Getting ready to go," I tell her.

"What?" she says. "Like that? You can't."

"I'm not going to sit here while my team goes off on some suicide mission to take you halfway across the country."

"Chase," she protests.

"Not happening," I say as I walk out into the hallway and begin looking around for some clothes to wear. A draft on my backside reminds me that my ass is literally hanging out in the breeze, but I'm determined not to be left sitting around in a hospital bed while the other men in my platoon risk their lives.

"Chase!" Claire calls after me. "Where are you going?"

A nurse comes out from behind the desk and gets in front of me.

"Where are my clothes?" I ask her.

"Mr. Graves," she says. "You should—"

"I just want my damn clothes!" I demand.

"I will get them for you," the nurse relents. "Please, just return to your room."

A couple of military police appear at the end of the hall. I give them a hard look as I turn around and head back to my room. Claire settles back in the chair once I resume eating my food.

"So what did you used to do here?" I ask her. "Or you probably can't talk about that."

She smiles to let me know I'm right.

"I see how it is," I say as I stuff a cracker in my mouth.

"I don't want to get locked in prison for the rest of my life," she says.

"In case you don't remember, it seems like nobody is locked in prison anymore."

"You have a point there," she says.

The nurse returns and rolls a cart with my fatigues and gear to the side of the bed.

"Sorry," I say as she turns to leave. "I didn't mean to be a pain in the ass."

"I understand," the nurse smiles. "Just let me know if you need anything else, darling."

She leaves and I return to spooning cold chicken broth into my mouth.

"Do you know what DNA printing is?" Claire asks me.

I look up at her confused.

"Synthetic biology?" she asks. "The Human Genome Project?"

I shake my head.

"You're gonna have to break it down Barney style," I tell her.

"So you know we're all composed of DNA strands that determine our traits," she starts.

I nod.

"Well, we've learned to map that DNA," she says. "We know more about which codified components affect traits, and we've even figured out how to insert artificial compounds into the DNA strands to change traits more drastically. I guess you can say my job here was to determine how we can modify human DNA to adapt it to a different environment."

"Doesn't sound so top secret," I say.

"Well it is when you're trying to bio-engineer humans that can survive on Mars."

"What?" I ask her.

"That was what I worked on here," she repeats.

"You were trying to make a Martian?"

She nods and holds a finger up to her lips.

"That's about the most fucked up thing I've ever heard," I tell her.

"You wanted to know," Claire says and sits back in her seat with a smile on her face.

"Why would anyone want to do that?" I ask her.

"You don't honestly think this planet can sustain us much longer?" she asks. "The population is exploding, we're draining our resources, not to mention the destruction and waste. Forget the zombies, another twenty years and we'd have wiped ourselves out."

I get up off the bed and pick up my boxers and pull them up under the hospital gown. Then I take the gown off and pick up my pants. I notice Claire watching me and she turns her eyes up to the ceiling.

"So did it work?" I ask her as I pick up my undershirt. "Did you ever make a Martian?"

"It would have worked," she says. "Given more time. Maybe another five years. Now, I will probably just have to wonder what might have been possible if it weren't for all this."

"As long as you're still alive it's possible, though," I tell her. "You can help figure out how to stop this thing and then you can get back to work."

"It might not even be necessary now," Claire says. "This catastrophe will probably send us back to the Dark Ages. That is if we manage to survive at all. Either way, Earth will be better off without so many of us here to destroy it."

"I don't plan on dying anytime soon," I tell her. "Don't worry. We'll get you to Los Alamos."

CHAPTER FOURTEEN

As soon as everyone is awake, we gear up and prepare to move out.

"So, what's the game plan?" Sarge asks the lieutenant.

"We're going to rendezvous with a team of Navy Seals that is transporting the doctor to Holloman Air Force Base," says Will. "Then we will proceed up to Los Alamos, secure the facility and provide security until additional support arrives."

"You make it sound so easy," says Mac.

"It will be," Sarge says. "As long as we don't all die.

"The word is Holloman is a hell of a stronghold," says Will.

"The population is sparse in that area," I say. "West of it is nothing but miles and miles of harsh desert. My dad was stationed there for a couple years when I was a kid."

"Some of the remnants of the Army personnel from Fort Bliss made it up to Holloman and are keeping the local population of the recently departed off the Chair Force," says Will.

The lieutenant glances at all of us.

"I know you guys have already been through hell," the lieutenant says. "I got family back home, too, and I don't know if they're okay. But I believe that the best thing we can do for all of them right now is help protect Miss Davies and this doctor so they can figure out a way to stop this thing. We are going to need their help to get it done."

The thought of staying behind never even crossed my mind, and I'm sure that no one else in the room had considered it either. We all want to see it through now.

"Let's get to work then, gentleman," says Will.

We pick up our gear and head out. Down the hall a guy dressed in slacks and a button-down shirt waits for us. He puts on a pair of sunglasses, checks his watch and then hits the button for the elevator.

"Who's this guy?" I ask Mac.

"Logan," says Mac.

"Something wrong?" asks our platoon commander.

"No, not at all," says Logan. "I'll be coming along for the ride."

"I appreciate the offer, but we can handle it, agent," Will says.

"I'm sure you can," he says. "However, some of the folks back in Washington felt this should be a joint operation."

Will hesitates for a long moment.

"Is that going to be a problem, Lieutenant?" Logan asks.

"No," Will says. "No problem. Good to have you aboard."

"Great," says Logan. He unbuttons his cuffs and folds his sleeves up around his forearms. "Let's rock and roll then."

The elevator dings and we get inside and ride up to the surface. Across the dried up bed of Lake Groom, the sun hangs just above the mountaintops. On the runway sits a CV-22 Osprey. The helicopter crew scrambles around as they prep for take off.

The flight takes nearly two hours in the blazing heat. I try to get some shuteye while we're in the air, but my hand is still in a lot of pain and the downtime leaves too much opportunity for my mind to wander and to dwell. The last thing I want do right now is to think, but sometimes you can't bury it down.

It's a relief to get back on the ground so I can just focus on the mission again. We get off the Osprey and are greeted by an Air Force captain with Walker etched on his nameplate. He waves us over and leads us to a hangar a couple hundred yards away. Walker shakes hands with Logan and the lieutenant. He seems a little paranoid and relieved to see us.

"What's the situation here, Captain?" asks Logan.

"A lot better than other places," says the Captain. "From what I hear anyway. We have continual friction from the small town of Alamogordo to the east. We lost most of our infantry in the initial wave, but Army forces have been able to keep the dead off of us. For now, anyway."

"This is Miss Davies," Logan says and introduces the scientist.

Walker smiles and shakes her hand.

"Our first priority is to provide her security," says Logan. "We go wherever she goes."

"Once the team from Chicago arrives we will step off to Los Alamos," adds Will. "In the meantime, if there is anything my men can do to help around here, just let us know."

"Actually there is something," Walker says. "We've got a bit of a situation brewing around here."

"Anything I need to be worried about?" asks Logan.

"No," Walker shakes his head. "Tensions have just been a little high since some of the guys from Fort Bliss arrived. Apparently they have taken it upon themselves to restructure the chain of command. The colonel is having a hard time keeping some of them in check. If you can have a word with the man in charge, Private Jenson, maybe try to bridge the divide here?"

Instead of answering, Logan looks at our platoon commander. Will nods and tells the captain that he will see what he can do.

"I appreciate it, Lieutenant," says Walker. "We have some room at the Holloman Inn for Miss Davies and your men if you need it."

"Thank you, Captain," Logan says, looking around the hangar. "We shouldn't be here very long."

"There's vehicles out front to bring you over when you're ready. Welcome to Holloman," Walker says to all of us. "Lieutenant," he jerks his head for Will to follow him back out the bay door.

"I'll meet you guys back at the inn," Will says. He gives Gunny a quick nod to let him know he'll be running the show in his absence, then he turns and heads back outside with the captain.

"The shit must have really hit the fan down in El Paso if a private has taken over command of the 1st Armored Division," I tell Mac.

"No shit," he agrees.

"What would you expect?" Gunny says. "It's the Army. Those guys had it too easy."

Gunny has never liked the Army. Not since he tangled with an Airborne Ranger that he believed to be making eyes at his girl.

Logan pulls out a satellite phone from his bag, powers it on and paces while he waits for the device to get a signal. I watch as he punches the number pad and then places the phone to his ear.

"Jess," he says. "It's Logan. I just touched down at Holloman."

He pauses.

"Who is Jess?" Mac asks.

I shrug.

"Probably his girlfriend," says Gibby.

"You better check in when you get there, honey," Mac says in his nagging wife imitation.

"What the fuck is with that man purse?" Gibby asks. "That shit is just wrong."

"It's the hottest fashion trend among cocksucking metrosexual douchebags," says Mac.

"I agree," Logan says. "We have the surviving Marines of 1st Recon providing personal security for Miss Davies here."

Logan paces back and forth as he talks with Jess. He is too absorbed in the conversation to notice us making fun of him.

"You guys are terrible," says Claire.

"What about the doctor?" Logan asks Jess. "Is he cooperating?"

Apparently, Jess isn't his girlfriend but is involved in this operation somehow.

A thundering explosion outside interrupts the conversation.

"What the fuck was that?" Logan asks us as he holds the phone to his chest.

Another explosion in the distance makes the ground tremble.

"Those are bombs," says Gunny.

We all walk over to the bay door of the hangar to see smoke drifting up to the sky to the east.

"They're using the drones," notes Sarge. "Just like in Nevada."

"Bombing civilians to save their own asses," says Mac.

"No everything is fine, Jess," says Logan. "Just some ordnance going off around here. Yes. I'll wait to hear from you."

He hangs up the phone and tucks it back into his pathetic looking man purse.

"That was my contact in Chicago," he says. "She is still on route to Great Lakes Naval Base with the doctor, but she should be airborne tomorrow morning."

"All right then," says Gunny. "Enough smoking and joking. Let's escort Miss Davies to her room."

CHAPTER FIFTEEN

"If you need anything, anything at all, I'll be right across the hall," Logan says as he opens the door to Claire's room for her.

"Thank you," says Claire. "I'll be fine."

She closes the door and then Logan turns to Gunny.

"I want two men on that door at all times," he says.

Gunny doesn't respond. He just scowls as Logan turns away and enters his own room. The last thing Gunny wants to deal with in a situation like this is some smug Washington asshole telling him how to do his job.

"I'm getting a bad feeling about all of this," Gunny grumbles. He pulls a cigarette out of his pocket and lights it up in the hallway.

Gunny is notorious for following his gut. It usually never steers him wrong, whether it is in combat or just in life in general.

"I hear that," Sergeant Lowe agrees.

The stairwell door opens and Will steps out into the hallway. He looks concerned to see us all standing around, especially since we're quiet.

"Anything wrong?" he asks.

"No, sir," says Gunny. He drops his cigarette and stamps it out on the carpet.

"I'm sensing some hesitation," Will says.

"The situation here seems a little disorganized," Gunny tells him. "Plus, that agency dick is getting on my nerves already."

"Duly noted, Gunny," Will says.

"Who has authority on this operation anyway?" Gunny asks.

"As soon as I get word on that, I'll let you know, Gunny," Will says. "For now let's just try to get along. I think we might have bigger problems here."

"Army?" Gunny says.

"Yeah," says the lieutenant. "I was warned off. Apparently, they've taken exception to the way the Air Force is running things."

"They planning a coup?" Gunny asks.

Will nods.

"I was assured that if we steer clear of any involvement that we will be allowed to remain on base."

"What a clusterfuck," Sergeant Lowe says.

"Are they serious?" asks Mac. "How soon are they talking here?"

"Imminent," says Will.

"This shit just gets better and better," I mutter.

"So what are your orders, sir?" Sarge asks.

"Rodriguez," Will says. "Have your men stay on Miss Davies. Gunny, Lowe, Collins, and Jax are with me. We'll post up by the front doors and keep an eye on things out front."

"What do we do if the shooting starts, sir?" Sarge asks.

"Keep your heads down and don't do anything unless Miss Davies is put in the line of fire," says Will.

"Copy," says Sarge.

The lieutenant leads the other members of Nightmare Company back to the stairs.

"This is some bullshit," Gibby says. "You all know that right."

"You having second thoughts about being here, Corporal?" Sarge asks him.

"No, I'm with you, Sarge," Gibby says. "I'm just being real right now."

"Gibby is right," I say. "Are we just supposed to stand around and let this happen?"

"That's your orders," Sarge says. "The lieutenant was clear, so I don't want to hear about it."

"The middle of all this," Mac says. "And people still got to start shit."

"Mac," Sarge warns.

"Sorry, sir," Mac says.

Sarge raps a knuckle on the door and waits for Claire to open it.

"Is something wrong?" she asks.

"No," Sarge says. "Not yet anyway. But there is a chance you might hear some gunfire in the vicinity. If that happens, I want you to take cover in the bathtub and don't open this door until the shooting stops. Can you do that?"

Claire nods her head and then looks apprehensively around the hallway.

"You'll be fine," Sarge says. "You're safe here."

She closes the door and we hear the chain locking on the other side.

"What do we do about the agency asshat?" I ask Sarge. "Should we tell him?"

"I'm not under orders to do shit for him," Sarge says.

It doesn't take long before gunfire disrupts the relative peace on the base.

Logan whips open the door to his room and steps out into the hallway.

"What is going on out there?" he asks Sarge.

"You might just want to go back to your room," Sarge tells him.

"What?" Logan says. He balls his hands into fists and puts them on his hips. "Sergeant?"

Sarge remains quiet until another burst of gunfire nearby breaks the silence.

"Fine," Logan huffs. "I'll go find out for myself."

As he turns to leave, the lieutenant returns with the rest of our squad and confirms our suspicions.

"It's happening," he says.

"What's happening?" Logan pleads.

RAGE OF THE DEAD

"The Army and the Air Force are having some tactical differences of opinion," says Will.

"Tactical differences of opinion?" says Logan.

"They're shooting at each other," Gunny translates.

"Fuck," curses Logan. "We have to try and stop this."

"I wouldn't go out there if I was you," says Will. "We can't afford to get caught up in the middle of this."

"We can't afford not to," Logan says. "This could put the security of the whole facility in jeopardy."

The door to the stairwell opens again and Walker appears in the hall holding a rifle. His face is flushed and stricken with a look of panic. We hold our positions outside of Miss Davies' room.

"Lieutenant," he says. "We have a problem. They've taken over the operations center."

None of us move.

"Lieutenant!" the officer yells.

"I'm sorry," says Will.

"The Army just executed the colonel," the man pleads. "How can you just stand there and do nothing?"

"I'm sorry, Captain," Will says. "We've got our orders."

Walker curses us before returning to the stairwell.

Sporadic gunfire continues outside the inn for the next several minutes. We stand around quietly in the darkened hallway and try not to think about what is going on out there.

"You think they're going to want us around here after this?" Logan asks.

"I talked to the man in charge of the Army forces," says Will. "He assured me that we will have no issue if we steer clear of the fray."

"Yeah?" says Logan. "And what happens if they don't come out on top? Then what?"

"That won't happen," Will says. "They have the upper hand."

"Jesus," Logan says. "I sure hope you're right. Otherwise, you just fucked us, Lieutenant, and I will make sure that everyone knows you were complicit in this act of treason."

"Hey buddy," Gunny interrupts and grabs the collar of Logan's shirt into his fist. "Instead of standing around here saying things that might result in me fucking up your face, why don't you get your goddamn phone out of your little purse and tell your friends to hurry the fuck up so we can get out of this mess."

Logan nods and mumbles in agreement until Gunny releases him. The agent reaches into his bag and grabs his phone.

The shooting outside tapers off until an eerie silence settles over Holloman. Sarge taps on Claire's door and waits for her to open it. She pulls it open as far as the chain allows and peers outside.

"All clear," Sarge tells her.

"What is happening?" she wants to know. "Was it the dead?"

"No," Sarge tells her. "It's nothing you need to be concerned about. Everything is under control."

The stairwell doors open at the end of the hall and we all look to see who is coming. Six guys in Army uniforms file into the hallway.

"Stay inside," Sarge tells Claire as he closes the door again.

The guy leading the squad has a shaved head and a smirk on his face. He walks down the hall with bravado, his rifle propped on his shoulder in an I don't give a shit fashion.

"Reasoner," he smiles at the lieutenant.

"Jenson," Will gives him a nod.

"It's all taken care of," Jenson says. "Consider this situation officially unfucked. I appreciate the cooperation, fellas."

"We're just trying to do our jobs," Will says.

"I know it might seem like I'm the bad guy here," Jensen says. "But I'm not. Those Air Force assholes left us to fend for ourselves down in El Paso when we had to deal with the dead and the fucking cartels from Juarez. They just sat up here watching their own asses."

"Times are tough everywhere," Will says.

"Yeah," Jensen agrees. "I guess they are."

His eyes scan all of us as he talks like he is sizing us up.

"You see something you like?" Mac asks him.

"Corporal," Sarge says. "Watch it."

"Sorry, sir," Mac says.

"You better respect the chain of command there, devil dog," Jenson smirks.

His squad behind him gets a good laugh out of that one. He grabs Mac by the shoulder and jostles him roughly.

"I'm just fucking with you, man," Jenson says to Mac.

"Is that all?" the lieutenant asks.

"Sure," says Jenson. "For now."

His squad turns and begins to make their way to the stairwell again, but Jensen pauses and glances back at us.

"Don't look so nervous, fellas," laughs Jensen. "We're all friends here."

He leaves the hallway and the door slams shut behind him.

"What a fucking psychopath," says Sarge.

CHAPTER SIXTEEN

In the evening, the lieutenant sends our squad out to recon the base a bit more and see if we can requisition some dinner from the mess hall. In the dusky light, the barren desert streets give me an apprehensive feeling.

We cross the road to the Holloman Club and open the door. Inside the darkened bar, ten guys in jeans and t-shirts look up from the beers in their hands and stare at us in the doorway.

"You guys know where we can still grab some grub around here," Sarge asks the men.

"Not here," a man with a thick beard says as he pulls a cigar out of his mouth. "Try the commissary."

"Thanks," Sarge says.

"You're with Recon?" he says as we turned to leave.

"That's right," Sarge says. "Just flew in yesterday."

"How's Miramar handling this?" he asks.

"It's gone," Sarge says. "Same as everywhere."

"Why don't you boys sit down and have a beer?" he says as he kicks out a chair from the table beside him.

"Maybe another time," Sarge says.

"Come on," the man says. "We will probably all be dead in the morning. Might as well."

Sarge looks at me and I shrug and tilt my head toward the bar. We might as well see what we can learn from this guy about the situation we're in here.

"I could use a drink," Mac says.

The four of us walk over and grab some chairs and sit down.

"These miserable drunks already drank most of the good stuff," he informs us. "There's plenty of that shitty Mexican beer left though. You're probably okay with that, right Rodriguez?"

Sarge doesn't say anything but he gives the man a flat, unamused expression.

"Dolly," he says. "Get these fellas four shitty Mexican beers."

A middle-aged woman with long blonde hair comes out from behind the bar with four bottles in her hand and sets them down on the table.

"Drink up," the man says. "It's on the house."

I pick up the bottle and take a swig of warm beer. They really did give us the cheap shit. I cringe as I swallow it down and set the bottle back on the table.

"I didn't catch your name," Sarge says.

"Rhodes," the man says. "You can just call me Trevor."

"So, what's the word?" Sarge asks Rhodes.

"I was about to ask you the same thing," says Rhodes. "Most of us haven't heard shit since this all started. It's been one long nightmare down here. So, when you got here I had to wonder what the hell anyone would want to come here for."

"We're escorting a civilian scientist," Sarge says. "She might be able to figure out how we turn the tide against these things."

"That so?" says Rhodes. He leans back in his chair and folds his arms across his chest.

Sarge nods.

"So," Rhodes says. "In spite of everything you boys are still running around trying to save the world. Doesn't that seem kind of, I don't know, pointless? No offense."

"Just doing our jobs," Sarge says.

"Under whose authority are you operating?" Rhodes asks.

"Washington," Sarge says. "Straight from the Pentagon."

"Hell, we haven't had radio contact with Washington since Monday. No official word from anywhere, other than NORAD. That place is still a fortress. The rest of the people we have heard from that are surviving out there are just a few well-prepared civilians."

"So you all just figured to hell with your oath to protect the country," Mac says. He takes a swig from his bottle and swipes his mouth with the sleeve of his uniform.

"More like we decided it was time to start looking out for each other," says Rhodes. He peels the label off his beer, leaving little bits of paper on the table beside it.

"It's all subjective," Mac says.

"You can say that," Rhodes says. "Our government didn't do shit to help us down in El Paso. We were already on our own before we realized it. You are, too. All of you. Whether you want to believe it or not. Just because you still wear the uniform doesn't mean it stands for much anymore."

"I think I'd rather keep trying to do something instead of sitting around on my ass," I tell him.

Rhodes smirks and shakes his head.

"I can respect that you're loyal to your brothers," says Sarge. "That's understandable. If you're all okay with Jenson calling the shots, good luck with that."

"You think it's just us?" he laughs. "Wake the fuck up, Sergeant."

"What do you mean?" Sarge asks.

"We've been in contact with dozens of militias across the country. Texas, Montana, Missouri... a whole network of highly-trained military elements are working together. They're the ones that are going to survive this thing because they realize the government has failed to adequately invest in our civil defense for decades. If you think the United States is going to come out on top, you got it wrong."

I can't really argue with his reasoning. I take another sip of the beer and set it back down on the table. Maybe we shouldn't be putting our asses on the line, but it is what we are trained to do.

"Thanks for the beer," Sarge says.

He sets the empty bottle down and gets up from the table. He makes a circle with his finger to tell us to get moving.

"Let's go check out the commissary," Sarge says to us.

We follow Sarge through the front doors and into the hot desert night. As we walk up the road, we hear the crackle of small arms firing several blocks away. None of us even react to the sound. It's been pretty much continual for the past couple of hours.

No matter how awful a situation may be, if you endure it long enough, it will eventually seem routine.

The commissary is still fully stocked with everything imaginable. They even have a generator running to power the lights and refrigerators and freezers. We grab a case of water, a few bags of chips, and some bread and meats for sandwiches. Instead of a cashier at the register, we just find a pair of guards in civvies holding assault rifles.

"Somebody here to ring us up?" I ask them.

"No need to pay," the guard tells me. "Money won't be good for shit soon anyway."

"We're just here to make sure no one gets too greedy," the other guard says.

We carry our dinner back to the inn and eat. Afterward, we spend the night taking shifts on watch in the hallway. For the most part, Holloman Air Force Base remains quiet and we are left alone. I eat my sandwich, pop one of the antibiotics I got from the medical facility, and grab a few hours of rack time until it's our turn to keep watch in the hallway.

"You think these guys are right?" I ask Sarge. "Is this really going to be the end of America?"

"Probably," he says. "Hell, I don't know anymore. I don't care either. If we weren't doing this, I don't know what else I would do."

"We'd get the fuck out of here," I say. "Go find Melissa."

"You know, the only thing I'm afraid of right now is what I might find if I go home," Sarge admits. "That's the real reason, I'm still here fighting, man."

"Don't think that way, Sarge," I say.

"I mean it," he says. "I look around and see everything, and I'm just like, there's no way, right? I should just accept that they are all gone."

Sarge rubs his index finger across his eyebrows and fights back the emotions that are about to overwhelm him. I want to say something to make him feel better, but I can only think of some meaningless nonsense that won't change a damn thing. Deep down, I know he is probably right. His family is most likely gone.

"Just hang in there, Pedro," I say. "If they are still alive, the best way we can help them is by doing our jobs. Give Claire and this doctor a chance to stop this thing."

Sarge nods, but I can tell he is just agreeing for my benefit, so I stop trying to say things to make him feel better.

"You're right," he says.

"I'm always right," I remind him.

"No," Sarge says. "You're definitely not always right."

"Come on," I moan. "One time, maybe, I was wrong."

Sarge cracks a smile.

"Thanks, Chase," he says. "You're a real friend."

"Don't get all goddamn mushy on me now," I warn him.

"Shut the fuck up," Sarge laughs. "Fucking asshole."

It makes me feel better just to see him smile and laugh again. After the past couple of days of tense situations, it's good to see we can still almost have a normal conversation.

"Hey," he says. "How's the hand doing?"

I hold it up in front of me and look at it as I turn it from side to side.

"I don't think they're gonna grow back," I say.

Sarge grins and rubs at his eye with his hand.

"Sorry," he says. "That should have never happened. Fucking Pittman."

"Don't worry about it," I wave my bandaged hand dismissively and lower it again.

"Does it still hurt?" he asks.

"Like a motherfucker," I tell him. "But I'm getting used to it.

CHAPTER
SEVENTEEN

When morning comes, Logan makes contact with the team in Chicago. He updates them on the situation at the base and urges them to hurry the hell up.

"I'm serious, Jess. We can't wait around here much longer. These guys are fucking nuts," he says as he hangs up the phone.

He paces up and down the hallway.

"How much longer are we going to be waiting around here?" the lieutenant asks Logan.

"I'd say it's about a six-hour flight," Logan says as he flexes the muscles in his hand by opening and closing it. "They will probably need to stop and refuel, but they should be here by sundown."

"We'll be ready to go by then," Will says.

"We may have another problem," Logan tells the lieutenant. "Apparently the pilot in Chicago is refusing to fly the helicopter."

"He what?" Will says.

"He won't fly," Logan repeats.

"Jesus," Will sighs.

"The rest of the crew is willing to make the flight, at least for now," Logan explains. "They're not as experienced. Hopefully, they should be able to manage without him, though. But you've seen firsthand how these things go. You just need one asshole that gets out of line and it's like a cancer. Pretty soon it spreads to the rest of the team."

"Let's just hope that doesn't happen," Will says. "Keep me updated. I want to know the minute they are in the air."

Logan seems to relax a bit and nods as he listens to Will. He might have thought he was in charge yesterday, but our platoon commander has a way of easily asserting his authority due to his superior ability to handle any situation that comes his way.

"Gunny," Will says. "Take Lowe and Collins and head down to the motor pool to secure some transport for us."

"Yes, sir," says Gunny.

"And Gunny," Will says as Gunny heads for the door.

The big man turns around and waits for his orders.

"Try to keep a low profile out there," Will says.

"They're all wearing civvies, sir," Gunny says. "We sort of stick out around here."

"Then we will, too," says Will. "Head over to the BX and see if you can grab some clothes first. I want to fly under the radar here as much as possible until we are ready to hit the road."

"Licken Chicken, sir," Gunny says to let him know he heard him loud and clear and then he makes his way down the hall with Lowe and Collins trailing behind him.

"Pedro," Will says. "If you're good here, I'm going to go hit up the rain locker."

"We're good, sir," Sarge says.

"Come get me if there is any trouble," Will says.

"Copy," Sarge says.

The platoon commander heads back into the room down the hall and leaves us to guard the scientist. Mac retrieves his notebook from his pack and opens it to a blank page and starts scrawling on it. Gibby takes out his phone and plugs his headphones into his ears.

"Motherfucker," he curses and yanks the cords to pull them out again.

"It broke?" Sarge asks.

"Nah," he says as he shoves it back in his pocket. "Battery is dead."

"Guess that makes this the day the music died," says Mac. "You know that song, right?"

"Bye, bye—" he sings.

"Shut up, Mac," says Sarge. "We know it."

"Come on," says Mac. "Poor Gibby just lost the only thing he cares about in this world. It's the least we can do for the guy. Besides, it's a classic. It'd be un-American not to sing it."

"No," Gibby says. "It's better if you don't."

"I agree with Gibby on this one," I add.

"You're like a bunch of fucking communists," Mac says. "Come on. Sarge?"

Sarge laughs and shakes his head.

"Comrade Rodriguez, please don't tell me you're a sympathizer," he continues. Mac tosses down his notebook and pen and raises his hands up toward the sky. "What is the world coming to?"

"Don't you got something you need to be writing, Mac?" I say.

"Fuck it," says Mac. "I'm gonna sing it anyway."

He starts humming the classic song again. It always amazes me how he seems to have the words to every song ever written memorized but forgets everything else. By the chorus, I can't resist. I start singing it too. Sarge joins in, too, and then Gibby gives in as well.

"What the hell is wrong with all of you?" Claire says.

We stop singing and turn around to find her standing in the doorway. Her eyes are hardly open and her red hair is a tangled mess.

"Sorry," Sarge says. "We, uhh—"

"We're just boosting morale," Mac says.

"By singing a song about a bunch of people dying in a plane crash at seven in the morning?" Claire sighs.

"That's not what it's about," says Mac. He looks at me. "Is it?"

I shrug. I thought it was about pie and pickups.

"I'm going back to bed," Claire groans before she slams the door.

"I'm sure you're wrong about that song," Mac yells after her.

"Let her sleep, Mac," Sarge says.

"If I could still Google shit, I'd totally prove her wrong," Mac mumbles.

"How many Rip Its have you had this morning?" Sarge asks.

"Only four," Mac says.

"Jesus," Gibby says and he leans back against the wall. "It's gonna be a long day."

As stupid as it might seem, the whole moronic exchange makes me feel better about our situation. If we can still act like we used to, then there is still hope that things can go back to normal someday. Or at the very least, we can still pretend to believe that it might be possible.

Mac may seem to be ridiculous at times, but he does what he does to try and hold on to what it means to be human. It's good to have someone like that on the team. Sometimes distractions are the only way to stay sane when it feels like the whole world is going to hell.

When we hear the stairwell door at the end of the hall, we expect to see Gunny and the guys returning but instead it is Private Jenson and his squad of steroid-infused gorillas. They look slightly agitated as they head straight for us.

"Where's the lieutenant?" Jenson demands.

Any good feeling we had quickly evaporated into the thin desert air.

"He's in the shower," Sarge says. "Everything okay?"

"No, asshole," Jenson snaps. "There are fucking dead people walking around. Everything is far from fucking okay."

"Easy, man," Sarge says. He reaches out a hand to try and calm the kid down.

"Shut the fuck up," Jenson shoves Sarge away. "Get your fucking filthy beaner hands off me."

My finger moves from the guard and rests gently on the trigger of my rifle.

"What do you need?" Sarge asks the man.

Jenson takes a deep breath and throws his hands up.

"Sorry," he says. "I didn't mean to say that. It's been a fucked up morning."

"It's fine," Sarge says. "What's the problem?"

"When the lieutenant gets out can you tell him I'd like a word with him? It's urgent."

"Sure," Sarge says. "I'll let him know."

"Thanks," says Jenson. "I'll be in the Ops Center."

He turns to leave and waves at his guys to come along with him.

"What the fuck is that about?" I ask Sarge.

He walks down the hall to the lieutenant's room.

"I don't know," Sarge says as he knocks on the door. "But it can't be anything good."

A minute later, Will opens the door a crack and peers into the hall. He has a towel around his waist and he brushes the damp curls off his forehead.

"What's up?" the lieutenant says.

"We got a problem," Sarge informs him. "Jenson was just up here. Wants you to go see him in operations. Said it's urgent."

"Gunny get back yet?" he asks.

Sarge shakes his head.

"All right," Will says. "Give me a couple of minutes."

He closes the door again but returns to the hallway a few minutes later in his undershirt and pants. Will crouches down and yanks the laces of his boots tight and ties them.

"Mac and Gibby. You guys stay posted up out here," he tells us. He looks at Sarge and me as he stands up again. "You two are with me. Let's go."

As we head for the elevator, Logan opens his door again.

"What's going on?" he asks Gibby as he buttons his shirt. "Where are they going?"

"Situation with Jenson," Gibby intercepts him as he tries to follow us. "The lieutenant has it under control."

"It's okay, Gibby," Will says. "I would appreciate having the agent come along with us on this one."

Gibby steps aside and Logan heads down the hall to catch up with us, rolling up his sleeves as he walks.

"What does that stupid Army fuck want now?" Logan grumbles.

"I guess we'll find out," says Will as we head for the stairs. "Everyone put on your nice faces."

He pushes the door open and we take the stairs down to the bottom floor. We step outside in the morning light with the temperatures already climbing toward a hundred degrees.

We walk several blocks across the base to get to the operations center. There is increased activity near the center of the base as fifty-cal machine guns, mortars, and even a pair of tanks are being positioned around a long three-story building on First Avenue.

"Looks like they're getting ready for something," Gibby says.

"Where can I find Jensen?" Will asks a guy hauling a sandbag over his shoulder.

The guy drops the sandbag onto a pile surrounding a machine gun and points us toward the main entrance.

"Go inside," he says. "Through the doors on the left."

We walk up the steps to the building and through the main doors. The lieutenant leads us to an office along the left side where Jenson and his team surround a set of monitors.

"No," Jenson tells a guy on his left. "It's not feasible. We don't have the resources for that."

"Jenson," Will says to get his attention.

The grunt turns around and seems glad to see us for once.

"Thanks for coming, Lieutenant," he says.

"Just call me Will," the lieutenant tells him. "I think we've established that formalities have gone out the window."

"Will," he says. "Sounds good."

"So, what's the problem?" Will asks.

Jensen directs his attention toward a monitor with an aerial image on the screen.

"We got drones up in the air," Jenson says as he gestures to a screen. "Look over here."

The screen shows a sizable force of the dead slowly making their way down a road.

"Where is this?" Will asks.

"Just outside El Paso," says Jenson. "Pan out."

The man operating the terminal adjusts the drone camera. Then we can see that the line of the dead extends for miles, with more and more following the horde onto the highways all the way down to Juarez.

"Holy shit," says Will. "Where are they going?"

"Here," says Jenson. "That highway leads straight to Holloman."

"How long do we have?" Will asks.

"A day," says Jenson. "Maybe a day and a half. Unless I get a team down here to Orogrande to divert them."

"Good plan," Will says. "Risky, but it should work. You sure your team is up for that?"

"I'm not going," Jenson says. "You fellas are."

CHAPTER EIGHTEEN

"We're not seriously considering doing this, sir, are we?" says Sarge.

We push through the front doors of the operations center and move down the steps toward the street.

"Hell no," the lieutenant says. "I just agreed to get him off my back. As soon as the helicopter from Chicago gets here we're Oscar Mike."

"Let's just hope they don't get held up along the way," I say.

"If they do hit any snags, then we are going to have to do whatever we can to help keep this base secure," the lieutenant says.

"Even if that means putting our asses on the line to divert the dead?" says Sarge. "I'm not okay with that."

"It won't come to that," says Will. "At least, I hope it doesn't come to that."

"We should just tell them to fuck off," I suggest.

"I'd like nothing more than to tell them that, Corporal," says Will. "But then what happens to me, to all of you, to Claire? These guys have already proven that they don't give a fuck about our orders, and they do not operate with any respect for authority."

I know Will is right. If we aren't somehow useful to these guys, they won't allow us to remain on the base. It's that simple.

"Logan," the lieutenant says. "Get on the phone and find out where that helicopter is at right now."

The agent pulls out the satellite phone from his bag and powers it on.

"When we get back we need to make sure we have everything we need," the lieutenant says. "We might be up at the laboratory in Los Alamos for weeks without any support, so we need to get some extra rations, ammo, and everything else. We need to plan ahead for any contingency."

"Damn it," says Logan.

"What's the issue, agent?" Will says.

"I lost contact with our team in Chicago," says Logan. "Hopefully it's just a communication issue."

"Keep trying," Will tells him.

"I am," the agent says.

We get back to the inn and find Gunny and the rest of the squad waiting for us in the hallway. For a second, I almost don't realize it's our guys since they're dressed in jeans and shirts from the base exchange. They even brought back a new pair of jean shorts and a pink tank top for Claire. Mac gives a soft whistle as he sees her in the hallway.

"What's going on?" Will asks. "Gunny, please tell me some good news."

"We got four Victors parked behind the hangar near the airfield," Gunny says. "It's such a clusterfuck around here we just walked in to the motor pool and took them."

"At least something has gone right today," the lieutenant says.

"What did Jenson want?" Gunny asks.

The lieutenant fills the rest of the team in on the situation.

"Is anybody else getting a bad feeling about this place?" Gunny asks.

"I am," Claire says. "It started right around the time I had to hide in a bathtub for a couple hours."

"Sir," says Sarge. "Maybe we should just get the hell out of here while we still have those Victors secured."

"We aren't leaving without the doctor," says Logan.

"I thought you said we lost contact with them?" says Sergeant Lowe. "We have to assume that something happened."

"Why don't we just talk to Jenson?" says Claire. "Maybe we can try reasoning with him."

"They're not really big on talking things out around here," Mac says. "You haven't met these assholes, Miss Davies."

The volume of the conversations increase as everyone begins arguing and talking over each other.

"Listen up," yells the lieutenant. "Everyone stay calm. We may not be able to unfuck the situation here and that is not our job. All we can do is focus on our mission and make sure we are prepared for anything that comes at us."

The lieutenant pauses to let everyone take a breath.

"Arguing with each other won't fix anything. We still have a lot to do before anything happens, so I need you all to focus," he says. "Logan, keep working on getting in touch with your contact. Gunny, take Lowe and Collins and see if you can get some additional supplies. Rations, medicine, batteries, anything else we might need at Los Alamos. Claire—"

"I know," she says. "Stay in the room. Got it."

"I'm sorry," says the lieutenant. "It won't be for much longer."

She heads back into the room and closes the door again.

"I'll keep her entertained if you want, sir," Mac offers.

"That won't be necessary, Corporal," says the lieutenant. Will glances at me and Sarge. "You two better get changed into some of the clothes that Gunny brought back. I want everyone ready to go as soon as we get word back from Logan."

"Yes sir," I tell him.

Mac waits for me while I grab a change of clothes from the selection that Gunny got from the BX. None of them are really my style, so I settle on a pair of black cargo pants and a black and white flannel shirt.

"Don't you ever wear any color?" Mac says, gesturing at the tropical shirt on the bed that matches his own.

"I'd just hate the thought of us getting confused by anyone," I tell him.

"You just don't think you can pull off this look," he says. "I get it."

"Don't you ever stop?" I say. I'm losing my patience with him a bit. Usually it's fine, but I'm still feeling edgy about our current situation. After I toss my uniform on the bed and put on the new clothes, I take a look at myself in the mirror. I push up the sleeves, but still feel like I look stupid.

"You know, when you don't have your uniform on you look like you're not even old enough to drive," he informs me.

"Shut the fuck up, Mac," I tell him.

"Just saying," Mac shrugs.

I head out to the hall and find Logan looking at his phone. I watch as he dials a number on the keypad. It's a different number than I remember seeing him dial to call Jess. Even seemingly little shit like this, I always remember.

"Who are you calling?" I ask him.

He holds up a hand as if to block the sound of my voice as he listens to the phone.

"Hey, it's Logan," he says.

There is a short pause. I try to hear the other end of the conversation but the volume on the phone is too quiet.

"I haven't been able to reach her," Logan says.

Another pause.

"Are you sure?" he says. "I need absolute certainty on this."

There is a long pause while he listens on the phone. The lieutenant comes out of his room, now wearing a pair of camo cargo shorts and a green polo shirt.

"Thanks," Logan sighs as he hangs up the phone. For a long moment, Logan stares at the device in his hands.

"Who was that?" the lieutenant asks.

"I couldn't get through to Jess," Logan says. "So, I put a call in to a friend of mine at NORAD. He was able to track the helicopter by GPS to an Army airfield in Missouri where they stopped to refuel. He was monitoring them by satellite."

"That's good news, then," the lieutenant says.

"No," says Logan. "They were ambushed by an unaffiliated group after they touched down. They tried to take off, but the helicopter went down in the forest a few miles away. No one has been able to contact them since. The area is swarming with the dead. I think we have to presume the doctor did not survive."

"That's it then," Sarge says.

"Game over," says Mac.

CHAPTER
NINETEEN

"L et's get the hell out of here," says Will.

He raps a knuckle against the door to get Claire. She opens it a few inches with an exasperated sigh and peers out into the hall.

"The doc is dead," Will says. "We're leaving."

"Hold on," says Claire. She grabs at his sleeve as he turns to walk away. "What happened?"

"The helicopter crashed," Will tells her. "I'm sorry. We have to go now. Get your things."

Several minutes later, we escort Claire out the front door of the inn and head up the block towards the airfield. The sun is sinking below the massive dunes to the west, casting shades of pink and orange onto the white sand. Several men patrol the street, walking along with assault rifles at a low ready. The lieutenant holds up a couple fingers when one of them waves and we swiftly pass by them.

We reach the airfield and Gunny directs us to a hangar at the far end of the runway. The area is quiet aside from the cool breeze kicking up sand on the tarmac.

"Just around the corner," Gunny says.

"You gassed them up, right?" Will asks.

"Yeah, we got more than enough to get to Los Alamos," Gunny says as they round the corner.

"Los Alamos?" Jenson says. I recognize the tone of his voice before I even come around the side of the hangar and see him sitting on the hood of the Humvee holding an apple in his hand with a big bite missing from it. After a quick scan of the scene, I count about twenty of his men surrounding the vehicles. He swallows, then takes another bite of the apple and waits for some kind of response from us.

Will opens his mouth, but he hesitates. In all the time I have known him, I have never seen him at a loss for words until now. He was not expecting a clown like Jenson to be a step ahead of him. Maybe we all underestimated him.

"You fellas wouldn't be running out on us?" he asks Will as he tosses the apple off to the side and slides off the hood of the Humvee.

"No," Will finally says.

"No?" Jenson asks. "That's kind of what it seems like."

I keep my rifle ready, just in case. I don't want to get into a shootout right here, but if they try anything I won't go down without a fight.

"Lieutenant, did you know there are still over one thousand women and children on this base right now?" Jenson asks. "You really going to leave them here to be eaten alive by the dead? Is that the kind of men you are?"

"I don't see you volunteering to drive down to Orogrande," Gunny says.

Will holds up a hand to tell Gunny to be quiet. He approaches Jenson, but keeps a casual distance. Jenson stands a good six inches taller than the lieutenant, and looks much more imposing in comparison.

"We are going to take those Victors and complete the operation, just like we discussed," Will says. "After that, my team will proceed with our mission to Los Alamos."

"Okay then," says Jenson. He holds out a hand to invite us to get into the Humvees.

Will jerks his head and we begin to pile into the vehicles as Jenson and his followers stand around watching. For a moment, I have to wonder if he is just a complete moron. Once we take the trucks, there isn't anything preventing us from taking off and leaving them to die.

"Oh," Jenson says. "Just thought I'd remind you, I'll be watching. You know... drones."

He gestures up toward the sky.

"If you get the urge not to keep your word," he warns. He balls his fists up and makes an exploding sound as he opens them up again.

"Let's move out," Will says.

Will turns around and climbs into the passenger side of the vehicle beside Corporal Collins.

"Good luck boys," Jenson waves after us as we begin to accelerate away from the hangar.

"I really want to kick his ass," I mutter.

"Even with two good hands, he'd bust you like a piñata," Mac says.

"Doesn't mean I wouldn't enjoy trying," I say.

I feel Claire looking at me, the whole situation seems to have her on the verge of tears.

"You okay?" I ask her.

"I never thought people could be this terrible to each other," she says.

"This ain't nothing," says Sarge. "People are capable of worse."

"I still don't understand how we got suckered into this shit," Mac says. "The lieutenant really fucked this one up."

"He didn't have a choice," says Sarge. "Besides, there are innocent people here. Kids. Families. Jenson wasn't lying about that. If he isn't going to risk his ass to help them, it might as well be us."

"It's not our mission," I say.

"Yeah," says Sarge. "But it still might be the right thing to do."

"Unless we all die," says Mac.

"Let's just focus then and make sure that doesn't happen," Sarge says.

We pull out of the base and onto a dusty backroad that winds through the rocky desert. As the skies turn black, I look up at the amazing number of stars in the sky around the glowing swirl of the Milky Way. I forgot how mesmerizing it is to look at. Like God is trying to remind you that your problems will never matter that much in the grand scheme of things. Even if this is the end of humanity, the universe will continue to expand and grow and change, and our entire existence will be nothing more than a tiny flicker in all of it.

Within a half hour, we reach the intersection at Orogrande. The vehicles pause in the middle of the road while we all scan the highway to El Paso that stretches into the dark night. Although we can't see the dead yet, we can hear them. The faint constant moaning of thousands and thousands of corpses travels across the desert.

"Do you hear that?" Claire asks.

The haunting sound sends a chill down my spine. I try not to let it show. Claire looks nervous enough already.

"Don't worry," I assure Claire. "They won't get anywhere near us. We just have to lead them up that road. It'll be fine."

"Unless this old Humvee dies," says Mac. "Or Jenson decides to drop a bomb on our heads."

"Corporal," Sarge warns him.

"I mean, it's probably going to all be fine," Mac says. "The lieutenant has assured me we're perfectly safe out here."

"Enough, Mac," Sarge says.

The dark figures of the dead appear in the distance as they shamble toward us down the highway.

"I see them," I say.

The trucks roll side-by-side along the empty highway.

Gibby lights the stiffs up with the fitty cal, spraying bullets into the oncoming horde that trails behind us. The barrage does nothing to slow them, but the noise ensures they chase after us.

The sight of all the corpses at our six is terrifying, but we keep leading them along for miles down the dark highway. At least until we come to an overturned tanker that blocks the road.

The scent of fuel fills the air. Gunny drives off the road to the left around the rear of the tanker. Mac steers off the road in the opposite direction. Bushes scrape the undercarriage and the wheels spin in the sand, but he gets us around the tanker. Mac pulls back on to the highway but stops when he notices the other vehicle stuck in a ditch.

"Fuck," Sarge says.

The immense amount of fuel from the tanker turned the sand into a quagmire on the other side of the road. We watch as Gunny gives it some gas and tries to push out of the sand, but the Humvee isn't going anywhere.

"Not good," says Mac.

The lieutenant yells for the rest of the squad to abandon the vehicle as the dead swarm around the tanker. Gunny and the lieutenant climb out and sprint toward the road, but Collins, Logan and Sergeant Lowe fail to get out before the dead surround the Humvee.

I raise my rifle, but I hesitate to shoot. One spark could create a massive explosion with all that gasoline in the area.

"Don't fire," I yell, but it doesn't matter.

One of the dead latches on to the CIA agent and he pulls his sidearm and fires in desperation. The air all around us catches fire. I raise my arm to shield my face from the heat of the fireball. When I lower it again, I hear the screaming.

Gunny is engulfed in flames, he flails his arms as he falls to the ground. The lieutenant swats at the fire that covers the back half of his own body. He drops and rolls around on the highway. I see the shapes of Collins and Sergeant Lowe ablaze inside the vehicle.

"Gibby!" yells Sarge. "Help me get Will."

The two of them jump out of the truck and race over to where the lieutenant is collapsed in the road. I fire at some of the dead to cover them, but we only have seconds before there will be too many. Sarge tosses his combat jacket over the lieutenant and tries to smother the fire. Corpses, some of them in flames, close in around the men.

"Hurry up!" Mac yells.

Gibby and Sarge lift the lieutenant up and carry him back to the Humvee, but the dead are too close. I pull the trigger again to try and hold the dead off, but my mag runs dry as the things encircle them.

Several of the dead grab on to Gibby first. He tries to break free of their grip and keep moving, but more of them lunge at him and latch on to his clothes. He yells at the top of his lungs as he lets go of the lieutenant and falls back into the horde.

I jump out of the truck and run over to help Sarge. He shoves the dead to keep them away from the lieutenant until I reach them and help drag Will back to the truck. I get in and Sarge lifts Will on top of me in the seat. His legs dangle out the open rear door, so I wrap my arm around his neck and hold onto him.

Mac hits the gas once Sarge gets into the front seat, but the dead are already swarming around us. I reach for my nine-mil and fire at their faces as they try to pull the lieutenant away and climb inside the Humvee. Claire screams and leans back into me when the dead reach through the window on the opposite side of the vehicle.

"Get us out of here, Mac!" I yell as I kick at the dead in the door and fire again.

The vehicle lurches over several bodies and then breaks free from the group. Some of them cling to the vehicle, hanging on to the hood and the bumper as we pull ahead of the pack. The Humvee swerves as Mac tries to shake them off of us to see the road ahead. I fire at the last of the dead that clings to the lieutenants leg. It falls away and tumbles on the pavement.

"We're clear," I say, but when I turn around, I see a corpse crawling through the turret from the roof. I lift the gun and fire my last round as the thing lunges down at us. Claire screams as the stiff falls headfirst into the Humvee and crashes to the floor between us.

"Everyone okay?" Sarge asks.

With the chaos and the surge of adrenaline and the continual pain from my hand, I have no idea if I am okay. I glance quickly to see if I have any new injuries. I take a look at Claire; her face is flushed, and she is panting so hard that she can't even speak, but she seems okay.

"We're good," I say.

Then I notice Sarge is inspecting a wound on his arm. He cringes at the sight of a missing chunk of flesh. Blood drips onto his jeans. It's definitely a bite. Sarge leans his head back against the seat as he wraps his tourniquet around the wound.

"How's Will doing?" he asks me.

I take a look down at our platoon commander. Half of his face is burnt to a crisp. I check for a pulse, and I finally find it.

"He's alive," I say. "But he's in really bad shape. We need to get him help soon or he won't make it."

CHAPTER TWENTY

"We need to drive faster," I urge Mac.

"I can't go any faster," Mac says. "If we get too far ahead of those things, Private Dickhead might decide to order a drone strike on our fucking heads."

"Will is dying, Mac," I plead. "He won't be able to hang on much longer."

"Mac is right," Sarge tells me. "We have to maintain our speed."

"Fuck," I curse. "This ain't right."

I can feel myself losing my grip. We have lost a lot of our brothers, but Will has been the glue that kept us together through all of it. As I look down at him, burnt and on the verge of death, I begin to feel the burden of everything we have been through over the last few days.

"Keep it together, Corporal," Sarge reminds me. "We can't afford to lose our shit now."

I decide right then and there that if we make it back to base, I am going to kill Private Jenson. It doesn't matter if I die in the process. All of the pain and frustration and rage that has built up inside me since this started becomes focused on that singular objective. I just want him to die.

Will starts to convulse in my arms. His body shakes so violently I nearly lose my hold on him.

"Shit," I curse.

"What's wrong with him?" Sarge asks.

"A seizure, or something," I say.

"He's going into shock," Sarge says. "Fuck."

"What do I do?" I can't remember any of my training in this moment. Besides, there probably isn't much I can do for him right now.

"Don't quit on us, Will," Sarge says.

"Hang in there, lieutenant," I plead.

Will trembles violently before he lets out a gasp, and his body goes still in my arms.

"Will," I say.

He doesn't respond. I pry open an eyelid and his pupil is fixed and dilated. He isn't breathing anymore.

"Damn it, Will!" I curse. I shake him violently. "Wake the fuck up."

Claire reaches a hand over and places it on my shoulder.

"Chase," she says. "He's gone. You can't do anything for him."

"Let him go," Sarge says. He grabs my hand that is clutching the lieutenant. "You've got to let him go."

I shake my head. Not just because I don't want to drop his body on the side of the road, but I still can't accept the fact that he is gone.

As much as I don't want to, I let go of the lieutenant, and his weight slides off of me as his body falls out of the truck and into the night.

My good hand balls up into a fist. I raise it up wanting to punch something so bad. Then I remember I already have one fucked up hand and can't afford to wreck the other one.

"This is fucking bullshit!" I yell.

In the front seat, Mac quietly drives the truck while Sarge wraps a bandage around his forearm. I take a breath and try to pull myself together. We still aren't out of this shit yet, and I'm worried that we will have even more problems soon.

"How's your arm?" I manage to ask Sarge.

"Don't worry about me," Sarge says. "I'll be okay."

I can tell by the flat tone of his voice, that he does not fully believe what he is saying. The truth is we have no idea what will happen. No one that has been bitten by one of those things has lived long enough to find out what comes next.

"What the fuck are we going to do now?" Mac says.

"We keep going," Sarge says.

"To Los Alamos?" Mac says. "No fucking way, man. You can't be serious. Everyone is fucking dead. I'm done with all this shit."

"Mac is right," I agree. "We can't keep going like this. We will all just end up the same way."

"I don't like our chances back at Holloman much better," Sarge says. "We finish the fucking mission. Otherwise all of this was for nothing."

"Sarge," I say. "We won't make it there."

Sarge looks down at his arm and considers our situation. He knows I'm right. I don't even need to tell him this time. Still, it is never easy to admit defeat, especially for a Marine.

"I don't know," Sarge says.

"Well, we better figure it out soon," Mac says. "We're ten miles away from Alamogordo."

It's not like we have a lot of options. Our backs are against the wall, and we only have each other left. As we reach the town of Alamogordo, the decision is made for us. The intersection at the highway is flooded with the dead. Mac brings the truck to a stop and we sit there in the middle of the road with the dead closing in on us from both directions.

"Guess this is the end of the line," Mac says. "It's been nice knowing you guys."

"Fuck that," says Sarge. "Let's go. Everyone out of the truck."

"Where are we going to go?" Claire wants to know.

"Anywhere but here," Sarge says as he slams the door.

We follow his lead and exit the vehicle as the dead converge on us. The area surrounding the highway is mostly mobile homes, a few small shops, and a border patrol office.

"This way," Sarge says. He runs for the left side of the street, heading toward a dark alley between a convenience store and a barber shop.

"We got time to stop for a happy meal?" Mac gestures at a fast food restaurant on the corner.

"If you don't shut up and keep moving, you're going to be a happy meal," Sarge tells him.

We reach the end of the alley, step over the trampled remains of a chain-link fence, and head for a row of mobile homes. I can see several silhouettes wandering between the trailers in the moonlight. I check back over my shoulder to see if the dead are coming down the alley behind us, but it seems like they did not notice us slip away in the dimly lit street.

Unfortunately, the scattered corpses that wander around in the dusty lot of the trailer park take notice of our approach. There aren't too many of them, but any sound we make will only draw more attention from the horde near the highway.

Mac raises his rifle and swings the stock at a corpse that gets too close, and it collapses on the ground. The thing reaches back up and grabs at his leg as he tries to step away from it. Mac hits it again as the thing tries to bite him. It latches on to him again with jaws wide open, but Mac swings the rifle around and puts a bullet in the thing.

Sarge tells him to cease fire, but the sound has already alerted every one of those things for miles. I glance back and notice some of the dead in the street are turning and making their way toward the alley.

"We need to get off the streets," I say.

We start running across the desert, weaving through the dead on the path to the mobile homes. Sarge tries the door to a trailer, but it is locked. One of those things inside starts raging and knocking over what sounds like pots and pans. I run ahead and try the next dumpy looking residence with pink flamingos sticking up in the yard. The unlocked door pops open and I stick my head inside. It is dark and quiet and reeks of years of smoke, mold, and sweat; the scent of years and years of misery.

I wave them over and we pile inside. After I shut the door and lock it, we wait in the darkness and listen to the dead moaning and bumping into shit as they approach our position. We duck down and crouch on the floor that smells like an old bathroom stall and hope that the tide of the dead will pass by us.

"Never thought it'd end like this," Mac whispers.

"If you can keep your mouth shut for more than five minutes, we might just get out of here alive," I tell him.

Mac finally shuts up. Even he realizes this is a time where fucking around at all will get us killed.

Hours go by.

The dead gather outside.

Hundreds of them.

Mac stares at a spider crawling across the ceiling.

Claire sits on the floor beside the couch with her arms folded across her knees so she has a place to rest her head. I thought she managed to sleep until she finally picks her head up, and I can see the tears in her eyes.

Sarge starts to look worse. Perspiration collects on his forehead and trickles down his temples as he stares at the picture of his family. He has to know he will never see them again. Maybe he is just hoping that he will be with them soon.

I finally manage to sleep a little by resting my face on my knee. When I open my eyes again, the faint morning light illuminates the trailer. The sun comes up, and the temperature immediately starts to climb inside the aluminum tomb. The dead still move all around us, moaning and bumping into the trailer every few minutes. No matter how many times they make a noise outside, I still get scared they are about to swarm the trailer. Finally, I decide to peek through a window and recon the situation outside to get an idea of how bad it is.

The dead completely surround the trailer. Hundreds and hundreds of them slowly trudge along in the same direction. I turn my head to the left to see where they are going and notice a distant trail of smoke drifting up to the sky.

"They're all going that way," I whisper as I gesture toward the kitchen area of the mobile home. "There is smoke in the distance. Seems like maybe that is drawing them."

"Holloman," Sarge says. "That's where they're all going."

"You mean all that and we didn't even steer them away?"

"I don't think so," Sarge says.

"All those people there," Claire says.

"Some of them might have made it out," I say.

"Nothing more we could have done for them," Sarge tells her. "We tried."

One of the stiffs outside bangs into the trailer again and we all quiet down and wait some more. We can move around a bit inside, but we have to be careful not to draw attention to ourselves.

Mac crawls to the kitchen and finds some lukewarm water bottles in the fridge and some stale girl scout cookies. That helps keep us going, but it doesn't take long to get really uncomfortable inside this metal box. The dead are starting to smell pretty awful, and it seeps inside through the open windows.

I notice Sarge keeps messing with his arm, trying to adjust the bandage and resisting the urge to claw at it with his fingernails. The blood soaks through the fabric. I reach in my bag and grab an extra bandage I had for myself and hand it to him. Sarge unwraps his arm and inspects the wound. Severe bruising surrounds the bite. Puss trickles from the tissue where the skin and tendons were ripped open. It looks bad, but Sarge is a tough motherfucker. He just cringes as he pours some water to flush the wound and wraps it in a clean bandage.

"I hate to say this," Mac whispers. "But I have to take a shit."

"Fucking hold it, Mac," I curse him.

"What do you think I've been doing?" he says.

He crawls by me and makes his way into the bathroom. Since he can't flush the toilet he just leaves it there to fester.

Fucking asshole.

Finally, night comes back around and most of the dead seem to have moved on. I push the curtain aside and take a look outside again. There are still a few dozen stragglers wandering around, but nothing like the horde that went through here earlier. If we hold out for a little longer, we may just be able to make it out of here.

"We should be able to move soon," I whisper.

"I don't think I'm going anywhere," Sarge says.

I look down at him again and notice that he is shivering and soaked in a layer of sweat even though the air around us is dry as can be.

"We'll get you help," I tell him. "We just need to hold out a little while longer."

Sarge shakes his head.

"I can feel it," Sarge says. "I'm not gonna make it."

CHAPTER
TWENTY-ONE

Within a few hours, Sarge struggles to form sentences and can only keep his eyes open for a couple minutes at a time. His forehead feels much hotter than it should, too. I know we're going to lose him soon, and it feels like there is nothing we can do about it.

"We got to try and do something for him," I tell Mac.

"Like what?" Mac says.

"I don't know," I say. "We have to help him. We can't just sit here and do nothing."

"Just leave me here," Sarge mumbles.

"We can probably make it to the truck," I tell Mac.

"Then what?" says Mac.

"He's right," says Claire. "There's no one out there that can help us anymore."

"What about you?" I ask her.

"Me?" she says.

"You know about all this zombie shit," I say. "Can't you do anything to help him?"

"I'm not a doctor," Claire whispers. "And even if I was, we have nothing."

"Graves," Sarge says loudly as he tries to sit up.

"Not so loud, Sarge," I remind him and put a hand on him to keep him from moving. He is becoming delirious and doesn't have enough sense to keep quiet at the moment.

"I'm serious, Corporal," Sarge says. "I'm not going to make it."

"Quiet, Sarge," I whisper. "You don't know what you're talking about."

He reaches into his pocket and pulls out the photo of his family and a note.

"Don't you even fucking try to give me that shit, Pedro," I warn him. "I'm not taking that."

"Just fucking take it," he growls at me and shoves the note in my chest. "If you get out of this fucking mess alive, you find Melissa, and you give it to her. Please."

I take the note with my shaking hand and tuck it in my pocket.

"Now, listen to me," Sarge tries to sit up but struggles to push himself off the floor. "There's no way I'm ever gonna make it out of here. You know it as well as I do. But I can still buy the rest of you some time."

Sarge tells us when the dead thin out enough for us to make a break for it, he will create a diversion to help keep them off us. I look at Mac and he shakes his head.

"We can't do that, Sarge," I say.

"I'm not fucking asking, Chase," he says.

"There has to be a better way," I insist.

"There's not," he says. "It's the only way you will ever make it out of here. You have to let me do this. I'm going to die anyway."

When I hear him say it out loud, the eventuality of his death hits home. I look down at the floor.

"You two need to get Claire out of here," Sarge says. "Find a way to get her somewhere safe. Finish the mission. Do it for the rest of us."

"Okay," I finally agree.

We wait until it is light out to make our move, so we have better visibility. The only problem is that Sarge barely has the strength to stand anymore by the time dawn breaks. In a way, I was hoping we'd have to carry him out of here so he couldn't insist on sacrificing himself to save us.

When it comes time to make our move, he finds enough strength to pick himself up and prepare to go. He gives Mac all his ammo except for one mag.

"I won't need more than this, but you will," he tells Mac.

"You sure about this?" I ask him one last time to give him an out if he is having any second thoughts. "We can just try to make a run for it."

"I got this," Sarge tells me.

I give him a hug and then Mac does the same. Then Sarge props the barrel of his rifle on his shoulder with the muzzle pointing to the sky and opens the door. He looks around at the sun coming up and casually walks down the steps like he was heading out for a relaxing stroll on a lazy summer day. It's probably the bravest thing I've ever seen, and even though I never thought I could have respected him more, I do now.

Sarge walks right up behind a corpse a few trailers down the road, before the topless dead man in filthy jeans notices and slowly turns around. Sarge holds the rifle a few inches from his face, fires a round, and the body falls to the ground.

"Come on, you motherfuckers!" Sarge yells.

Another corpse turns and stumbles toward him.

"You want to play?" Sarge yells in his best Cuban gangster impression. "Okay."

He fires at the corpse as it reaches for him. More of them start moaning and wandering in his direction. Sarge drops to a knee for a moment and lowers the rifle to brace himself by placing the muzzle in the dirt. He turns back to look at the trailer, and I see a smirk on his face before he rises to his feet again.

"Let's go," Mac urges me.

"Come on!" Sarge yells at the dead as they close in around him. "I'll send you all to fucking hell!"

I resist the compelling urge to stay and watch Sarge die. It might sound morbid, but I kind of feel like I should be there to witness his final moment of bravery. Instead, I follow Mac through the door as Sarge limps in the opposite direction of the highway, firing at the dead from the hip.

"Say hello to—" I hear Sarge scream, but he suddenly stops yelling and resumes firing his rifle at the dead.

"Stay close," I remind Claire as we crouch and run across the lawn back toward the alley. Sarge continues firing while we make our way back to the Humvee. As I open the door, the shooting stops. I stand there holding the handle. In the distance, Sarge screams.

Mac fires up the engine and yells at me to get inside. I glance around the street. The dead are rushing toward us from every direction. Mac hits the gas before I even get the door closed.

"We ain't getting very far," Mac reminds me while pointing out the gas gauge.

"Just get us out of here," I say.

He makes a right at the intersection and heads north through town. There are still scores of the dead wandering aimlessly through the streets, but not nearly as many as two nights ago when we were forced to abandon the truck. Most of them have probably made their way over to Holloman, drawn by the fire and smoke. We can only imagine how bad things got there, but we don't want to.

"Do you think we have enough to make it to the next town?" I ask Mac as he weaves down the road, swerving through the dead that mindlessly throw their bodies at the truck like flies to a bug zapper.

"How the fuck would I know?" says Mac. "Probably not. These dinky towns are all like twenty or thirty miles apart."

The only thing that might be more likely to kill us than the dead is the desert. I don't want to risk getting stuck out there. As we drive, I scan the streets for any place that we might hole up.

Unfortunately, the stiffs are all over the place. If we stop now, they'd just surround us again. We need to find some place where there aren't more of those things around than we can handle quietly. We have to get farther away from the center of town.

"Make a left up ahead," I tell Mac when I spot a residential street.

He steers us down the road a little too quickly and the tires squeal when they skid over the pavement. We follow the long street and pass by several intersections, until the road curves to the right. I peer between the houses on the left and see nothing but desert behind them. There are a couple of stiffs wandering the street, but nothing we can't handle if we are smart about it.

"Stop here," I tell Mac and point to a house on the left side of the road with the front door left wide open. There is a body visible on the front porch, but it appears to be motionless on the ground.

We step out of the Humvee and run up the driveway. I help Mac drag the body out of the way and then we close the door and slide the deadbolt into place.

I catch my breath as we listen to the silence inside the house.

It sounds clear.

Claire climbs on the couch in front of the windows in the family room, pulls the curtain aside and looks up and down the street.

"Still just those same ones out there?" I ask her.

"Yeah," she says.

"How many?" I ask, just to be sure.

"Four of them," Claire says.

I walk over to the fireplace and grab the poker from a stand.

"We got to take care of them," I tell Mac. "Quietly."

I wait while he goes to the garage and returns with a sledgehammer.

As the first of the dead stumbles into the sandy yard, we open the front door and rush back outside. I swing the poker around and crack a grey-haired man with a mustache on the side of the head. He lurches to the side and falls to the earth but reaches his arms up right away and grabs at me. I jab him in the skull as hard as I can again, but with only one arm that is still worth a shit, I don't generate the force needed to inflict any real damage. I put my boot on his chest, smash the poker through his eye until the tip penetrates his brain, and then he finally stops moving.

When I look up, Mac is already walking away from a trio of bodies in the street. The sledgehammer smashed their skulls leaving gory patterns like red inkblots on the pavement.

"You okay?" he asks.

"Yeah," I say as I get back to my feet.

"You better just shoot them next time," Mac says.

"Maybe you're right," I agree.

CHAPTER
TWENTY-TWO

"If we're going to stay here, we need to secure this place," I say once we get back inside.

"Here?" Claire says looking around the modest house. "For how long?"

"Until we're dead, probably," Mac says.

"The lower level has a lot of windows," I say. "But at least the fence will keep them out of the back. We just need to focus on the front."

We search the house from top to bottom, but there are no unwanted surprises. Then we gather up materials to secure the building.

In the garage, I locate a few pieces of plywood propped up against the side wall behind a pickup. Mac digs through a tool chest and pulls out some screws, nails, a hammer, and a battery-powered drill. I follow him toward the door but pause and stare at the truck in the garage.

We could take it. Try to make it to Los Alamos. Complete our mission.

For what?

To save the world?

It feels like it is too late for that bullshit.

All that's left out there is more violence and death.

I push the thought away and shut the door to the garage. As much as I don't want to accept the fact that we have lost this fight, I know it's true.

All we can do now is survive.

Within twenty minutes, we have all the exposed windows on the lower level relatively secure. If we get a whole shitload of them coming at us at once, it won't hold. Only a couple more of the dead have wandered down this road so far, and they seem oblivious to our presence for now.

After days on the move, I collapse on the couch in the living room of random strangers. It is the most at ease I've been since this whole thing started. I kick my boots off and put my feet up on the armrest and stare at the ceiling.

Mac sits down on the loveseat across from me, and Claire takes the recliner in the corner of the room. She picks up a family photo off the side table beside her and studies it for a long time.

I don't know what we're going to do now. Everything has gone to hell. All that matters for the moment is that we don't have to keep running. I stare up at the ceiling and the nothingness of the white painted drywall and savor the emptiness of it for a few moments. The only thing that could make this any better would be some air conditioning.

Mac takes out his notebook and opens it up and starts scrawling in it again.

"What are you always writing in that thing?" Claire asks him.

"Words," Mac says. "Poetry. Stuff like that."

"Poetry?" Claire says. "It's the end of the world and you're writing poetry?"

"The world is poetry," Mac says. "Everything happening out there, the end of the world, if that's what you want to call it, is really just poetry. Poetic justice. That's my take on it."

"Such a renaissance man," says Claire.

The two of them ramble on for a few minutes, talking like a couple of nerds while I just kind of space out. It's not that I can't keep up with the conversation, I just don't really give a shit about philosophical or scientific explanations anymore. There doesn't seem to be much point in it. Everyone is dead. End of story.

"I'm going to see what they got to eat," I say and force myself to get off the couch. "Don't steal my spot."

I don't even bother opening the refrigerator. After a few days with no power, any of the food left inside there would just make me sick. That's the last thing I'd need right now. Luckily, the pantry is stocked with enough food to last us at least a week. They even have a couple cases of bottled water stacked on the floor. It may not be much, but right now it feels like we hit the jackpot.

I grab a bag of nacho cheese tortilla chips and pry it open. Then I notice a six-pack of soda in the cabinet, and I crack one of those open as I sit down at the kitchen table. I munch the crunchy chips as I glance around the room at the belongings and decorations of the people that lived here.

They were probably older, since everything is dated. The walls are painted in a mucus yellow color, and the wallpaper in the family room is decrepit. There are no photos of themselves. Old people never like to see how young they used to be or how old they've gotten on a daily basis. There is only one photo on a cherry cabinet in the corner of a cute blonde girl in a wedding dress, which I'd guess was probably their daughter.

I don't really know why I'm curious about the people that lived here. They're dead now, probably. Maybe I'm just trying to distract myself from thinking about all the bad stuff I don't want to think about, or because even though the people that lived here are gone now, they are still saving our lives.

"What's for dinner?" Mac asks as he wanders in from the family room. "Anything good in here?"

I'm about to tell him not to check the fridge but he grabs the handle before I get a chance. He opens the fridge and then slams the door shut again and covers his nose.

"You might want to try the pantry," I tell him. "There's enough in there to last a while. Give us a chance to figure out what the hell we do next."

"There ain't nothing to do now," Mac says. "Except probably die at some point."

"I'd still like to put that off a while," says Claire.

"Then we better make this food last," Mac says.

So that is what we do. For the next week, we conserve as much as we can. We stay inside to avoid attracting the dead. By the end of the first week, the pantry is nearly bare, and the water stops working, so we have to resort to drinking out of the tank in the back of the toilet.

Eventually, we have no choice but to start scavenging from the other houses on the block. That comes with a significant risk. We never know what might be coming at us once we smash in a window to get inside.

In this one house, we run into an entire family. The mom, dad, kids... baby.

All dead.

We deal with them, but I don't sleep so well that night.

The boredom is by far the worst part. Mac keeps busy writing in his notebook for hours on end, so I spend a lot of time listening to Claire talk because she doesn't have much else to do. She seems like a sweet gal, but me and her come from different worlds.

I hear all about how she had a hard time going to private school, how hard she had to work so hard to earn her second college degree by age twenty, and how she regrets it all because her parents died in a car accident when she was eighteen, and she wished she had a normal life and could have spent more time with them while they were here.

I mostly just listen, because hearing her go on and on about her upper-middle class struggles mostly just makes me feel like a piece of poor, white trash. Her definition of a rough childhood is a lot different than mine. That doesn't mean she doesn't try to ask me about it.

Whenever she gets curious about my past, I change the subject. I taught her to play poker, just to have something else to do besides talking. But she mostly continues to talk about herself while I pretend to be concentrating on my cards.

Finally, she convinces me to talk one night.

Earlier in the day, we had tactically acquired a stash of expensive Kentucky bourbon whiskey from a house on the next block over.

"It'd be a damn shame to let this go to waste," Mac tells me as he cracks open the bottle and fills three glasses.

A couple hours later, Mac is busy writing on the sofa, while Claire and I are piss drunk playing poker on the floor.

"Why don't you ever talk about yourself?" she finally asks me.

"There's not much to tell," I deflect.

"Come on. By now you know like everything about me. But all I know is that you're Corporal Chase Graves from Wichita Falls, Texas," she lowers her voice and does her best imitation of my accent. It makes me laugh, but mostly because it's so bad and I'm pretty drunk.

"Well, what do you want to know?" I ask her.

She seems so surprised that I'm agreeing that she can't think of what to ask me right away.

"I don't know," she says. "What was your family like?"

"Just a regular shitty family," I say.

I'm pretty content to leave it at that, but she stares at me until I finally go on.

"My pop is in the Air Force. We don't really get along."

"What about your mom?" she says.

"She died," I say. "I never really knew her too well."

"How old were you when it happened?" she asks.

"Eight or nine," I say. "I don't really remember."

"I'm sorry," she says. "What happened?"

"She overdosed," I say.

"Oh my god," says Claire. "I can see why you never wanted to talk about it. I'm so sorry."

"It's okay," I tell her. "I never really knew her. She up and left when I was a year old. Just walked out one day. Left my dad to take care of me. I never really knew why."

"That's terrible," Claire says.

I don't really want her pity, but it makes me want to explain the rest, so she doesn't feel so bad for me.

"I think my pop might have resented me for it, like it was this baby she was trying to get away from and not him. Maybe it was. But from what he told me later, she went off to Mexico and got involved with some biker down there. She got addicted to some junk then the biker bailed on her.

She wound up on the streets. Prostituting herself. Eventually, she died of an overdose. She was kind of a shitty person."

"Chase—" she says.

"It's alright," I assure her. "I never told anyone about that."

"I can't even imagine how hard it was growing up with all that," Claire says. She stares at me, but differently now, like a kid staring at a broken toy.

I suddenly feel irritated with myself for saying anything.

"No," I say. "You can't."

I grab the bottle off the table and fill my glass.

"You and me are from different worlds," I say. "We don't have nothing in common. If we weren't trapped in here together, we probably wouldn't have nothing to talk about."

"That's not true," Claire says.

"It's fine," I say. "There's nothing wrong with that. It's just reality. That's how it's always been."

"No," Claire shakes her head.

"You know, I'm right," I say.

"You're not," she insists.

"Suit yourself," I tell her. I down my drink, get up off the floor, and head toward the bedroom.

"Chase," she calls after me. "Don't leave."

"I'm going to sleep," I tell her. "Goodnight."

I leave Mac and Claire downstairs and head up to the bedroom. I take my shirt off and toss it aside. Then I lay down in the bed and try to get comfortable.

I regret the whole exchange with Claire already. Even though she is probably just bored, I'm not looking to be her friend. I definitely don't want her pity either. I manage to fall asleep but wake up a short time later when I hear a noise.

The floorboards creak and groan in the hallway. I decide to get out of bed and check it out. I need a drink of water anyway.

When I open the door, I notice a light on in the other room.

"What do you want?" Mac sighs.

"Make love to me, Mac," Claire whispers.

I knew it was just a matter of time before it happened. Maybe it's been going on for a while. It's probably better if I don't stand there listening to them, but my curiosity gets the better of me.

I walk over to the door and can see Claire sitting on the bed beside Mac. She touches her forehead with her hand, and I can tell she is really feeling the whiskey. She slides her feet onto the bed and lays down on her side and props her head up with her hand. Her eyes look at his face, then down his chest.

"Claire—" he starts to say but she lets out a hiccup and interrupts him.

"Excuse me," she laughs.

"You should probably get some sleep," he tells her.

She reaches up and touches his chest with her fingertips. Mac grabs her hand. It startles her, so he lets go and she retracts her hand. She rolls onto her back and stares up at the ceiling and sighs.

"What's wrong with me?" Claire asks.

"You clearly had too much to drink," he tells her.

"No," she says. "I mean why don't you care about me?"

"I never said I don't," he says.

"You act like it," she says. "Do you hate me because of them? The guys in your squad that died to rescue me?"

"That's not it," Mac sighs.

She turns her face away from him and starts to cry. Mac swipes his palm across his face in frustration.

"Claire," Mac says. "I do care about you. But... love? I'm just not that guy."

"I don't want it to end like this," Claire says. "To die like this. All I ever did my whole life is study and work. I've thought the right guy would come along one day. There will be time for all of that. But I was wrong. There isn't going to ever be time. Nobody is going to love me."

"Easy," he tells her. "Calm down."

She buries her face in her palms and sobs. Mac finally relents and reaches his arm out and pulls her toward him. Claire scoots her body closer and lays her head on his chest.

"I don't want to be alone until I die," she says.

"You're not alone," he assures her.

She lets out a deep breath and then she reaches up and puts a hand on the back of his neck. Claire pulls him closer to her, and Mac leans down and kisses her. His hand reaches up to cup her breast.

I feel awkward standing in the hall, so I retreat to the bedroom, careful not to make any noise that might disturb them. As much as I try to forget the whole thing and go to sleep, I can hear them having sex across the hall as I stare up at the ceiling. I can't blame them, but something about it still bothers me. If there is one thing life taught me, it is that relationships never end well, so it's best to just look out for yourself. Maybe it will be different for them. I'll hope I'm wrong, even if I know that I'm not.

CHAPTER TWENTY-THREE

In the morning, I wake up to Mac running up the stairs in a panic.

"Chase, wake up!" he says as he rushes into the bedroom.

"What's wrong?" I ask him.

"We may have a problem," he says.

"Stiffs?" I ask him as I get out of bed and pull my shirt over my head.

"No," he says. "Looks like some of the Army made it out of Holloman."

He hurries back across the hall to look out the window. I get out of bed, follow him, and do a double take at Claire clutching a sheet to her naked body on the bed. In my groggy state, I wasn't sure if what I remembered from last night was not just some strange dream. Instead of saying anything, I just head to the window and peek through the blinds at the street.

Mac points out the vehicle up the road. A team of six men work their way from house to house. Too bad for them we've already ransacked the entire block. I watch the men moving from the houses to the truck and try to spot Jenson, but from this distance it's not possible to tell if he is among them.

"What do you want to do?" I ask.

Mac rubs a hand along the facial hair that covers his jaw.

"We can just try talking to them," suggests Claire.

"I don't know if they'll be so happy to see us," Mac says.

"Probably not," I say. "I'm not exactly happy to see them either."

"Two against six," says Mac. "Don't really like those odds."

"Three," Claire says, pulling a shirt over her head.

Mac looks over his shoulder at Claire.

"I meant three," Mac lies.

"Give me a gun," Claire says. "I want to be able to defend myself if something happens to you guys."

Mac walks over to the bedside table and picks up his nine-mil and hands it to Claire. She will likely end up shooting herself in the foot, but she has a right to do that if she wants.

We grab our rifles and head downstairs to the front door. The truck pulls up to the neighboring house and four of the men get out to search the building while the other two keep watch on the street.

"Let's go," I say to Mac.

"What are we doing again?" Mac says.

"Just going to try and talk with them," I say.

"Sure. This will go great," Mac scoffs.

"Stay inside," I tell Claire. "If something happens, go out the back patio and run like hell."

I open the door and walk down the driveway beside Mac. We approach the truck casually but keep our rifles at a low ready.

"Don't look so nervous," Mac says.

"I'm not nervous," I tell him.

"You look nervous," Mac says.

"How do I look nervous?" I ask him.

"I don't know," Mac says. "But you do. Put on your nice face or something."

I try out a smile and Mac looks at me and shakes his head.

"Never mind," he says. "Don't do that. You look like a psychopath."

"Hey!" one of the guys on the truck spots us approaching and raises his rifle. "Stop right there!"

We stop walking in the middle of the road, and I raise a hand to acknowledge the man.

He squints his eyes at me and Mac.

"How's it going?" I ask him.

"Who the hell are you guys?" he asks.

"Nobody special," says Mac. "Just a couple guys out for a stroll."

"What?" the guy asks. He continues to point his rifle at us with a confused look on his face. "Drop your guns. Both of you."

"This isn't working," Mac mutters to me quietly out of the corner of his mouth.

"Just take it easy," I say to the man. "We're not looking for any trouble. I just thought I'd let you guys know we already cleaned out the houses on this street. Save you all a little time."

"Rhodes!" the man calls.

"Shit," I mumble.

Rhodes steps out of the house next door.

"What's wrong, Davis?" Rhodes asks.

Davis points to me and Mac in the street. Rhodes blinks his eyes as he tries to place us. I can't be positive what day it is anymore, but it's been maybe six weeks since we left Holloman. Both Mac and I have longer hair than before, and Mac has a beard now. I hold out hope that he won't recognize us until he looks down and notices my hand.

"You," Rhodes says. "Holy shit. I can't believe you're still alive."

"Most of our guys weren't so lucky," I say. Even though I attempt to hide my hostility, it probably still shows.

"So, it's just you two?" he asks.

I decide not to answer him. Maybe it's better to let him wonder if we have additional support.

"Well," he finally says as he takes a few steps toward the street. "That's how it goes now. The world ain't the same as it was."

"They said they cleaned out this block already," says Davis.

"Is that right?" Rhodes asks.

I nod slightly when he looks at me.

"You guys must have a lot of shit then," he says. I watch his hands as he shifts his grip on his rifle. "Don't suppose you fellas would be willing to share the wealth."

This guy has some fucking nerve. After everything, he shows up here trying to intimidate us into handing over our shit.

"Not a fucking chance," I tell him.

"I had a feeling you might say that," Rhodes says.

He turns his head to the side and spits in the dirt. I can tell this is going to get ugly. Even if they leave now, they will not just leave us alone. If anything, they will come at us with more guys and probably when we least expect it.

"I'll get the guy in the truck," I whisper to Mac as I pretend to swipe my sleeve across my face like I'm wiping away sweat.

"You sure you want to do this?" Mac mutters through clenched teeth.

"It's going to happen either way," I whisper. "You with me?"

"I'm with you," Mac says.

"You know, I'd invite you gentleman to come back with us, but Jenson is still pretty pissed," Rhodes says.

"Is that right?" I say.

Rhodes nods.

"Says your guys fucked up that whole operation," Rhodes tells us. "Got a lot of innocent people killed."

"That wasn't on us," I say.

Rhodes fixes his stare on me and Mac as he slightly adjusts his grip on the rifle. He tilts his head back without taking his eyes off us. I watch his every movement closely.

"Let's go," he calls to the rest of the team inside the house but makes no move to head toward the truck. He just stares at us as he waits for the other men to exit the house.

I get the feeling Rhodes will make a move as soon as the numbers are in their favor.

I could be wrong. It's possible they might just walk away and never come back.

Let bygones be bygones.

I'm not about to take my fucking chances on that happening.

"Kill," I say to Mac, and I raise my rifle and start firing.

The Honey Badger spits a round that hits Davis in the chest and knocks him back against the rear bumper of the truck. Mac takes shots at Rhodes as he tries to raise his rifle. A round tags Rhodes in the thigh and staggers him. He tumbles and starts crawling through the dirt toward the house. The driver in the pickup opens the door and I hit him in the chest and the leg before he even makes it out of the truck.

"Get to cover," I tell Mac as the hostiles in the house take aim at us from the front door and windows.

I put some suppressive fire on the building and sprint for the truck in the road. I slide to safety behind the rear tire and look back as Mac runs back towards the house. He fires while sidestepping up the driveway as he heads for cover on the front porch. Then a 5.56 mm round tears through his mid-section and sends him face-first into the dirt. He manages to drag himself a few feet as bullets punch the dirt around him. Finally, Claire runs out the front door and grabs his arm to pull him out of the line of fire.

Even though Mac has to be hurt bad, he grabs his rifle, adjusts his grip, and gets ready to give these bastards some hell. For several seconds, nobody fires. Rhodes grunts in the dirt as he tries to drag his ass to safety. I could kill him right now, but I wait.

He is just a piece of bait to draw out the others.

When I hear the rest of his team coming out to help, I pivot around the back of the truck and open fire. Mac manages to lean around the side of the house and unloads his magazine at them before collapsing to the ground.

I step around the truck and scan the bodies on the ground. The only one still moving is Rhodes. He sits up, trying the get his rifle into a firing position, but I lift the Honey Badger and pop him in the shoulder, and he falls back again and writhes in the dirt.

I'm not done with him yet.

I cross the lawn and stand over Rhodes on the ground. He reaches for his gun, but I put a boot on his wrist.

"Fuck, man. It didn't have to go this way," Rhodes says.

"Where the fuck is Jenson?" I question him.

"I don't know," Rhodes says. "We bailed on him weeks ago and never looked back."

"You're full of shit," I say.

"You think I'd lie to protect him?" Rhodes scoffs.

"Chase!" Claire yells.

"You're even crazier than he is," Rhodes smirks at me.

I lift the rifle up and fire a round into his head. The gunshot echoes off the aluminum siding of the houses as his body falls still in the dirt.

I run over to where Claire crouches beside Mac and checks his gunshot wound. The bullet hit him above the hip, and he is already losing a lot of blood.

"Hang in there, Mac," I tell him.

"How bad is it?" he asks me.

"It ain't nothing man," I tell him. "You're gonna be fine."

"You're a shitty liar, Graves," Mac coughs.

I check the street again and spot the dead up the road. No doubt all the gunfire will draw a lot more stiffs to this area soon. We will have to abandon our refuge.

"Help me get him inside," I tell Claire.

She grabs his feet, and I pull him up by the shoulders to get him inside and onto the kitchen table. I check his back and locate the exit wound near his spine. This is way beyond my training. I keep pressure on the wound and try to keep Mac still while I figure out what to do. The bullet probably tore through his intestines, but I can't see anything with all the blood.

"Grab me some towels and water," I tell Claire. "And there should be some morphine in my bag."

She runs into the other room and returns a minute later.

"Soak one of the towels," I tell her, as I keep my hand clamped on the wound.

She does, and I cover the wound with it. Mac cringes from the pain.

"Try to keep still," I say to Mac.

"It fucking hurts like hell," he curses, clutching the table.

I grab the morphine from Claire and inject it into his leg. Within a few seconds his body relaxes on the table.

"That's better," he says. "That's a lot better."

I check his pulse and it is still pretty strong, but there isn't much else I can do for him here. He will at least need some fluids, antibiotics, and surgery unless by some miracle the bullet didn't destroy any of his organs.

I collapse into the chair beside the table and try to think.

"What else can we do for him?" Claire says.

"I don't know," I tell her. "I don't have anything here to even try and help him."

"Well then where can we find what we need?" Claire says.

I think about it for several seconds.

"Holloman," I say. "They have a hospital on base. We'd have to go back there."

"What are you sitting around for then?" she says. "Let's go."

CHAPTER TWENTY-FOUR

I find the keys to the pickup left hanging from a nail next to the door in the garage. I pack enough food and water to last a couple days in a cardboard box and toss it on top of the tools in the bed of the pickup. Then we load Mac into the backseat of the truck. The thought hits me that maybe this is crazy. Even if we make it to the hospital, we might not be able to do anything to keep Mac from dying. There is a chance we might even run into Jenson there.

It still doesn't make me think twice about it. The rest of my platoon is gone. Mac is all I have left. I don't know if I can handle losing him, too.

Besides, we can't afford to sit around. The dead are converging on the area and it's just a matter of time before Jenson figures out that something happened to his team.

I don't believe a word Rhodes said about abandoning his brothers. It had to be bullshit.

Jenson would eventually come looking for them either way, and my chances of facing them alone and coming out alive do not seem very good.

So, in spite of the sense of impending doom, I unlatch the garage door and lift it open. I hop in and shift to reverse and back out of the driveway. Several shambling dead bodies smash against the rear gate, and their bones crackle beneath the tires. I shift to drive and plow over a couple more as they rush the vehicle.

"Jesus," Claire says. "You can drive around them, you know."

I could, but I'm angry right now. No, I'm not angry. I'm fucking pissed. I'm pissed at Rhodes, at Jenson, at Claire, at the dead, and the whole fucked up world for being so fucked up all the time.

"Shut up," I tell Claire.

The woman is cursed. Everything was going fine before, but then she showed up and my whole world immediately started going to shit.

"Chase," she says.

"I said shut up," I snap. "This is all your damn fault. If we didn't have to help your sorry ass none of this would have ever happened."

She leans back against the door, putting as much space between us as possible as though she is afraid, I might try to hurt her. Maybe I'm an asshole, but it makes me feel better to see her react that way. It's exactly what I want right now.

The truck speeds down the backroads, probably faster than it is safe to drive. I steer between the dead bodies on the road but can't help cutting it too close and hitting some of the dead as they approach the vehicle.

"Slow down," Claire pleads with me.

My foot presses down on the gas pedal a little more.

"You're going to get us all killed," she says. "Is that what you want?"

I turn around the corner and head toward the highway. The dead flood the streets. There really is no alternative but to slow down to navigate through them. Unless I really do want to die, and I guess what I come to realize is that I am still not ready for that.

"I'm sorry," I tell her, even though I don't feel all that sorry. Right now, it feels like the weight of the world has been dumped on me while everything that matters has been methodically ripped away by forces beyond my control. Mostly, I tell her I'm sorry because I want her to forget everything and leave me alone.

We make it out of Alamogordo and drive along the short stretch of desert highway to Holloman. The corpses are more dispersed outside of town, but hundreds of them wander along the entire ten miles of road that leads to the Air Force base. The closer we get, the more the dead crowd the highway. When we finally reach White Sands Road, I pause at the intersection and stare at the sight of tens of thousands of corpses wandering the road up to the entrance of the base.

Claire looks at me. Her eyes are filled with terror as she shakes her head. Right now, I think she is mostly afraid that I might just be irrational enough to try and drive us through that nightmare.

"There has to be some other way in," I say. I take my foot off the brake and keep driving. I speed down the highway another mile or so until I reach the road for White Sands National Park. I make the right turn into the entrance and roll up the empty lane into the parking lot outside of the derelict visitor center.

"Where are we going?" Claire asks me.

"Going to see if I can follow one of these trails and get a look at the back of the base," I say. "I don't know what else to try."

"You saw how many of those things there are," she says. "We can't possibly go in there."

"I have to," I tell her. "Unless you can come up with some better idea."

"We can drive to the next town or something," Claire says.

"The next town is fifty miles from here," I tell her. "Mac ain't going to make it. We don't have a choice."

I follow the road through the mounds of brilliant white sand beneath the midday sun. We circle around to the first trail, and I steer the truck off the sandy streets. There isn't any road to get where we need to go from here.

"Do you have any idea where we are?" says Claire.

I ignore the irritating questions and keep driving north along the dunes at the edge of the park and scan the eastern horizon until I get a glimpse of the base in the distance. We're still at least half a mile away.

"I have to get us closer," I say.

I steer the truck through fields packed with creosote and cacti. Eventually, the remains of the chain-link fence surrounding the base comes into view, and in the distance, I can see the back of the complex. I park the truck and get out to recon the area. When I look through the scope of my rifle, I make out the shapes of the hangars along the runway, and the dark specks of the dead wandering all over the area. The place is completely overrun.

Claire gets out of the truck and shields her eyes from the sun to try and see as well.

"We can't go in there, Chase," Claire says.

I leave her surveying the base and walk around to the other side of the truck to open the rear door and check on Mac. I reach down to check his pulse, but I can't find it.

"Mac," I say. I shake him gently. His body is completely limp. His eyes stare up at the clouds drifting across the blue sky above us, but he can't see anything now.

I could try to resuscitate him, but it seems pointless. Nothing I can do will ever be able to keep him alive at this point.

"Chase, there are too many of them," Claire repeats.

"It doesn't matter now," I say. "He's already gone."

Claire hurries around the truck and cups her hands over her mouth when she sees Mac lying there lifeless. I slide my arms beneath him and hook them under his shoulders.

"Let me help you," Claire says.

I ignore her and haul him out alone, his weight carries both of us to the ground. Claire bends down to help me up, but I shrug my arm away from her. After I pick myself up from the dirt, I crouch down to check him for a pulse one more time.

I have to be sure.

Staring down at his lifeless body still doesn't seem real to me. I keep expecting his eyes to move, and then he would laugh at me for buying that he could really be dead.

Finally, I give up and get back to my feet again. I grab my rifle from the front of the truck and then I stand over Mac and shoot him, so he doesn't come back.

Claire turns her back, so she doesn't have to see him anymore and lets out a sob. My head starts to spin as I drop my rifle and take a knee beside him.

"Chase!" Claire says when she sees me drop to the ground with my hand clutching my face. She goes inside the truck and starts digging around in the supplies.

"I can't fucking do this anymore," I plead.

I'm just done with all of this shit. Everyone is dead. It's just a matter of time for us now, too.

"Here," she says. "Drink some water."

I take the water from her, but I just hold it in my hand for a while before I calm myself down enough to pour some back into my parched mouth. As hard as it is, I turn my head and look at the body of my brother in arms on the ground beside me. The desert sun already feels like it is burning my skin, but I know what I need to do next. I can't just leave Mac sitting out here.

I get to my feet and walk over to the truck and grab a small shovel in the pile of supplies. Then I turn and trudge back toward the desert until I find a softer patch of sand and begin to dig. I toss shovel after shovel of white sand aside as Claire watches me from the truck.

It seems like it takes forever to get a couple feet down; then I look down and decide I can't do anymore. I sit down on the edge of the grave and take another gulp of water. Claire notices how tired I am, and she walks over. I stand up and pick up the shovel as she approaches me.

"I'll give you a hand," she says.

"I got it," I say as I throw another shovel of sand aside.

"I cared about him, too, Chase," she says.

I pause for a moment and look at her. I can tell she is broken up over this, but that's what happens when you start caring about people.

"I know," I tell her. Then I bend down and scoop up another shovel of sand.

"At least take a break," she says. "You're going to kill yourself."

"I'm fine," I insist.

She sighs and turns to the side and looks across the vast empty desert.

"What are we going to do now, Chase?" she asks me. I can hear the hopeless despair in her voice.

"I'm going to finish digging this hole," I say and toss more sand.

"I mean where are we going to go?" Claire says.

I stop digging for a second to catch my breath and impale the pile of sand next to the hole with the shovel.

"We can't go back to the house," she says.

"I know that," I say.

She doesn't seem to realize I haven't been thinking about anything except putting my friend in the ground. I lost everyone. The only thing I can do is to make sure I take care of Mac now. Lay him to rest. Maybe it's too late to do anything for the rest of my brothers. But at least I can do this one last thing for Mac. It might not be much, but at least it is something.

"I really don't know," I tell her. "I'll figure something out."

I pry the shovel free and continue digging as she goes back to the truck to get out of the hot sun. Once the hole is several feet deep, I climb out and walk over to drag the body of my friend toward the grave. I reach down and take his dog tags off his neck.

I am too exhausted to pick him up, so I just roll him into the ditch. He lands all twisted up with his face in the dirt, so I drop back down in the hole and shift him onto his back. Then I climb back out and take a look at him, but it's still too hard to see him like this, so I immediately start covering him with white sand.

After I cover the grave, I shove his rifle in the ground and prop his helmet down on top of it. I take his dog tags and wrap the chain around the barrel, so they hang there.

I take a step back and look at the ground one more time.

"Sorry, brother," I say. "I did the best I could.

CHAPTER
TWENTY-FIVE

As the fiery sun descends below the desert, I climb into the truck and take a sip of water. I have no idea what to do now. We were lucky enough to find a quiet place to lay low for a couple of months. It wasn't much, but we got by. Now we're back out in the world, with a few days' worth of food and water between us and death.

I know we will have to figure something out, but it is already getting late and after everything that happened, I just can't handle dealing with all our problems right now.

So, we decide to spend the night in the truck. There isn't much out here, and we can see for a couple miles in every direction. We're as safe here as we'll be anywhere for the night.

Claire tries to make conversation, but I don't feel like talking. After enough of my one-word answers, she eventually just gives up. We eat some stale chips and split a can of baked beans in the quiet night. Then I tilt the seat back and try to get comfortable enough to fall asleep while Claire keeps an eye on the desert.

In the middle of the night, I wake up after having a dream where I saw the rest of my platoon as shambling corpses walking toward me through the ghostly white sands of the desert. As I open my eyes and take a deep breath, I notice Claire snoring quietly in the seat beside me. I only managed to get a couple of hours of sleep, but I choose to stay awake and let her rest. It's not like I want to go back to dreaming after that nightmare.

I just sit there in the quiet of the truck and stare at the stars until the sun starts to rise and I can't see them anymore. After dawn breaks, I get out of the truck and start checking our supplies.

We're down to our last couple bottles of water. We still have a cardboard box full of food. Nothing that looks particularly appetizing. There is some jerky, stale cereal, animal crackers, saltines, peanut butter, and some assorted cans of fruit, veggies, beans, and tuna.

I grab Mac's pack, but I open it and see his notebook on top and then I close it back up and set it aside. I can't bring myself to look through his stuff yet.

At least we have a full tank of gas in the truck. That ain't much, but at least it's something. I check how much ammo we have left and break down and clean the Honey Badger. Then I sit in the bed of the truck and refill my empty magazines while I wait for Claire to wake up. Finally, as I climb down from the truck, she opens her eyes and groans from the pain of sleeping sitting upright in the seat all night long.

"Good morning," I say to her. I pass her a water through the window to rinse the taste of sleep out of her mouth.

"Thanks," she says. She grabs the bottle and takes a drink.

"Go easy," I tell her. "We only got a couple bottles of water left."

She lowers the bottle and puts the cap back on.

"Do we have anything to eat?" she asks.

"Not much," I tell her as I reach into the bed of the truck and grab the box of cereal. She takes it and stares at the box. Then she opens the top and reaches a hand inside and pulls out a handful of colorful fruit-flavored loops.

It's already late in the morning. We probably should have gotten on the road hours ago, but the fact is I still have no clue where we should go.

I look around us at the harsh desert. The terrain surrounding White Sands is stark and unforgiving and now it belongs to the dead. Claire hands the water back to me and I swallow down the last drops before tossing the bottle back inside the pickup.

"What do we do now, Chase?" she asks me.

"I don't know," I admit.

Hundreds of soulless creatures trudge across the desert. It appears the dead at the base have spotted us. It will take them quite a while to reach us, but we will have to get on the road soon.

The scorching sun glistens off the sand and slowly cooks our bodies. No human can survive very long in conditions like this. But those things out there aren't human. They're relentless. Remorseless. And they're everywhere now.

I listen to the endless moans of the dead carry on the wind, but then I hear another distant noise.

"You hear that?" I ask Claire.

"What?" she asks. "I don't hear anything."

I hold a finger to my lips, so that she will stop talking. The unmistakable whirring of a helicopter cuts through the stifling air. After listening for a few more seconds, I'm sure I'm not just imagining things. As the sound of the bird gets louder, I scan the horizon.

"A helicopter," I say to Claire. "Heading this way."

The Osprey emerges through the clouds hanging over the eastern horizon and circles around Holloman Air Force Base and the swarms of dead below. The sight of the military aircraft is surreal. I have to wonder who could possibly be on board.

Maybe they are just more of the fractured remains of our armed forces, like the Army units from El Paso. It probably just means more shit to deal with.

The bird peels away from the overrun airfield and turns towards the Tularosa Basin.

"What is he doing?" Claire wonders.

"It looks like he is trying to find a spot to touch down," I say.

The engines on the Osprey shut down as the pilot circles above the desert. The fool must have run out of fuel up there. Claire and I watch as the aircraft wobbles down to the ground and spews up a cloud of sand as it makes a hard landing. I hold my breath for a long moment, expecting an explosion that doesn't come. The corpses in the area begin to converge on the crash site. If anyone managed to survive that landing, they won't be alive very long.

"We should get moving," I say to Claire. "That crash will draw every walking stiff for miles."

"They could still be alive," she pleads as she watches me load my gear back onto the truck. She folds her arms across her chest when she sees my indifference. "They're probably with the military. We have to do something."

"They're probably dead," I say. "And we will be, too, if we don't get the hell out of here."

Gunfire from the direction of the helicopter proves me wrong a moment later. I bring up my rifle to scope the area again and see a big ass guy dressed in SEAL fatigues hauling a woman out of the cargo bay. A long-haired brunette and a man dressed in black tactical uniforms follow him out into the white-hot sands and cover him as he runs into the Osprey and retrieves another person. The big guy returns carrying a kid in his arms and is trailed out by a scruffy dog.

As the man in the black uniform scans the desert for threats, he spots our vehicle parked on the dunes. He waves an arm in the air to show he is friendly but keeps his rifle at a low ready. I don't move to return the gesture.

These people aren't military. Not all of them anyway.

"Get in the damn truck," I growl at Claire.

She ignores me and waves her arms over her head.

"They need help," Claire says. "And we do, too."

"Claire!" I yell.

Before I can stop her, she is heading down the hill, skidding down the hot sands. This woman is hell bent on getting me killed. I decide to leave her ass to die out here in the desert with them.

She made her own damn choice.

I walk around and get in the pickup and start the engine. After I shift the truck in drive, I look back to see Claire running toward the chopper through the sand as the dead from Holloman swarm toward their position.

"Dumb bitch," I growl.

I slam a fist on the steering wheel, then I crank it to the right and drive down the hill.

I slow down alongside her and tell her to get her ass back in the truck. She ignores me and keeps walking toward the crash site.

"I can't believe you would let them die out here," she shakes her head.

"I'm just trying to protect you," I tell her.

"Yeah, yeah, the mission," she scoffs.

"It's not about the mission anymore," I say.

"We did it your way last time," she says. "That didn't work so well. This time we do it my way."

"Damn it," I curse.

Claire turns her head and keeps walking as I roll along beside her.

"Fine," I relent. "Just get in the truck, Claire. We'll go help them."

She stops walking and stares me down before she finally gets in the passenger seat.

I hit the gas and the truck rumbles over the sand until we reach the helicopter. We get out and the big guy in the SEAL uniform looks me up and down as he heads inside the bay of the Osprey again.

The man in the black fatigues approaches the vehicle cautiously.

"We came to help," Claire tells him.

The man shifts his gaze to me and my finger hovering over the trigger of the Honey Badger. He gives me a nod and then smiles at Claire.

"I know you were taking a chance just by coming to help," he tells Claire. "Thank you."

"Who are you guys?" I demand. "How'd you get all this shit?"

"I'm Blake," he says. "Not sure you will believe me if I tell you how we ended up here, but I will. After you give us a lift out of here."

He looks to me for agreement. My eyes shift from his face to the kid crying beside the body of a woman that looks to be dead. These people don't seem very threatening, but they don't exactly seem very capable either. Still, I am curious how they ended up here, and I know that Claire

will continue to give me shit unless I offer to help them.

    "Fine," I agree as I open the door to the truck again. "Just hurry the fuck

up."

CHAPTER
TWENTY-SIX

"Oh my god," says Claire.

"What?" I pause with my hand on the door of the truck and turn back to look at her.

"That's him," she says.

"Who?"

"That's Dr. Schoenheim," Claire says.

She runs over to an old man in a lab coat and boxer shorts that is being helped off the helicopter by a young blonde woman. Claire gets in front of them, and the doctor looks up at her with a smile as he seems to recognize her.

"No fucking way," I mutter to myself.

"She knows him?" Blake asks me.

"Yeah," I say. I'm so stunned I can hardly get the words out. "They worked together. We brought her out here a couple of months ago to meet up with him."

"We?" Blake asks me. His eyes search the area around us.

"My platoon," I tell him. "I'm the only one left now."

"I'm sorry," he tells me.

Claire hugs the doctor and then she turns and helps him as he makes his way toward the truck. A smile crosses her face as she waves and points to me and says something to the doctor. She looks more alive today than the entire time we've been together.

"This is fucking unbelievable," I mumble.

"Let's hurry up," says the Navy SEAL. "We still got a bunch of shit to move."

I wait by the truck while Blake and his crew load everyone and all their supplies into the overloaded pickup. Maybe I should have helped them to speed things along, but I decide to keep an eye on the truck. They seem okay, but I don't know them, and it's better to be safe than dead.

"I'm sorry," I pull Blake aside when he returns to the truck. My head feels like it's spinning. "We thought everyone from the team out of Chicago was dead."

"You did?" Blake says.

"We heard the helicopter crashed months ago," I tell him.

He seems as confused as me.

"Really?" he says. "How did you hear that?"

"This guy," I say. "Logan. He was some moron the CIA sent to tag along with us. He was in satellite contact with Cheyenne Mountain."

"What happened to that guy?" Blake asks.

"Bought it back in the first few days," I tell him.

"So, you've been out here waiting for us all this time?" he asks.

"Not exactly waiting," I say. "More like just surviving."

"Blake," the brunette woman interrupts. "We should probably get moving."

With everyone piled into the truck, I start the engine. Rolling through Alamogordo with the cab overflowing with people is probably not the best plan. If I have to swerve to avoid the dead, that might be all it takes to send someone tumbling out of the truck bed. We're going to need to secure another vehicle. I start driving in the direction of the welcome center near the entrance to the White Sands National Monument.

"Where are we going?" the big Navy SEAL asks. "You guys have a safe place you've been staying around here?"

"We did," I say. "But I don't think it will be safe there anymore."

The sight of so many unfamiliar faces make me nervous after everything we have been through. I'm not sure I'm ready to trust people. I keep checking the rearview mirror, looking at the men in the backseat and the rest of the group in the bed of the truck.

"You were military," the Navy SEAL says. It is more of an observation than a question.

"Yeah," I say.

"What unit?" he asks.

I tell him.

"You the only one left?" he asks.

"Yeah," I say. "What about you?"

He doesn't say anything, which I take as an affirmative.

"Recon," he says. "What's your name, Marine?"

"Chase" I tell him.

"Chase," he says. "I'm Hoff."

"You in charge?" I ask him.

"That's a laugh," Hoff says. "Like these people would actually listen to me just because I served."

"They probably should," I tell him.

"That's not how it goes, though," he says.

I pull up in front of the visitors center and park the truck out front. Several abandoned cars sit in the parking lot.

"We should check these cars," I say. "Probably going to be hard getting through those things with this many people in the truck."

"Good call," Hoff says.

He opens the door and hops out of the pickup and approaches the SUV with his rifle ready. Once he makes sure the front seat is clear, Hoff smashes the driver's side window. He pokes his head inside and checks the back seat. After he reaches in and unlocks the door, Hoff inspects the dash. He pulls out something from his bag and starts messing with the steering column.

I am finally over the shock of everything that happened today and can consider the situation rationally. I scan around the empty parking lot and the dark visitor center and then glance at the clock in the dashboard of the truck. My fingers wrap around the keys and I cut off the engine and open the door.

"What are you doing?" Claire asks me. "We should start driving toward Los Alamos. Maybe we can still try to do something to stop this nightmare."

"I know you want to get to Los Alamos," I tell Claire. "But we are staying here. Just for the night. We have no idea what might be waiting for us in Los Alamos. I don't want to be going into an unknown location in the dark."

I take a look back at the truck bed and all the strange new faces with their eyes on me. They look like they have been through hell already. I realize they must be just as apprehensive about me as I am about them.

"You folks can leave if you want, but I'm telling you we should wait. You have no idea what it's like around here," I tell them. "The situation is kinetic. Getting up to Los Alamos is not going to be easy. We must exercise caution."

"Sounds good to me," says a guy with dark hair and a slight southern accent. "We could use some time to catch our breath."

"Okay," agrees Blake.

"Say young fella," says the southern man. "Give me a hand getting the lady inside."

I cock my head to the side as I try to figure out if this guy is trying to be funny or not. He glances back at me when I don't move and notices my missing fingers.

"Oh shit," he says. "I didn't see that, brother. I'm sorry."

"It's fine," I say. "I can help you."

I walk around to the rear gate and wait for everyone else to climb out of the truck. The woman on the bed of the pickup looks beat to hell. Her face is swollen and bruised. She has matching black circles around her eyes.

The dead didn't do this. Someone beat the hell out of her.

I help lift her out of the vehicle, and she groans slightly as we carry her toward the front door.

"Easy with her," the man tells me. It isn't hard to see he cares for her by how he looks at her.

She opens her eyes a bit at the sound of his voice.

"Fletcher," she says.

"I'm here, Scout," he says. "You're gonna be okay."

"I'll take some of that joint now," she smirks. Her eyes close again, and her head lolls to the side.

"Sorry, doll," he says, even though she probably can't hear him. "I'm all out."

She closes her eyes again as we carry her through the doors of the welcome center.

"What happened to her?" I ask Fletcher.

"More than you can imagine," is all he says in response.

We get everyone inside the lobby and sit in the hot shade. I help bring Scout over to a bench and set her down. Then I step away from the group and take a minute to hang back by the door and get another look at all of them. I'd been so shocked when Claire recognized the doctor that I hadn't paid a whole lot of attention to the rest of these people, but now I'm trying to get a feel for who the hell they might be and how they all could have possibly ended up together. It's about the most ragtag looking group of people imaginable.

The half-naked doctor with his unruly gray hair and taped glasses sits next to Claire who seems to hang on to every word he says. A little kid in a Captain America backpack clings to his dad and watches over Scout while a short, bulky gal with auburn hair treats her injuries.

Across the lobby from the rest of us, a young blonde girl with cold, jaded eyes sulks by herself on a bench. Something about her catches my attention. I can't help looking at her. She seems like an outsider, keeping her distance from the rest of them. When she turns her head and looks at me, our eyes lock for a moment until I overhear my name.

I turn to see Fletcher, Blake, Hoff, and that brunette having a discussion on the other side of the room. They watch me lingering by the doors for a moment, and then they approach me. I shift my weight from one foot to the other.

"Hey," says Blake. "Everything okay?"

"Yeah," I tell him. He seems harmless enough. Kind of like some dorky history professor or something, but not like anyone I'd especially like to talk to right now.

"Take it easy, kid," says Fletcher.

"I'm fine," I tell him.

"You don't look fine," he says. "Looks like—"

"It's been a rough day," I tell him without bothering to hide my annoyance.

"Why don't you sit down with us?" the brunette says.

"I think I'm okay where I am, Miss," I say to her.

"Danielle," she corrects me.

"Let me have a word alone with him," Hoff tells the rest of them.

The group leaves us alone, and Hoff puts one of his big hands on my shoulder, turns me around, and walks me outside.

"I realize you've probably been through the wringer out here," Hoff says. "But I just need to know if you're good."

"Yeah," I say.

"Good," he says. "I know it will be hard, but you can trust these people. They are some of the good ones, and lord knows there aren't enough of those left now."

I nod my head in agreement. This guy seems like somebody I can relate to.

"In the meantime," he says. "How about you just give me a rundown of the situation out here as much as you can. Can you do that?"

"Yeah, sure," I agree.

"Okay then," Hoff says.

I lay it all out for him. I tell him what happened in El Paso, about the Air Force and the Army and how Holloman was overrun. Then I tell him about the countless dead in Alamogordo and finally about Jenson, Will, Sarge and Mac. By the end, I'm choking back tears and trying not to completely lose it.

"You did good, though," Hoff says. "You kept that redhead alive. That's a miracle right there. We get this turned around, and you'll be a hero when it's all over."

I know he's trying to make me feel better, and it almost does. We head back inside, and they share some of the MRE's they have with us. While we eat, they tell their stories. They talk about Chicago, the CIA agent that was with them named Lorento, and about some conflict they had with a militia in Missouri. They get quiet when they talk about the friends that they lost but seem mostly to be relieved to finally be here, which does surprise me. They only feel relieved because they don't know just how bad it is here yet.

The only one that doesn't really talk much is the blonde girl. As the sun sets and we sit in the darkness around a lantern, I can't help but steal a glance at her from time to time. During one such moment, she turns, and our eyes meet again before she quickly looks away. She avoids looking my way after that, and I feel like maybe I scared her a bit. Women have never exactly made much sense to me.

I stay awake most of the night. Everyone else is tired, but Claire and I had weeks to rest at the house. Besides, after losing Mac yesterday, I doubt I will sleep very well.

So, I convince Hoff that I can take watch while the rest of them catch up on some sleep. After our talk, he seems to trust me, and the two of us have quickly developed a mutual respect for each other.

As much as I can't help but like the guy, part of me does not want to get to know anyone now. It is just a matter of time before they are going to end up dead.

CHAPTER
TWENTY-SEVEN

Early in the morning, we load everyone back in the vehicles and get ready to leave. I've been up for a full day now, but I still probably feel a lot better than most of these new people. They smell. Their clothes are filthy and torn. Every single one of them looks exhausted. They manage, though.

Even that woman, Scout, with her face all beaten and one of her eyes swollen shut, manages to get back on her feet, limp out to the pickup, and climb in alongside the redheaded guy and his kid. He keeps trying to help her but mostly just ends up pissing her off until she snaps at him and shoves him away.

I get in the pickup truck with Claire in the passenger seat beside me. As she pulls her hair back into a ponytail, I get the urge to apologize for how hostile I've been since we left the house, but I struggle to find the words. Finally, she looks back over at me. I can tell she is not exactly happy with me still. Instead of trying to be the nice guy, I just stick the keys in the ignition and start the engine.

"What is it?" she asks me.

"What?" I say.

"You look like you wanted to tell me something," she says.

The accusatory tone of her voice makes me glad I didn't apologize.

"Let's go," Fletcher says. He lifts the dog into the truck bed and then climbs in along with Blake. Once the two men are ready, Fletcher bangs on the hood of the pickup to urge me to move.

"When I got something to say to you, you'll know about it," I say to Claire as I shift the truck into gear and drive toward the highway.

"Chase," she says. "I don't know what I did—"

"You didn't do anything," I insist.

"Then why are you being like—"

"Fuck!" I curse. "I'm trying to drive. Will you just shut the fuck up?"

I glance back and notice the dad covering the ears of his little kid with his hands. Then I get mad at myself for losing my shit.

"Is there a problem?" the man asks me.

"Just mind your own business, pal," I tell him.

He starts to say something, but Scout talks over him.

"Steven," Scout says to him. "Just stay out of it."

In the rearview mirror, I notice her putting a pair of sunglasses over her black eyes.

"He's never learned when to shut up," Scout mumbles through her swollen cheeks.

He gives her a wounded look, but she just turns and stares out the window.

"This is going to be fun," she mutters. "I can tell already."

Steven slumps down in his seat and watches the road out the other window.

I steer the truck onto the highway toward Holloman. The dead swarm the roads. It seems like there are even more of them now than yesterday. Maybe our trip down the highway drew them out.

Blake and Fletcher fire at the dead as they get close to our vehicles. It keeps enough of the corpses off us so that we don't get too bogged down. Once we make it through Holloman, the road clears up a bit and I continue our drive toward Alamogordo.

"You weren't kidding," Blake yells through the back window of the truck, as he loads a fresh mag into his rifle. "There really are a lot of those things here."

"Shouldn't be as bad once we get through town," I say.

At least I hope it won't be that bad. I loosen my grip on the steering wheel and navigate through the corpses and abandoned cars on the highway.

We reach the trailer parks and junkyards along the outskirts of Alamogordo a few minutes later. I keep an eye out for any remnants of the Army while I drive, but it takes all my concentration to avoid crashing the truck into the abandoned cars or the clusters of the dead in the streets.

"Keep an eye out," I say to Claire.

"For what?" Scout asks.

"Trouble," I say.

"What kind of trouble are we talking about here?" Steven asks.

"Military," I say. "Well, ex-military. They're more like soldiers of fortune these days."

"Great," Scout sighs. "More assholes. Everywhere I go. I'm beginning to think I'm cursed."

"Better get used to it," I say.

She brushes her hair out of her face with her fingers, and then she reaches down to her bag and pulls out a Glock and loads a mag.

"I know we just met," she says. "But you'll find out soon enough. I'm kind of an expert in dealing with assholes by now."

Ugly as she might be right now, I have to say this gal is growing on me already. I can't help but smirk at her cocky attitude.

"Just make sure you don't turn into one of them," she warns me.

I turn my gaze back to the road and swerve between a toppled shopping cart and a pair of dead bodies in a heap on the ground. We reach the entrance to the expressway that runs north toward Los Alamos, and I make the turn on to the ramp. I get a bad feeling as I merge into the road. The last time I was on this highway, most of my team ended up dead.

My nerves settle by the time we leave the small town and cruise along the mostly empty highway. For the next hour, we continue north and enjoy the air conditioning in the pickup as we drive beneath the scorching sun. It helps to calm me down.

I learned in boot camp, and then witnessed on deployment in the Middle East, that hotter temperatures or climates can impact your ability to think, especially in stressful situations. Just being in a nice cool car makes me feel better than I have in a long time. I even look over at Claire because I feel bad for snapping on her earlier. Though, I still can't bring myself to say I am sorry to her. When she turns her head and looks back at me, I give her an apologetic smile.

We've been through too much together. She is my oldest friend in the world now. The only person that knows anything about me. That has to be worth something.

A flash in the mirror catches my eye, and I notice Hoff flashing the headlights of the SUV behind me. I keep an eye on them for a minute, and then I notice the pattern.

Two long flashes and a short flash.

A short flash and a long flash.

Three short flashes.

Gas. He needs to refuel.

I hold the brakes down lightly with my foot to acknowledge him and he stops flashing his lights. Our chances of finding a gas station with a working pump are pretty slim, so we will probably have to siphon some fuel from another vehicle. Hopefully, he has enough to make it to the next town because any cars abandoned along the way are most likely there because they ran out of gas.

No one in their right mind gets out of a working car and walks in the middle of the desert unless they have no other choice.

We come to a place called Corona a few miles later, and I pull into a gas station at the edge of town. I park the pickup next to one of the pumps, and Hoff pulls up to the fueling station behind me.

I get out and take a look around.

The streets seem empty and quiet. It might seem like the place is completely abandoned, if not for a pair of dead bodies wandering outside a restaurant up the road. Blake gets out and tries the pump but gets no juice from it.

"I'll go check and see if they have a generator," Fletcher says after he hops down from the truck.

"You need a hand?" Blake says as Fletcher jogs up to the door.

"Nah, I got it," Fletcher waves, and then he cups a hand to the glass, peers through the windows, and heads inside.

"Ugh," Scout groans in the backseat.

"You have to pee again, don't you?" Steven says.

"Shut up, Steven," she says. She opens the door, gets out, and limps toward the entrance.

"She has to pee," Steven smirks. "Every time we are on the road. Every single time. It's like clockwork."

He finds it amusing, but I just turn around and scan the streets again. Fletcher opens the door on his way back out and holds it for Scout. He watches her limp inside and then calls back to us.

"They got a generator but she's dry," Fletcher says.

"I can pull some gas out of the truck," Hoff says.

"There's a hose in my bag," Fletcher tells him. "Just don't be playing around with it. I don't usually let guys touch my hose, but I'll make an exception for you, big guy."

"Go find me a gas can you goddamn degenerate," Hoff yells at him. "And a pair of sunglasses. The good kind. None of that hideous aviator shit."

Fletcher disappears back inside the shop. Beneath his golden beard, Hoff grins as he shakes his head and walks over to the pickup. He retrieves the hose and then slides it into the open gas tank.

"Fletcher will get on your nerves from time to time," Hoff warns me while holding the end of the hose in his hand. "But he's mostly harmless."

"Unless you're a female," Blake adds.

He smirks but then he looks at my unamused expression and thinks about what he said.

"I didn't mean you are a female," he explains. "I just meant he's only dangerous—"

"I knew what you meant, smart guy," I say.

"Sorry," he stammers. "Just clarifying."

Fletcher comes back out with a gas can and hands it to Hoff. Hoff sets it on the ground and prepares to fill it up with the gas from the truck.

"Don't tease me big guy. Put it in there," Fletcher says. "I ain't got all day."

Hoff just ignores him and begins to suck on the hose. He coughs on the fumes but gets enough suction to get gasoline flowing.

I glance back over my shoulder and notice the corpses from the restaurant are closing in on the station. A couple of stiffs emerge near an intersection further up the block.

"Let's move this along guys," I urge them. "Looks like we're starting to attract the attention of the locals."

As soon as I say it, the door to the restaurant crashes open and more of the dead pour out into the street.

"Hold them off, Chase," Fletcher says.

"I got them," I tell him. I crouch into a shooting position and take aim at the dead. "Just hurry the fuck up."

I can't hear if he answers due to the report of the rifle after I pull the trigger.

Even though this town can't have more than a couple hundred people in it, the dead always seem to know when you're least prepared. We got two vehicles in need of fuel, and I'm the only one with any actual training that is not dicking around with gasoline right now.

Blake opens fire from the bed of the truck as well, but it is pretty obvious he can't shoot for shit. I almost want to turn around and tell him to just save the goddamn bullets instead of wasting them.

The closest pair of corpses fall to the ground, as I methodically take aim and work my way toward the back of the pack. At first, I think I have it under control, but then more of them appear from the neighborhood behind the gas station.

"Look out," Scout yells from the truck. She pushes open her door and takes up a firing position next to me. Steven covers his kid in the backseat, using his body like a shield.

I reposition myself and focus on the ten or twelve of them coming around the building. The blonde girl gets out of the SUV and runs over to help Blake and Scout hold off the crowd from the street.

Fletcher finally gets the generator going and switches on the pumps. As soon as Hoff spots him sprinting out the door of the shop, he turns and grabs the nozzle off the pump. He starts filling the truck and then runs over to the SUV.

"Better move fast," I urge him. With all the shooting, we are likely to draw out every stiff for miles, and even with most of us laying down fire, the dead steadily close in around us.

I'm honestly mostly terrified that one of these idiots is going to shoot a gas pump on accident and blow us all up. Most of them have zero training. It's amazing that any of them have survived this long.

I kill another one of the stiffs coming around the building, but then my mag runs black with the last one shambling right towards me. I fumble with the rifle as I eject the magazine and grab a fresh one from my pocket. No matter how much I've worked on it, I'm still a couple seconds slower than I used to be when I had two good hands.

I start to panic as I sense the dead woman closing in. By the time I slap a fresh mag home, the old hag wearing a straw sunhat is just a few feet away from me. I raise my rifle up to get a shot off before she can fall on me, but before I squeeze the trigger, her head snaps to the side and sends her stupid fucking hat flying off her head. The rotting woman collapses on the ground beside me.

I glance back to see Hoff standing in front of the SUV. He takes aim at the dead while the pumps fill the gas tanks. He may have just saved my ass.

I'm about to turn around and start shooting again when I notice movement between the pump and the SUV.

"Behind you!" I yell.

As soon as I realize what is happening, the corpse lunges in the passenger window and bites the gal with the auburn hair that was taking care of Scout. Blood spurts out of her neck. She howls in pain and swats feebly at the mangled face of the rotting man. Crimson splatters across the windshield and conceals what happens next inside the vehicle.

We were so focused on the ones coming up the road, that none of us spotted the one creeping up on our six.

"Fawn!" Scout screams as she turns and realizes what is happening to her friend. She stops shooting and turns to limp back and help Fawn.

I raise the Honey Badger to fire, but I don't pull the trigger. The doctor is in the seat right behind Fawn. I don't want to risk hitting the gas pump either. Besides, the fact is, that gal is already dead.

Fletcher intercepts Scout before she can make it back to help Fawn. "Scout," he says. "You can't."

She tries to fight him off, but she gives up quickly and collapses into his arms, erupting into tears.

Hoff hurries around the truck, grabs the lanky corpse by the collar, and flings it back against the pump. It lunges at him, so Hoff raises his arm to fend the thing off. He pivots and shoves it down on the ground and then raises a big boot to stomp down on the decomposing face of the thing until it stops moving.

"Let's get the hell out of here," Hoff yells as he yanks the nozzle out of the tank and tosses it aside.

I climb back in the truck and start the engine and wait for the rest of them to get in their seats. After Fletcher climbs aboard, I stomp on the gas and peel out of the station. Dozens of dead gather in the middle of the road, so I swerve into a parking lot on the opposite side of the street to get around them.

Then we're gone. We speed out of town and back onto the highway in the quiet, desolate desert.

CHAPTER TWENTY-EIGHT

The sign alongside the highway tells me we are still a hundred miles from Santa Fe, but my knuckles are already clutching the steering wheel after leaving Corona. If we ran into problems in a dinky little town like that, what chance will we have in a major city with a population in the hundreds of thousands?

This isn't like before when I was with my platoon. Most of these people are pretty fucking useless, at least as far as I can tell.

Steven consoles Scout as she mourns the loss of Fawn. It must hurt to cry with her face in the shape that it's in, or maybe the pain is just making her cry even harder. It gets on my nerves pretty bad after a few minutes, but I guess it would be rude to say something about it, so I just grip the wheel harder and keep driving down the empty highway.

The dog hangs his head out over the side of the truck and opens his mouth and catches the desert air on his tongue. The shaggy thing must be dying in this heat. Although if he has managed to survive this long in the apocalypse, I imagine he must be a little fighter, too. It almost makes me smile to see how carefree he looks back there until I notice the blood on the windshield of the SUV behind us.

"I'm sorry about your friend," Claire says to Scout.

"Her name was Fawn," Scout says.

"She seemed like a very kind woman," Claire offers.

"She was," says Scout. "That gal wouldn't ever even hurt a fly."

Claire smiles. She probably feels like she is helping.

"I guess she had this coming," Scout sniffles as she wipes away the drips from her nostrils. "Some people just aren't cut out for all of this."

Claire's smile falters. Maybe she realizes she is one of those people. Not knowing what else to say, she turns back around and stares at the road ahead of us.

"I don't mean to sound like a dick," I say. "But everyone needs to find a way to set that all aside. We're going to be hitting Santa Fe in a little over an hour."

"Don't worry, kid," Scout tells me. "I've had a lot worse days than this."

"The day ain't over yet," I remind her. "Don't jinx us."

Scout sits back in her seat and rubs the little boy's messy hair with her hand. He snuggles up against her and she winces as he lays his head in her lap, but she lets him do it anyway. I know right then that the only thing that might ever really kill this woman would be losing that kid.

"Your son is really cute," Claire says to Scout. "How old is he?"

Scout hesitates for a second. I'm pretty sure that kid is not hers, but I choose to pretend I'm not listening. I don't really feel like talking anyway. The less I know about these people, the less it will bother me when they all die, too.

"I'm seven," Stevie says without lifting his head.

It's the first thing I've heard the kid say since they got here. I was actually starting to wonder if he was deaf or mute or something. Just thought it would be rude to ask.

"It gives me hope to see a whole family still together through all of this," Claire says.

I glance over at her. She must not have noticed the way Fletcher and Scout look at each other. It isn't hard to see there is something between them. Claire does seem even a little more clueless about people than me. That's what spending your entire life in a lab will do, though.

Scout lets out a laugh.

"What?" Claire says.

"Steven is just my friend," Scout tells her.

"Well, it's a little more complicated than that," Steven says with a wink.

"No," Scout says, swatting Steven. "It's not more complicated than that at all actually."

Claire turns back around. She leans back in her seat with her fingers laced together on her lap. Then she stares at the dwindling highway in the vast desert that seems to disappear into nothing when it reaches the horizon.

The tension begins to mount as we near the city. I mess with the air conditioning to try and cool down the cab, but it still feels warm to me no matter how high I turn it up. It isn't bad enough that we have to deal with the dead, but I'm not even entirely sure how to get to Los Alamos.

All I know is Los Alamos is somewhere in the mountains on the opposite side of the city. I don't want to get lost and go too far west because that would bring us too close to Albuquerque. We'd risk running into half a million of those things out there.

To hell with that.

"Check the map," I tell Claire. I grab the road map off the center console and toss it in her lap. "I'm going to need you to help navigate me through this."

Claire unfolds the map and scans the area around Santa Fe.

"Looks like it will be easiest to go around the west side of the city," Claire says.

"East," I tell her. "East is better."

"Okay," she sighs. "I guess we're going east then."

She runs her fingers along the lines on the paper, then brings her finger up to her lip and searches the page again.

"Make sure you have alternate routes in mind, too," I tell her. "Something tells me we're going to hit some traffic along the way."

"Yes, sir," Claire mocks me.

"Hey," I snap. "Don't fuck around. Screw this up and we all die."

"I know," she sighs. "You don't have to tell me that."

"He said fuck," Stevie says as he sits up in the backseat.

I keep forgetting there is a kid around.

"Sorry," I say, glancing at him in the rearview mirror. "You probably should try not to listen whenever I'm saying something, kid."

"Is he a bad guy?" the kid asks Scout.

"No," Scout says. "He isn't bad. He just talks like he is."

The kid looks at me, and then he lays his head back down in her lap. Scout gives me a small smile and then turns her head and stares out the window. I turn my attention back to the road, but the way the kid looked at me lingers with me. It was like he sensed something nobody else realized when he looked into my eyes. He looked afraid of me.

Maybe I have just been awake too long.

"Stay to the right up ahead," Claire tells me.

I snap out of it and notice several abandoned vehicles sitting alongside the road. Traffic means we're getting close. Instead of turning on to the highway, Claire points me to a smaller road that runs adjacent to it.

"You sure about this?" I ask her.

"Yes," she tells me as she points to the map. "It goes the right way."

"It's the best route though?" I say.

"I don't know, Chase," she throws her arms up in the air. "How am I supposed to be sure about that?"

"I'm just asking," I say.

Maybe I'm being too hard on her, but she is supposed to be the smart one here. It isn't that hard to read a map and find a route that won't run us into any major clusterfucks.

I follow her directions and take the road that runs alongside the mountains to the east of Santa Fe. The dead wander among the houses and strip malls along the outskirts of town. The best way to do this is to get it done as quickly as possible, like pulling off a band-aid. If we stop in the middle, it may just end up being more painful.

The pickup weaves between stranded and wrecked vehicles in the road. Most of the shops and homes appear to be abandoned and long ago raided for anything of use. The only thing left in this town are the dead.

"Turn up here," Claire points to an intersection ahead.

I follow the finger she is pointing and turn on to a wide road with a large sandy median separating the traffic. The nearby houses are elevated and set back from the road, so I can keep the truck above fifty miles per hour and avoid the obstacles in the street.

I check the mirror to make sure Hoff is keeping up and see him back there. His face is focused as he eyes the road through the blood-smeared windshield.

"Take the next exit," Claire tells me. She points to the sign to clarify. "Saint Francis."

"You're doing fine," I assure her.

I steer the truck up the ramp and follow the road that curves around to the north. The small houses over here are more tightly packed together and run right up against the street. It feels claustrophobic immediately. Corpses wander along the road and on every side street that we pass. I tap the brakes and reduce my speed as I focus on the possible threats before we get too close to them.

The feeling comes over me that things are about to get very bad, as I swerve through the gauntlet of death and destruction on the road.

That scruffy mutt starts barking while Fletcher and Blake open fire on the dead. They better be sure to hang on back there because I'm not getting through here without smashing through some shit along the way.

A woman up ahead is on her hands and knees devouring a dead body between an armored truck and a pair of wreck sedans. I have no choice but to plow over her. She turns and snarls just before her face smashes into the grill of the truck.

The crack and thud as the truck hits her is strangely satisfying as a small measure of revenge, but along with it comes the fear of messing up the truck. The last thing I want is to get stranded in the middle of a fairly large city.

The dead flood toward the gunshots and the growling engines of our vehicles. They emerge from the side streets and shops alongside the road. I hit the gas and drive fast enough that most of the dead arrive too late and merely raise their arms as they watch us speed away.

In the back of the truck, that stupid dog continues to bark at all of them. It's almost like it is trying to taunt them. It is hard enough to concentrate without that thing annoying the fuck out of me.

"Shut that damn thing up," I yell.

"Quiet, Stitch!" I hear Blake holler at the dog.

The dog keeps barking like an asshole back there. I have to wonder why they keep that thing around.

It almost seems like we will be able to slip right through this town, until we hit a crowd of several hundred corpses that clog the road between the capital building and a large shopping mall.

I bring the truck to a stop.

"Where do I go?" I ask Claire.

"Straight," she says.

"I can't fucking get through that," I inform her.

"We're not moving!" Fletcher reminds me as he fires at the dead that are quickly closing in on the truck in the middle of the road.

"Umm," she stammers and scans the map. "Left."

"Are you sure?" I ask.

"Yes," she doesn't seem sure, but I spin the wheel and steer down the side street.

Blake nearly tumbles out of the back of the truck. Fletcher stops shooting and grabs on to him to keep him from landing in the arms of the dead. They crouch back down in the truck bed and resume clearing away the corpses that grab on to the vehicle. The two men kick at the dead or smack them in the face with the rifle stocks. When all else fails, they shoot them in the head to get them to release their grip on the pickup.

Hoff has to work extra hard to avoid the bodies we leave in our wake. The sport-utility vehicle swerves from one side of the road to the other, but inevitably ends up bouncing over the bodies as they fall to the pavement behind us.

"Talk to me, Claire," I remind her. All of the threats on the street keep pulling her eyes and attention away from the map.

"Right! Right!" She yells as we enter an intersection.

I take a hard right, bouncing over the curb as I swing around a burned-out sports car in the street. The guys in the back of the truck are knocked around and I can hear the dog's claws scraping the metal as it slides from one end to the other. I steer onto the road and steady the truck again.

"I'd appreciate it if you'd stop driving like a dang lunatic," Fletcher yells through the back window.

I shoot a glance in Claire's direction, but she is busy trying to find the best way out of the city.

"Go left in two blocks," she tells me.

I make the turn and let out a relieved sigh. The roads clear again as we head out of the city center. After a few more blocks, we reach the entrance to the highway and leave Santa Fe behind us. The road opens up. Fewer structures are situated close to the pavement and the number of abandoned cars and corpses diminishes. I finally relax my grip on the steering wheel as we start our climb up the mountains toward Los Alamos.

"You did good back there," I tell Claire.

She smiles and looks back down at the map.

"I mean it," I say. "We couldn't have gotten through there without you."

"Thanks," she says.

"So," I say. "Any idea how we get to this lab from here?"

"Not exactly," she says. "But we'll figure it out."

CHAPTER TWENTY-NINE

The convoy rolls through several miles of barren desert until we come to a massive resort casino. It looks like a luxurious pueblo surrounded by unkempt golf courses. Hundreds of corpses wander across the massive parking lots. The lavish facility slowly withers away like an enormous monument to a lost civilization.

Towering pillars of imposing rock rise out of the earth in gravity defying formations along the road. Massive escarpments along the east side of the highway turn crimson in the afternoon light.

"This place is amazing," says Claire.

Stevie leans over Scout so he can get a better look at the landscape out the window. His elbows hit her ribs and cause her to grunt in pain.

"Wow!" Stevie says. "Mountains!"

"That's the Sangre de Cristo mountains," Fletcher says through the window. "This is just the southern tip. They run all the way up into Colorado."

"Kind of makes you forget everything has gone to hell," Scout adds.

While everyone else is distracted by the rock formations, I keep my eyes on the road. Good thing, too, because I spot a sign for Los Alamos just before the upcoming intersection. We pass by another pair of rundown casinos along the outskirts of a town with a name I can't pronounce.

"This must be an Indian reservation," Blake says into the back window.

"You guessing that because you can't pronounce the name of the town either?" Steven says.

"No," Blake says. "This whole area is casinos. Seems kind of obvious."

I round a curve and head out of town, but I slam on the brakes when I spot a pair of vehicles on the road ahead. It isn't like it is out of the ordinary to come upon vehicles blocking the roads now, but these trucks are different. They weren't wrecked or hurriedly abandoned. They were parked sideways at the edge of a bridge to create a blockade. I squint my eyes but can't see anyone around the vehicles.

"What's wrong?" Claire asks me.

"I know a trap when I see one," I explain. I gesture to the trucks in the road. "That's a trap."

I hit the gas again, crank the steering wheel around, and wave a finger around as I pass by Hoff in the SUV to tell him to follow me. He nods and starts to turn back, but then I stop when I see another pair of vehicles on the road back the way we just came.

We're boxed in.

Trapped.

"What do we do now?" Claire asks.

"Get ready to kill somebody," I say.

Scout loads a new magazine into her Glock as a group of men get out of the trucks and start walking toward our vehicles. More men on horseback ride out from the surrounding buildings. All of them are armed, mostly with guns, but a couple even carry spears or bows and arrows. Still, we're out numbered. There must be thirty or forty of them.

"Hold on," Blake says. "Let me try to talk to them first."

"You want to get yourself scalped, go right ahead, buddy," I say.

"I like my chances," Blakes smirks. He turns and hops down from the truck and starts walking toward them with his arms raised. Dumb ass didn't even take his rifle along with him.

I decide I better get out there. He might like his chances, but I'm willing to bet he is going to need my help.

Sure enough, the guys raise their weapons as we get close.

An older man with long black hair steps out in front of the group. The rest of the guys are in worn jeans and filthy shirts, but the man who approaches us wears a dress shirt and pants. I'm guessing he is the one in charge.

"You're trespassing," he tells Blake. "This land belongs to the nation of the Pueblo Indians."

"This is still America last time I checked," I say. "Dumb fuck."

Blake turns around and glares at me.

"Damn it. Shut the hell up," he tells me.

Coming from him it takes me by surprise. So much so, that I actually listen to him.

"We're just trying to get to Los Alamos," Blake explains to the man. "We have scientists with us. They are going to try and stop the things that are happening."

The man looks at him disdainfully and the group behind him keep their weapons pointed at us.

"We're not here to harm any of you," Blake says. "We just want to stop this. Do you understand me?"

"This scourge," the man finally says, "is just the most recent crime against the Earth that has been committed by your people. Ever since your people colonized and stole our land you have spread one disease after another."

Blake listens to the man rant about bullshit that happened centuries ago. It takes every ounce of willpower I have to resist making a move.

"We don't have to stand here and listen to this shit," I gripe.

"Jesus! Shut up, Chase," Blake repeats.

"Now the time has finally come. The Pueblo nation is taking our land back," the man says. "The white man is no longer welcome here."

"You better check your tone there, old man," I snap as I raise my rifle.

"Hold it!" Blake says. He raises his arms up and steps between me and the tribe; then he turns and glares at me.

I lower the rifle, so it isn't pointing at his chest.

"Get back in the truck," he orders me.

I spit on the ground near his feet in disgust, but then I remove myself from the situation and make my way back to the truck. If they decide to shoot his ass in the street, it will be his own fault now.

Stupid dick.

I climb back in and watch from behind the wheel as Blake attempts to resolve the situation.

"What did they say?" Scout asks me.

"White people aren't welcome here anymore," I tell her.

"What?" Claire asks.

"It's all bullshit," I tell her. "These fuckers have the nerve to blame us for destroying the planet when they got a mile high pile of fucking hot garbage right there."

I point to a junkyard off to my left. Hell, I can even smell the stench from here.

"This is insane," Claire says.

"Didn't you explain what we're trying to do?" Scout asks.

"They can't be reasoned with," I tell her. "They just want blood."

I stare at Blake talking with the chief up the road. I'm kind of amazed they haven't killed him already. He must be begging for mercy. The chief just stands there with his arms crossed, listening. His expression never changes. Probably learned that by playing hours of poker in the damn casino.

"Just be ready when the shooting starts," I say to Scout. "Don't let them get the drop on us."

"Take it easy, killer," Fletcher says. "Let's just see how this plays out."

I wait for it. The moment one of these guys loses their patience and drops Blake in the street. He might somehow be stupid enough to believe you can be civil with people, but I've seen firsthand how well that goes. The chief holds up a hand, and then I know it's only seconds away.

His hand falls to his side again. The men lower their rifles.

Blake turns around and jogs back to the pickup with a relieved smile on his face.

"It's okay," he says.

"What did you say to them?"

He ignores my question and moves toward the bed of the truck.

"Hand me that box," he says to Fletcher.

Fletcher picks up the box of food that Claire and I brought from the house in Alamogordo.

"Hey," I say. "What are you doing with that?"

Blake takes the box from Fletcher and turns to walk back toward the tribe.

"Peace offering," he says.

"What?" I say.

He just continues walking away with the cardboard box.

"Don't you give them that!" I say. "That's my food!"

"Let it go, man," Fletcher says. "We got plenty to eat still."

"Fuck that," I tell him. I open the door, but Claire grabs my arm to keep me from getting out of the truck.

"Chase," she says. "Just let them have it. It's better than all of us dying out here when we're so close."

My blood boils beneath my skin as I sit and watch Blake hand over the box to the fucking bandits, but I stay in the truck. I don't do it for myself, or for Claire. It's just because I don't want to do anything that will make all the sacrifices of my platoon be for nothing.

Still, my way would have been easier. We should have just shot those scumbags.

Blake climbs back into the truck as the vehicles blocking our route pull onto the shoulder to clear a path. I start the truck again and spin us back around.

"All we had to do was give them a little food," Scout says. "This could have gone a lot worse."

"Not exactly," Blake says. "I had to promise to never bring Chase back, too."

They all get a kick out of that.

"Ha, ha, ha," I say as I shake my head. "Real fucking funny, smart guy."

"That's what they said," Blake tells me. "I'm not even joking."

CHAPTER THIRTY

By the time we start driving up the mountains, I manage to quit complaining about Blake giving away my food. Mostly just because everyone in the truck is begging me to give it a rest. I'm still sore about it, but I finally just stop talking.

Nobody ever takes my side. Even when I know I'm right.

We finally reach the outskirts of Los Alamos, and since I have no idea where the lab is from here, I pull off at an overlook about a half mile from town. Hoff pulls the SUV up alongside me and rolls down the window.

"Does anyone know how we find this place?" I ask him.

"Doc says he does," Hoff says.

"Him?" I ask.

"This is gonna go just great," Fletcher laughs.

"He seems pretty sure," Hoff says. "At least for the moment."

"Well then," I sigh. "Take the lead. I'll follow you."

Hoff nods and then pulls out of the gravel lot and back onto the road. I pull the truck out behind him and trail the SUV the rest of the way.

I have no idea what to expect in Los Alamos. To be honest, I originally thought that was the name of a facility before and not a whole town. It can't be that big then, I reason. But still, following a guy who walks around with no pants all day and thinks nothing of it, doesn't exactly seem like the best way to go about things.

Let's just hope his mind isn't completely gone.

Instead of heading up the main road into town, Hoff leads us down a backroad that runs farther south along the mountain.

"This doesn't seem right," Claire says. "The town is over there."

"He's probably going to get us lost in the mountains," I agree.

The road curves around a bend and then we pass a small pond. Just as I am convinced we're going the wrong way, we drive around another hill and a vast complex of buildings comes into view. Most of them are nondescript industrial buildings shaped like giant blocks, but in the center sits a tall structure with a curved facade and steel blue windows.

The lab probably once seemed like a monument to science and technology, though now it looks like it might just collapse. Half the windows are shattered or cracked. Scattered papers, broken equipment, and debris litter the ground surrounding the building.

"No," Claire mourns. "It's destroyed."

"I don't know what you were expecting," Scout says. "Everything is destroyed."

There are bodies all over the ground. A couple of deceased scientists and security guards wander amongst the structures, but the complex is essentially vacant.

Bullet holes and blast shadows mar some of the buildings. Other walls are tagged with graffiti, primarily indecipherable letters or crudely drawn dicks, but one wall has an ornate skeleton wearing a black cloak and holding a scythe next to the words, "Don't fear the Reapers."

Plural. Capitalized.

Reapers.

I don't think it was just carelessly written.

So, I have to wonder, who the fuck are the Reapers?

"This was all for nothing," Claire says and interrupts my train of thought. Her voice wavers, and she struggles not to cry.

I was not completely surprised to find the facility like this, especially considering how long it took us to get here. For Claire, seeing one of the most advanced laboratories in the world destroyed like this must be devastating.

"Maybe we can still salvage some equipment," I offer. "Try to fortify this place."

It sounds ridiculous. But I get it. It's hard to believe we did all this for nothing. I can't accept that either. Not after watching so many people die to get us here.

Claire buries her face in her palms as the tears begin to flow from her eyes.

"Let's just wait until we see how bad it is inside," I say.

We park outside the front entrance. Several corpses limp out of the building at the sound of our vehicles.

Most of the dead are in bad shape by now, but these stiffs were clearly shot to shit. One guy is missing an arm. Another man with a bloody goatee stumbles over his intestines as they drag along the ground.

Fletcher and Blake hop off the back of the truck and walk over to take care of the corpses on the front steps. The mutt hops down behind them and runs at the dead, snarling and baring his teeth, then turning and running away to hide behind the humans as the corpses lunge for him.

Instead of shooting, the two men approach the dead. Blake takes out a knife and jabs it upward below the jaw of the one-armed stiff and impales his skull on the blade. Fletcher swings the rifle around and smashes the man that tripped over his intestines until his skull shatters. Blake finishes off the last one, a blonde in a bullet-riddled lab coat, by grabbing a fistful of her long hair and jabbing the blade through her eye. He pulls the knife out, lets her fall to the floor, and wipes the blade on his jacket.

Maybe Blake isn't a total pussy after all.

We climb the steps and enter through the smashed doors of the lobby. More bodies are scattered across the interior floor of the building. Half the furniture and equipment around the reception area is gone, and what is left is completely destroyed. The place has been stripped of anything useful.

"Well," Fletcher says to Blake. "You ready to admit that I was right?"

Blake waves a hand at him and walks away.

"We come all this way, and for what?" Fletcher asks. "Told you this was stupid. We should have never listened to Lorento."

I hear a noise. Like a trickle of water running.

I turn my head toward the source and find the mutt with his leg up in the air, peeing on a potted plant across the room. Doctor Schoenheim wanders by the dog and continues toward a darkened corridor next to the elevators.

"Hey Doc," Hoff says. "Hold up."

"Where is he going?" Fletcher sighs.

We follow him down the hall and into one of the ravaged laboratories. He wanders over to a table covered with papers and bits of broken glass.

"Why would someone do this?" he wonders. "I don't understand. I can't possibly work like this."

"No shit, Doc," I mutter. I pick up a broken piece of a microscope or some shit and toss it on the floor. "Look at this place. We ain't going to find shit here."

"The state of this laboratory is completely unacceptable," Doc rambles on.

"Is he off his meds or something?" I ask the others.

"He's been through a lot," Scout says.

"He's all chewed up," Fletcher says, twirling a finger around his ear.

"So what are we going to do now?" Danielle wonders out loud.

"We should stay here tonight," says Blake. "Figure out what the hell we do next. It's too late to leave anyway. We might as well have a look around and see if we can salvage anything."

"You want to keep wasting your time? That's up to you, smart guy," I tell him. "I'm done with this bullshit."

I leave them all standing in the lab and wander back out to the hallway. I'm not really sure where I am even going, but just being around all of them is more than I can handle right now. I head back out to the lobby and look around at the wreckage again. I right a toppled, broken sofa that only has legs on one end. Then I drop my pack on the floor beside it before laying down on the lopsided surface. I let out a deep breath and close my eyes.

Instead of falling asleep, I feel something wet brush against my cheek. I flinch from the sensation and open my eyes again and find that damn dog licking me. I sit up and try to shoo the thing away.

"Get out of here!" I tell it and point at the door.

It chases its tail around in a circle and looks at me.

"Go away!" I tell it, still pointing.

It does another excited circle and stares at me again. Stupid dog.

"Go!" I yell.

The damn thing just spins around again and wags its tail.

"You're like the stupidest dog ever," I tell it.

The idiot lies down on the ground, stares at me, and growls playfully.

"Shut up," I warn it.

It gives me a little bark.

"Quiet," I tell it.

The dog barks again.

"Oh my god," I sigh in exasperation. I lay back down on the sofa, and the dog hurries over to lick my face again.

"No," I tell it, but it just gets up in my face even more.

"I'm gonna fucking shoot you, dog," I warn it. "I ain't playing."

Someone giggles behind me and I turn to find Claire standing by the front desk across the lobby. Scout, Steven, and his son follow her out from the hallway as well.

"Kid, come get your dog out of my face," I say.

"His name is Stitch," Stevie says.

"Whatever," I say. "Get him away from me."

The kid calls the dog, and it runs over and circles around him. He reaches out a hand to pat the dog's head and the pup looks up and licks his palm.

I realize I'm not likely to get any sleep, so I sit up again. As the rest of them come over to the couch, I decide to get up and offer Scout my seat. She probably needs it more than me anyway, considering the shape she is in.

Scout pulls off the satchel around her neck and drops it on the couch. Then she shrugs her backpack off and sets that down beside it. Scout collapses on the cushion beside them with a sigh and rolls her head from side to side massaging the muscles in her neck.

"Thanks," she finally says.

"Dog wasn't going to let me sleep anyway," I lament. "You doing okay?"

"I'll live," she says. She opens up the satchel and starts to remove the contents and inspects them before setting them down on the sofa. "Are you okay?"

"Yeah," I say. "I'm alright. It's just kind of hard to accept that everything I have been through since this all started has been for nothing."

Scout sets down a worn-out paperback, a map of Iowa, and a satellite phone.

"What's that?" I ask.

"This bag belonged to Jess," Scout says. "She was the CIA agent that was with us in Missouri."

"Jess," I say. I remember the conversations that Logan had with her.

"Can I see that?" I ask Scout.

"Sure," she says, and then she picks the satellite phone up and hands it over to me.

I hold down the button to see if I can power it on.

"I already checked it," Scout says. "Jess told us that she was in contact with someone, but there are no numbers or messages in there. Nothing. She was always real secretive."

The phone hardly has any power left in the battery. I may only have one shot at this. I stare at the keypad and start entering numbers.

"Who are you trying to call?" Scout asks.

"Logan had a contact, too," I say. "Someone at NORAD."

"You remember the number?" she says.

"Pretty sure I do," I tell her. "I sort of have like a photographic memory."

"Really?" Scout says.

"It's really more of a curse than anything," I say as I enter the last number. "But it comes in handy sometimes."

I place the phone to my ear. The other end of the line is picked up within seconds.

"Jess?" says a man on the other end. "Thank god. I thought we lost you."

"No," I say. "This isn't Jess. She is dead."

"Who is this?" the man demands.

"My name is Corporal Chase Graves," I say. "I'm with Doctor Schoenheim and Claire Davies at the lab in Los Alamos."

"You are?" the man seems skeptical.

"Yes," I say.

"How did you get this number?" the man asks.

"Agent Logan," I tell the man. "My unit was with him at Holloman."

"I see," he says. I can hear the relief in his voice.

"The laboratory here has been destroyed," I say.

"I know," the man says. "I have been monitoring your movements by satellite for two months now. I've been attempting to warn you away from Los Alamos but this phone has been offline for the past two days."

"Listen," I say. "This battery is about to die. I don't have much time to talk."

"I understand," he says. "It is imperative that you get the doctor and Miss Davies to Cheyenne Mountain. I will be monitoring your progress. Good luck, Corporal."

CHAPTER
THIRTY-ONE

"Who was that?" Scout asks me.

"I don't know," I say. "He didn't give me a name. Probably CIA or NSA."

"What did he say?" Claire says.

"He said that we should head for Cheyenne Mountain. There's an underground facility there," I tell them.

"So that's who she was talking to," Scout says.

"How far away is that?" Claire asks.

"Probably about six hours," Fletcher says.

I turn my head to see him walking back out of the hallway with the rest of the group.

"That was before," he says. "Now it's probably about a day. Maybe two."

The thought of getting back on the road again makes me anxious. Especially since we have no idea what we could be heading into.

Cheyenne Mountain is supposed to be the most secure facility in the entire country. By now we've come to accept that no place is ever really safe anymore. Still, we don't exactly have any options left. We just have to take our chances and hope it keeps us alive a while longer.

"So when do we leave?" Steven says.

"Hold on," Scout says. "Who says we should go there? I've had my share of underground bunkers. I'm not so sure I can handle going back into another one. How do we even know it's safe there?"

I think she is referring to what happened to them back in Missouri; the militia that was in some underground commercial facility.

"What else can we do, doll?" Fletcher asks her. "We can't stay here. We're out of options."

"I don't know," Scout sighs. "I don't like it, though."

"We've been on the road for too long," Fletcher says. "I mean, hell, look at yourself, Scout. We can't keep doing this."

"I'm going in the morning," I say. "I'm taking Claire and the doctor with me. The rest of you can do whatever you want. It's your choice."

"What exactly do we know about the situation there?" Hoff says. He seems skeptical.

"Not much," I say. "There wasn't enough battery left to have much of a discussion. But he knew Jess. I think we can trust him."

Hoff considers this for a moment.

"Okay," he agrees. "I think we should go. But we need to be prepared for anything. We've already walked into enough situations that seemed on the level and ended up paying for it. It's not happening again on my watch."

"I'm with you," I tell him.

"If we are staying here tonight, I think we should move upstairs to the top floor," Blake suggests. "It'll be safer."

"I think I'll stay down here," I tell him. "Keep an eye on the Victors."

"The what?" he says.

"Vehicles," Hoff explains.

"They're not going anywhere," Blake says.

"I'm not taking any chances," I tell him.

"Suit yourself," Blake says.

He takes Danielle by the hand and heads into the stairwell. I don't know what it is about that egghead, but he really just generally gets on my nerves. It's like he thinks he is smarter than everyone else in the room. Maybe he is. Maybe I'm just jealous because I know, in reality, he is a lot smarter than me. Either way, I still can't help wanting to beat his ass. I just might when this is all over with, but for now it's probably better to avoid starting any trouble.

Most of the others wander upstairs as well, but I don't mind. It's been a long time since I didn't have to deal with anyone else, and to be completely honest, I'm kind of sick of hearing about their problems.

As the sun sets, and the lab descends into darkness, I sit by myself in the lobby. A corpse wanders up to the entrance and spots me on the sofa. It moans as it shuffles through the broken glass and scattered papers on the floor.

I wait and let it approach me.

Part of me wants to just lie here and do nothing, and see if the thing might just lose interest and go away.

But these things don't operate like that.

They don't just go away.

It never ends.

I groan as I get to my feet and snatch up my rifle off the floor; the thing closes in. I raise the rifle and crack the stiff in the side of the face. It stumbles to the side and falls to the tile floor. It tries to sit up and reaches out to grab me, but I raise the rifle and bring it down on the damn thing. It moans, and the haunting noise reverberates off the empty walls of the lobby. Then, it goes silent as I hit it in the face again, driving its skull into the hard surface of the floor.

Even though it's been almost two days without sleep, I know that falling asleep down here alone is not an option. Not if I want to live anyway. Even though I don't want to, I'll have to head back upstairs. I turn around to pick up my things, and then I hear the click of a door opening across the room.

Not another one.

I pick up the rifle and walk toward the hallway wondering how it got inside. Maybe there is another entrance. It's possible the thing was in the building all along and we just missed it. The figure steps into the moonlight and I raise the rifle.

"Jesus," says the blonde girl as she walks around the corner and finds me ready to bludgeon her to death.

"Sorry," I say as I lower the rifle. "Thought you were one of them."

"You scared the shit out of me," she holds a hand over her chest and laughs.

"I'm sorry," I apologize again. "You had it coming, though. Creeping around in the dark like that."

"I was just coming to make sure you were okay," she says.

"You don't need to worry about me," I tell her.

"I wasn't," she says. "Well, I really just needed a break."

"A break from what?" I ask her.

"From people," she says.

I don't say it, but I have to wonder what that makes me then. At the same time, I kind of understand where she is coming from.

"I think I know what you mean," I say turning around to head back to the dilapidated sofa.

"I didn't mean to bother you," she explains. "I thought you would probably be asleep already."

"I had a friend stop by," I gesture to the corpse on the floor.

"You really should treat your friends better," she says.

"Well," I sigh and sit down again. "He really should have had the decency to call first."

She smirks and continues to stand next to the couch. I gesture to the other end to invite her to sit down.

"Don't worry," she tells me. "I'm not going to talk your head off or anything."

I grab an extra shirt from my bag and ball it up.

"You aren't bothering me, Miss," I say.

She makes a face when I call her that.

"I'm sorry, I never caught your name," I say.

"Natalie," she says.

"I'm Chase," I tell her.

"I know," she says. "I mean, they mentioned it." She gestures toward the upper floors.

"Of course," I say.

The moment feels awkward. Neither of us seems to really know how to talk to the other, and yet that kind of makes it all seem okay somehow.

"Go ahead," she tells me. "Get some sleep. I'll keep an eye on things."

I tuck the shirt behind me and rest my head against it. It's definitely not the most comfortable position I've slept in, but I'm so tired it probably won't matter. Besides, I'm not planning on resting for very long. These days, three to four hours is about as much as I get in before my dreams wake me back up again. Most of the time, the thoughts that come during sleep are far more frightening than what happens when I am awake.

I close my eyes and stare at the dark undersides of my eyelids for several minutes, but I can't fall asleep. Natalie sits quietly beside me. Even though she isn't doing anything, her presence keeps me awake. She isn't talking or moving around, but I can feel her there beside me. It's almost what I'd imagine sitting in a room with a ghost would feel like.

I resist the urge to open my eyes and turn and look at her again. Partly because I don't know what to say anyway, but also because I don't want to get close to anyone now, especially someone like her.

Finally, I open my eyes again and turn my head to look at her beside me. She stares outside at the empty, moonlit streets. Maybe she senses me watching her before she turns to look at me.

"Sorry," she says.

"You didn't do anything," I say. "I just can't sleep."

"I thought I might have been talking to myself out loud," she says.

"You weren't," I tell her.

"Good," she says and lowers her eyes to the floor.

Then I think about what she said.

"You usually talk to yourself?" I ask her.

"No," she says. "I mean I don't think so. Sometimes I feel like I'll be like thinking, you know, and I'm just not sure if the voice is in my head or if I'm actually saying it."

I nod politely, but then I start to wonder if this girl has some issues.

"You're looking at me funny," she says. Her blue eyes almost seem to glow in the darkness. "That probably made me sound weird."

"No," I say. "It's not weird. Well, maybe it's a little weird, but everyone is a little weird, I guess."

She almost smiles as I'm talking, but instead, she looks away from my eyes and stares out into the moonlight again. The glimmer I momentarily saw in her eyes vanishes and her eyelids seem to narrow again.

"Damn it," she curses and drops her gaze to the floor.

"Did I say something?" I ask.

"No," she says. "Not at all. I just didn't expect you to be nice."

"I'm sorry?" I say. "I didn't realize that was a problem. I can act like more of a dick if you like."

"No," she says. "I mean I thought you would be someone I could be around without really feeling anything, you know?"

I think I understand what she is getting at, but I'm also wondering if she is just crazy.

"I make an effort to keep to myself, and it isn't because I don't like those people upstairs," she explains. "It's because I'm trying not to. That way it won't hurt so bad when something happens to them."

"I know what you mean," I say.

"You do?" she says.

"Yeah," I say. "I've kind of felt the same way my whole life. Might not be as methodical about it as you, but it's all the same."

We both get quiet as a corpse wanders down the road in front of the entrance to the lab. It doesn't take notice of us in the darkness, so we just stay quiet and watch and wait for it to pass on. It seems to take an eternity, but honestly, it's a relief, too. As long as the corpse is out there, it means we have a reason to avoid talking to each other. When it finally leaves, I tilt my head back and close my eyes again.

I can still feel Natalie beside me, sitting there quietly, wanting to be near someone but also remaining disconnected.

"Don't worry," I tell her. "If something happens to you, I doubt it will really bother me too much."

"Thanks," she says.

I can't tell if she means to sound sarcastic or not, but I'm tired enough that I don't really care.

"Now, if you don't mind," I say, "I might actually try to sleep now."

"Go ahead," she says. "I'll be right here."

CHAPTER
THIRTY-TWO

It is still dark outside when I open my eyes again. I lift my head up and find Natalie sitting exactly as she was a few hours ago when I fell asleep. As I stretch out the godawful kinks in my neck from sleeping in one of the worst positions imaginable, I remember the incredibly awkward conversation we had earlier in the evening.

"How long was I out?" I ask.

"Just a few hours," she says.

I check the trucks in the empty street and then turn my head to look at Natalie again. She yawns and stretches her back a bit.

"Go ahead," I tell her. "Get some sleep. I'm good now."

I get up off the couch so that she can stretch out if she wants, and then I crouch down and search through my bag for something to eat. The food in my bag is all gone. Blake gave away what I had in the truck, too.

Dumbass.

"Something wrong?" Natalie asks me as she settles on the sofa.

"Blake gave away my food," I say.

"There's a Pop Tart in my bag," she says as she twists her body on the cushion to rest on her side. "It's all yours if you want it."

I pick up her backpack and open it up. I try to locate the silver wrapper without digging through all her stuff, but the inside of that thing is a nightmare of crap. I move a couple of things around, but all I find is more stuff. She notices me struggling and sits up on the sofa.

"Give it to me," she says and holds out her hand.

I pass her the bag and she reaches down in there, shoves something aside, and brings out the shiny package a second later like some kind of fucking magician.

"Thanks," I say as I open the crinkling wrapper. I sit down on a small end table beside the couch and start to eat. It's the first thing I've had since yesterday morning and eating it makes me realize just how hungry I am. After I finish, I look back over to the couch, but I can tell by her slow, deep breathing that Natalie has already fallen asleep.

Even though I told her before I passed out that I would not be upset if something were to happen to her, I don't know if I believe it myself. That is not what matters though. I just said it so that she would hopefully believe it.

As much as I feel drawn to this gal, I don't want to be getting close to anyone. Not before and certainly not now. I keep telling myself that, but I can't help watching her sleep until the sun begins to rise over the buildings to the east.

Shortly after dawn, the rest of the group comes down from the upper floors. The sound of them coming through the stairwell door stirs Natalie from sleep, and she sits up on the couch. Blake gives me a wave and walks over.

"Everything okay?" he asks. The question seems to be directed toward Natalie more than me, so I let her answer.

"Yeah," she says.

"I was a little worried when I woke up and realized you never came back up," he says. His eyes dart between Natalie and me. I don't know why the hell he is acting like an overprotective father all of a sudden, but I don't appreciate the implication.

"Everything's fine," she tells him. "It was just a little crowded up there."

"She's a big girl," I tell him. "I think she can look out for herself."

"You don't know the first thing about her," Blake informs me; then he turns and carries his bag to the truck.

"He always like that?" I ask Natalie.

"No," Natalie says. "Just with you."

As I watch him walk away, I notice Claire looking at me and Natalie. When our eyes meet, she averts her gaze, climbs into the pickup, and closes the door.

I pick up my rifle and my pack off the ground and get myself ready to leave as Natalie stretches on the sofa.

"Thanks," I tell Natalie. "For helping keep an eye on shit. And the food, too."

"Don't get all mushy on me," she smiles.

"Right," I say. "My bad."

I leave her to get herself ready to go and head for the pickup. I toss my pack in the bed of the truck and then look up at Fletcher sitting on the tailgate next to the annoying dog.

"You got an idea how to get to Cheyenne Mountain from here?" I say. "You seem to know this area a bit."

"Yeah, I grew up around there," he says. "I can't draw you a map or nothing, but I still got a pretty good idea."

"So, what kind of resistance are we looking at?" I ask him.

He thinks about it for a few seconds as he stares off at the sky.

"Well," he says finally. "Once we get through Española, it shouldn't be too bad. Bunch of small towns the rest of the way. At least until we get up near Pueblo and Colorado Springs. Then all bets are off."

"No way around those areas?"

"We can avoid Pueblo," he says. "It'll be safer but will probably add on a few hours of travel time. Still have to go through Colorado Springs, though. No way around that."

"We'll take the scenic route then," I say.

He nods, and then I open the door and climb into the driver's seat, stowing my rifle between my leg and the center console while I avoid making eye contact with Claire again. She probably is assuming something stupid about Natalie, because women generally assume the worst when it comes to men.

"Good morning," she finally says.

"Morning," I say as I stick the keys in the ignition.

"Did you get some sleep?" she asks me. It's one of those questions that seems like it is really asking something different than the words actually mean.

"Best night I've had in a while," I say and start the truck.

Maybe that seems cruel. I don't know why it matters to her anyway.

We get on the highway and navigate the winding roads through the Sangre de Cristo mountains. When we reach the Pueblo territory, we veer north on a highway that runs alongside a steep canyon far above the rocky waters of the Rio Grande.

"We just keep following the river up north," Fletcher says. "Takes us straight up to Colorado."

I give a thumbs up and continue rolling down the highway. Brown shrubs dot the downslope of a mountain along the right side of the road. Eventually, the dry brush gives way to trees that throw shade on the neglected houses. Only a few of the dead wander through the rocky, rust-colored dirt and thickets alongside the road until we reach a small community on the outskirts of Española. More and more of the dead stumble out of the woodwork toward the vehicles on the highway, moaning and flailing their arms in a futile attempt to catch us.

The small town comes in to view ahead as we crest a hill. I can see the highway runs right into a maze of tight streets lined with shops and shitty single-story homes. It reminds me of some of the towns I saw in The Stan. Except this place is crawling with walking corpses.

Fletcher didn't seem too concerned about this area, but I am. It won't be easy to navigate down these narrow lanes and all it takes is one wrong turn and we could find ourselves boxed in and surrounded by the dead.

Claire scans the map and looks up at the small town.

"It doesn't show all of these streets," she says. "Just the highway."

"This might get messy," I warn everyone.

Stitch starts growling and barking in the back of the truck.

To make matters worse, as we come down the hill, every stiff in town can hear our vehicles. Before we even reach the first intersection, there are corpses all over the road. I couldn't even avoid hitting them if I tried, so I just try to keep the pickup moving and hope we can make it through this hellhole before the thing is completely destroyed.

Dead bodies smash into the hood, grab onto the mirrors, and try to pull their decaying bodies up into the truck bed. Most of them are too weak and fall off, but some of them cling to the chassis until Fletcher puts a bullet in them.

I stay along the main street as long as I can and only turn at the closest thing I see to a major intersection. The only problem is I can't see a thing.

A decayed corpse splits in half as I run into the thing and the upper body crashes against the windshield. The man with long, dark black hair snaps his jaws at the glass. I swerve to try and shake him free, but the stiff somehow ends up impaled on the windshield wiper.

More of the dead crash into the grill and crunch beneath the tires as the truck rumbles over their withering bodies. The thing on the windshield bangs on the glass. Teeth crack off its decomposing jaws as the corpse tries to bite through the barrier. It smears dark sludge and decayed bodily fluid on the window, which obscures my view of the street more each time the thing moves.

I think I spot a road to the right. It might possibly be a bridge that crosses the river.

I crank the wheel but cut the turn too close to a garbage truck in the road. The rear fender of the trash hauler scrapes along the side of the pickup and damages the rear tire. It goes flat within seconds. The truck swerves down the pavement with the corpse still blocking my line of sight, but the powerful engine drives us forward.

"Come on," I say to the truck as if I could will it to get us through this mess.

I push the gas down more and run down anything in my way. We won't make it very far in this truck, but maybe we can at least get out of town. I glance back in the mirror to make sure Fletcher is still hanging on and Hoff is still behind us. Sparks fly off the rear rims of the pickup as they grind on the asphalt.

Then I plow into a wall of the dead. There are so many of them the truck skids off the road, smashes through a streetlight, and then rumbles through some bushes down a hill. Water splashes the windshield and the corpse that is somehow still attached to the wiper.

For a moment, I am terrified we're being pulled down a river. I turn my head to look out the side window and see it's only a small creek.

"Everyone out," Fletcher yells as he climbs out of the back of the truck. "Hurry up."

I grab my rifle, pop open the door, and hop down into the creek. I wade around the truck and grab Claire by the arm. We stomp up the hill through the bramble of shrubs behind Scout and Steven as he clutches his son in his arms and struggles to climb to the top of the ditch.

I look around as we get back to the road. The dead are coming at us from every direction except for the small, wooded area around the creek where the pickup crashed.

Hoff has the other vehicle idling in the middle of the street. He gets out and takes a couple of shots at the approaching dead as he makes his way around the back of the SUV. Natalie and Danielle begin firing from the rear windows as Blake slides over to get behind the wheel.

The mutt runs circles around Fletcher, barking and growling at the dead, the hair on his neck bristling. Fletcher opens the rear hatch of the SUV, and the dog immediately shuts up and hops in the back. Steven puts his son inside and then climbs in as well.

The vehicle is crammed full except for the passenger seat.

"Get in, Scout," Fletcher tells her.

"We're not leaving you," she says.

"Go on," Hoff urges her. "Get them out of town."

"We'll be right behind you," Fletcher assures her. "Go!"

I can tell Scout still doesn't want to go, but Stevie is in the vehicle. She turns and opens the door and climbs into the passenger seat. A second later, Blake hits the gas, and the tires squeal as he speeds off, leaving us stranded in the middle of a town that is overrun by the dead.

CHAPTER
THIRTY-THREE

J ust when I started to convince myself that I might make it through this
shit alive, reality comes back and bites me in the ass.

"Let's get moving," Hoff says.

We start running up the road in the direction the others left. My feet
squish in the soggy soles of my waterlogged boots with every step.

I can't even see the edge of town from where we are, but I know it can't
be too far. As long as we keep moving, we stand a chance. There are a lot of
these things but they are dispersed across the road, so we maneuver through
the slow-moving corpses without too much trouble.

As much as I want to plant my feet and shoot every last one of them, I
know that would only get us killed. Right now, our rifles only serve as melee
weapons to keep them from getting too close. Trying to fire from the hip
while on the move would just waste bullets and draw even more attention
to ourselves.

So, we keep running.

"We need to find another ride," says Fletcher.

"No way," Hoff pants. "We're not fucking around out here. Too risky."

"We can't fucking walk to Colorado," I agree.

Up ahead the street expands to four lanes. The stretch of road is lined with fast food chains and strip malls. It still must be at least a mile or two before the edge of town because all I see in the distance are more buildings and corpses.

"Look," Fletcher says. He nods his head toward a hotel on the left side of the road. Outside the entrance, a shuttle van is parked in the roundabout.

"Don't even think about it," Hoff says.

"I'll just run in and grab the keys," Fletcher says. "You won't even know I'm gone."

"Fletcher," Hoff gasps.

Fletcher pretends not to hear him as he veers left and starts sprinting across the opposing lanes of traffic. He dodges around the outstretched arms of a pair of corpses that attempt to grab him before he reaches the sidewalk. The guy has got to be ten or fifteen years older than me, but I have to say, he still has a lot of juice in the tank.

"He can really move," I say.

"Fucking hotshot," Hoff gasps.

The two of us pick up the pace and run after him. By the time we reach the entrance to the parking lot, Fletcher has already disappeared through the revolving door to the lobby. Hoff and I trot up the driveway and post up by the shuttle. I take up a firing position at the rear bumper and scan the parking lot for targets while Hoff opens the shuttle bus door.

"What are you doing?" I ask him.

"This thing is old as hell. I can probably hotwire it," Hoff says. "Would have told his dumb ass that if he didn't run off before I got the chance."

I fire off a round at a cleaning lady coming up the sidewalk, then I twist around and unleash another burst at a couple of teenage kids in bloody tank tops and swim trunks. Even though the hotel parking lot isn't nearly as bad as it was in the center of town, it's still a target-rich environment. I take aim at a man wearing a torn shirt that exposes the mangled ruins of his sternum. My finger squeezes the trigger, and the Honey Badger sends a round through his skull.

It seems like it's taking Fletcher too long. Even though I'm not even sure how long it has been.

Thirty seconds. Maybe it's been more like two minutes. I really have no idea.

Time becomes subjective when you're fighting for your life.

"How's it coming, Hoff?" I ask.

"Almost got it," he says.

"It's getting a little too crowded out here," I warn him before I pull the trigger again.

A couple seconds later, the engine turns over and the shuttle bus rattles to life.

"Hurry up," he says. "Go grab Fletcher."

I hop up to my feet and run around the back of the shuttle and push the tinted glass pane of the rotating door. The thing spins around, and as I come out the other side, I nearly walk right into the arms of the dead.

Several of them come at me in the lobby and I stumble back toward the door. My eyes dart around the room, but I don't see Fletcher. All I see are countless dead faces coming at me from behind the counter, in the lounge, and down the hallway. Their eyes are all fixed on me. As I back away from them, I catch sight Fletcher's rifle on the floor near the front desk.

The dead must have gotten him.

I retreat to the rotating door and lean my back against it to get it to move. The doors turn around and then I'm back outside. For a second, I just stare at the door in shock, unsure what to do. Then the things start shoving their way outside, so I turn and run for it. Hoff opens the door and I leap up the steps as the dead stagger out onto the sidewalk behind me.

"Go!" I yell.

"Where's Fletcher?" Hoff says.

"Fucking go!"

Hoff hits the gas and the tires squeal as he cuts the vehicle sharply around in the driveway. We both look back at the entrance where the dead pour out of the building.

"Is he still alive in there?" Hoff asks me.

"I don't know," I say. "There were fucking zombies everywhere."

"You didn't see him?" Hoff says.

I shake my head.

"We got to go back," Hoff says.

"We can't," I say. "You saw how many of those things there were."

Hoff brings a hand up to his brow and rubs it aggressively.

"No way he could still be alive," I tell Hoff. "Not in there. And even if he is, there's nothing we can do for him now."

Hoff clutches the steering wheel with white knuckles. His eyes dart back to the side mirrors to watch the dead swarming around the hotel as we speed down the road.

Once we get to the edge of town, the dead thin out, and the road clears again. I collapse into the seat behind Hoff and take a deep breath. It is hard to grasp that Fletcher is gone, but part of me can't help but feel like he did it to himself.

It takes a real cocky asshole to run off like that. He could have just as easily gotten all of us killed. All it takes is one wrong move and then it's game over. Fletcher should have known that by now.

We travel for another mile on the highway until we spot the SUV in the parking lot of a shooting range.

"There they are," I tell Hoff.

"I see them," he says as he steers the shuttle bus onto the shoulder.

Danielle waves to us from the open doorway, then turns and looks inside. We pull to a stop and the tires kick up a cloud of dirt. The rest of the group gathers out in front of the building. The sight of us returning in a shuttle bus brings smiles and excitement as they walk over to greet us.

"You better let me tell them," Hoff says. He pulls the lever to open the passenger door. "Just keep your mouth shut."

I can tell he doesn't want to, but he feels like he needs to be the one to break the news. It wasn't exactly like I was hoping to do it anyway.

"All right," I agree.

Hoff grabs the railing and grunts as he hauls himself out of the seat. I wait while he climbs down the steps, and then I follow him out into the warm sun.

"This is great," Blake gestures at the truck. "How the hell did you pull this off?"

Hoff walks around to meet them in front of the vehicle and raises his arms out in front of him to urge them to calm their excitement.

They see me approach behind the big guy. Then everyone gets real quiet. Scout gets on her tiptoes and cranes her neck to look around us at the empty bus.

"No," Blake drops his shoulders and tilts his head back and looks up to the sky. He lets out a long sigh as he comprehends the situation. Danielle blinks away the tears in her eyes and pinches her lips together.

"Where's Fletcher?" Scout asks.

Hoff just looks at her and shakes his head.

"No," Scout says. Her bottom lip quivers as she speaks.

"I'm sorry," he says.

"What happened?" Scout demands. I can see her hands trembling at her side.

"We got separated," Hoff says.

"How?" Scout yells.

"Fletcher went in to look for the keys to the bus," Hoff says. "Never came back out."

"And you left him there?" Scout scolds him.

"I tried to get to him," I tell her. "But the dead were inside. There were just too many. They were all over the place."

"I'm going to get him," she says.

"There is no way he could still be alive in there," I say.

"You don't know him," Scout says to me.

She walks over to the SUV and grabs a gun and her pack and starts walking back toward the road.

"You can't go back there, Scout," Hoff says. She tries to walk by him, but he grabs her firmly by the arm. "You will just end up getting yourself killed. I'm not going to let you do it."

She tries to shrug her arm free, but Hoff grabs ahold of her and doesn't let go, even as she tries to shove him away.

"Damn it, Hoff," she says. "Let go of me."

"We'll wait here," Hoff says. "Let's just wait. We can't do anything else."

He wraps his arms around Scout, and she buries her face in his chest and starts to cry.

"We'll wait here as long as we can," Blake says. "Hopefully, he'll show up."

Only I know he won't show up.

None of them saw what I saw inside the hotel. I am sure Fletcher is dead. There isn't a doubt in my mind.

Even if I told them that, it probably wouldn't make a difference. They're going to believe what they want either way. It's better to let it sink in slowly and they'll accept it when they are ready.

As much as I know that it is a waste of time to wait around here, I just keep my mouth shut and follow the rest of them inside.

CHAPTER
THIRTY-FOUR

Most of the guns and ammunition in the shop at the rifle range has been cleared out. There aren't any 5.56 mm rounds to be found, but I discover several boxes of ammo for the Honey Badger.

It figures.

Most people figure having a weapon that fires the most common ammunition would be their best bet if the shit hits the fan, which is exactly why that ammo is long gone. No one wants to haul around a different caliber ammo and different barrels.

It's too much of a pain in the ass.

Plus, you run the risk of someone that doesn't know shit having a rifle blow up in their hands. So, plenty of the most expensive ammunition on the market just sits around in shops like these collecting dust.

It's kind of a shame that people are that stupid.

Works out okay for me, though.

After a couple of hours of being stuck here, I start to get restless. I refill all my empty magazines and break down the Honey Badger to clean it again. Maybe I'm just trying to keep busy so I can avoid dealing with anyone. Or it might be that hearing Blake, Danielle, and Scout going on about Fletcher starts to get to me and I just need to find a distraction so I can block it out.

"Fletcher was always so alive," Blake says. "Just never a dull moment with him. I always thought that he would somehow make it through all this without so much as a scratch."

"I think he felt the same way," Scout agrees.

Hearing them talk about Fletcher makes me think of Mac. I didn't know Fletcher all that well, but he seemed to have the same kind of effect on those that knew him. It isn't easy to lose someone like that. The most valuable people are those that provide a spark when all anyone around them can see is darkness.

No matter how much it might seem like someone is above the fray, none of us are anymore. We're all in the shit, and there is only one way out of it. The rest of these people are just coming to terms with that.

I sit there listening as I load and count my rounds of ammo, but there is only so much sorrow I can handle. I need to extract myself from the group.

I walk to the front of the store and lean against the doorway. Across the parking lot, I spot Hoff. The Navy SEAL stands next to the hood of the shuttle and spits sunflower seeds in the dirt while he eyes the road. He might be hoping to see Fletcher, but he is really just waiting to see the first of the dead that will inevitably follow us down the highway from Española. It's not a question of if the dead will come. The only uncertainty is how long it will take them to drag their broke-ass bodies this far.

We don't have to wait long before the dead appear on the horizon. As soon as Hoff sees them, he lowers his eyes and rolls up the package of sunflower seeds and tucks them back into the pocket of his camo fatigues. He sees me in the doorway as he turns around and waves his arm to let me know we need to go. Then he climbs into the shuttle bus.

"Start packing up," I announce to everyone inside. "We're out of time."

Everyone grabs their things and heads back outside into the afternoon heat. We load up the trucks as the horde shambles toward us. Hoff waits behind the wheel of the shuttle watching Scout, Steven and his son climb in with the doctor and Claire. Natalie opens the rear hatch on the SUV and lets the dog hop inside while Blake and Danielle climb in the front.

I decide I'd rather not listen to Blake talk out of his ass anymore, so I head for the crowded shuttle. If the shit hits the fan again, at least I will have a chance to help the doctor and Claire. At least that's how I reasonably justify the decision to myself.

We are all set to go by the time the dead are within a hundred yards of the truck, but Hoff holds the wheel and stares at the road for a long minute. I give him time, but eventually the dead get close enough to make me anxious.

"He ain't coming, Hoff," I tell him. "We need to go."

Hoff silently shifts the shuttle into drive and pulls out onto the highway again. We keep driving north through the mountains. No one is really very certain where we are going now that we don't have Fletcher to help us navigate the roads to Cheyenne Mountain.

"We should pull off at a gas station," I tell Hoff. "We could use a roadmap."

"Probably come in handy," Hoff agrees.

"You think we can make it there by nightfall?" I wonder.

Hoff shrugs.

"Maybe," he finally says. "Maybe not."

I can take a hint.

He doesn't really feel like talking right now. I can hardly blame the guy. I have been in the same place myself too many times since this all started.

The somber mood makes for a quiet drive through the mountains. It doesn't seem like anyone feels like talking now except for Claire and the doctor. They discuss something quietly in the back row. I make my way to an empty seat near them. Claire turns to glance at me for a moment as I sit down before she returns her focus to the doctor.

I had not really paid much attention to him since he arrived, but now as I take in the old man in his boxers, dress socks, and lab coat, I have to admit, I'm a little curious to know what is going on with the guy.

"It was terrible," he says. "Inhumane conditions."

"How long were you held there?" Claire asks him.

"I cannot say for sure," the doctor says. "Many months."

"What is he talking about?" I ask Claire.

Claire turns to look at me. She seems annoyed at the interruption.

"The doctor was just telling me what happened to him," she says. "He's been held against his will in a secret Russian laboratory for several years."

"Why?" I wonder.

"They forced him to work on developing new weapons to use against us," she says.

I look up again at the doctor, and he smiles at me.

"I don't think we've met young man," he says. "I'm Dr. Charles Schoenheim."

"Chase," I tell him.

"Oh," the man smiles. He seems thrilled to meet me. Too thrilled. "I had a dog named Chase when I was a boy. A little beagle."

"That's great," I nod, before I turn back to Claire. "What the fuck is wrong with him?"

"He's been through a lot," she defends him. "It's a miracle he's even alive. He is one of the most brilliant researchers in his field."

I look at the old man and have to wonder how the hell he is going to be of any use to anyone. He certainly doesn't look like he is as brilliant as I was led to believe. Not anymore at least.

"Why doesn't he put on some pants then?"

"Chase," Claire says. "The doctor needs his medication."

"Medication?" I say.

"Donepezil," she says. "For dementia."

"What if we can't find him any?" I ask.

"We have to," she says. "If he is going to help us."

This is just another monkey wrench thrown in to fuck up the gears even further.

Not only do we need to get the doctor someplace safe and get the equipment he needs to do his research, but now we need to get our hands on a supply of a very specific medication so that he has enough mental capacity to do anything at all. Even if we get to Cheyenne Mountain, all of this might have been for nothing. Calling this a long shot would seem too optimistic at this point.

My eyes focus on the doctor. The senile man smiles at the sights alongside the road like this is some sort of amusing theme park ride. I can't help but resent the imbecile a bit, even if none of this is really his fault. It still bothers me to see anyone so oblivious to all the horrible things happening all around us. He better be able to make all of this matter somehow.

"What were they forcing him to work on anyway?" I ask Claire. "The Russians."

Claire studies my face for a long time. She doesn't seem like she wants to answer the question.

"I'm not sure," Claire says. "But it might have been something related to all of this."

The news sends a cold chill up my spine. I could be sitting with the man that took an active role in bringing about the death of my entire platoon. Claire raises her eyebrows and inhales sharply. She panics when she sees the look of rage on my face.

"Chase—," she holds a hand up, but I shove it out of my face.

"You mean to tell me that this fucking guy might have been the one that started all this shit?"

I stand up from my seat, even though I'm not sure what I'm doing. My instincts tell me to just shoot the asshole and avenge my brothers. Claire gets out of her seat as well and puts her body between the doctor and me.

I can feel everyone in the vehicle watching me. I glance over my shoulder and see Hoff looking up at me in the mirror above the windshield. I don't think he would do anything to stop me, but then again, I don't know him all that well yet.

"Chase," Claire says. "I'm not even sure."

"Move, Claire," I warn her.

The doctor continues to stare out the window, completely oblivious to everything that's happening.

"Stop!" Claire yells. "He didn't have a choice. He was just trying to survive. I know him. He isn't some monster. He didn't want any of this to happen."

"Damn it, Claire," I growl at her. "Get out of the fucking way."

She shakes her head as she lowers her arms.

"He is a good man," she says. "We need him. Without him, we're all dead. If you want to shoot him, you might as well shoot me right now, too."

"I'll do it," I warn Claire.

"Then it will be the last thing you ever do," Scout says. I look over my shoulder and find her behind me with her Glock pointed at my head.

CHAPTER
THIRTY-FIVE

I lower the Honey Badger to diffuse the situation, and I look back and see Scout lowering her weapon as well. If Claire and Scout hadn't tried to stop me, I don't know that I would have actually shot him. I just know I wanted to. I was willing to find out if I'd go through with it.

"You all done fucking around back there?" Hoff asks as he steers the wheel. "There's a gas station up ahead."

I move back up to the front of the shuttle bus and crouch down to see through the windshield. Up ahead, I spot the gas station where the road intersects with a highway. Everything looks quiet as we approach the area. Several vehicles rest beneath a thick layer of grime and dust. A lone corpse wanders in between the fuel pumps. It may appear deserted, but trouble lurks everywhere now.

As intense as the situation in the shuttle might have been a few minutes ago, we shift gears and grab our weapons in anticipation of whatever the stop at the station might bring. I can feel Scout watching me, though. It won't surprise me if she keeps a close eye on me for a while since we were just pointing guns at each other. She might be the one person here I know would not hesitate if she thought I needed to be dealt with.

Hoff brings the truck to a stop along the front of the store, and I step out the door and raise my rifle to quickly take out the corpse of the gas station attendant wandering by the pumps. I scan the inside of the store through the shattered windows and see the empty shelves and beverage cases.

We might not find anything of use here at all. The only thing I really want is a map to make sure we don't get ourselves lost on the endless mountain roads of Colorado, but it looks like even that might be asking for a little too much.

"I'm going to check it out," I say to Hoff. I raise my hand and look at Blake in the other vehicle to tell him to stay in the car. "Keep it running. I'll just be a minute."

"Famous last words," Hoff warns me.

I've already had to deal with Fletcher getting himself killed. I don't need anyone else to get out and make a stupid mistake as well. At the moment, the only one I have any confidence in is Hoff. The rest of them are all just a liability.

I step through the shattered door and into the dim light of the storefront. The glass cracks beneath my boots and causes me to pause and check the shop again. It sounds quiet at first, but then I hear sounds coming from the hallway at the back of the store.

Of course, there had to be at least one.

I walk slow and steady down the aisle to try and minimize the noise I make, but with all the debris on the floor I'm unable to avoid making a racket. The thing starts moaning and banging on something. I reach the front counter and turn to look around the hall to the right. One of the bathroom doors rattles on the hinges, but the corpse seems to be stuck inside. Then I notice the graffiti on the walls.

The Reapers.

I lower the rifle and take a quick look around the store, but there isn't much left inside here to take. There is a sour smell emanating from the thawed-out ice cream freezer and the beverage case full of pungent milk cartons, so I steer clear of that. The only things I walk out with are a dented can of soda, a roll of breath mints and a travel size tube of toothpaste. No map.

"Just another disappointing waste of time," I say as I climb back in the truck.

Only it wasn't.

Now I know for certain that what I saw was not just some random graffiti in Los Alamos. There is another group out here calling themselves The Reapers, or at least they were out here not too long ago. And they are taking everything they can get.

"It's getting pretty late," Hoff says. "Sun will be going down soon."

"Think we should stay here for the night?" I ask him.

"Doesn't seem like a bad spot," he says.

I look around the area again and check how low the sun is getting in the sky as I consider it.

"We should probably try to get some more miles behind us," I suggest. "We still have a long ways to go. Besides, it fucking stinks in there."

Any hope we had of making it to Cheyenne Mountain before nightfall is gone. We could go for it but driving through any town would be too risky in the dark. And we can forget about going anywhere near a place the size of Pueblo or Colorado Springs. So, we will have to find somewhere else to stay for the night.

We pull back on to the highway and continue heading north as the sun descends below the mountains to the west. More snow-capped peaks appear on either side of the road as we ascend further into the Sangre de Cristo range.

Hoff brings the vehicle to a halt at the gates of a large ranch that is miles and miles from anywhere. In the dim light, I see an impressive mansion set back a few hundred yards from the road.

"Now we're talking," Steven says.

"Think anyone is home?" Hoff asks me.

"Only one way to find out," I tell him.

The chances of running in to any survivors is pretty low these days. But out here, in a place like this, I'd say the odds are slightly higher. It's just a guess, but I'd be willing to bet that whoever bought this place might have had the apocalypse in mind.

"I'll get the gates," I tell Hoff.

He opens the door and I climb down the steps and walk up the dirt driveway to the security gates. Tall wooden posts on each end of the fence hold up a wrought-iron sign that says Twilight Ranch. I open the simple cattle gates that block the road and climb back into the shuttle as Hoff steers up the driveway.

He follows the long gravel road around an enormous barn and up to the darkened house. The cedar exterior gives the home a modest log cabin kind of feel, but the sheer size of the structure and solar-paneled roof make it pretty obvious that the owner had a lot of money.

We park the vehicles out in front of the house and look around. Across a meadow, I can see a barn and another large log home. Must be the guest house.

I try not to get my hopes up as we walk up the steps of the creaky porch. The place could be trashed inside. I twist the handle and am startled when lights come on in the entryway. I nearly start shooting before I scan the room and realize it is empty. In the corner, I notice a motion sensor on the wall.

My jaw drops as I look around.

The place is immaculate. I hesitate in the doorway as I take in the spiral staircase, the motorcycle parked in the den, and the massive stone fireplace.

"Chase," Hoff whispers. "Chase."

Someone pushes through the doorway behind me when I don't respond. I just can't believe my eyes at the moment. Everyone moves inside quietly and stares at the amazing home in awe. Even before the world went to shit, I never stayed in any place half as nice as this.

"Well, at least something finally went right for us," Blake says.

"This place is incredible," Danielle says.

I walk into the impressive kitchen and the lights turn on in there. I turn to look into a massive living room and then I spot the owners. The wife and the husband exhibit matching self-inflicted gunshot wounds to the head.

I cover my nose and turn my eyes away from the bodies. They've been dead at least a few days judging by the smell. The rest of the group follows me down the hall, but I turn around and stop them.

"Might want to stay out of there," I warn them although I don't need to. As soon as the smell hits them, they turn around and head back toward the foyer.

We clear the rest of the house. It takes us quite a while. The place has seven bedrooms. Downstairs we discover a bar, a game room, a sauna and hot tub. Hoff calls me over when he opens the door to what I thought was a hall closet. A set of stairs leads down to a solid steel door. I follow him down the stairs and through the doorway into a sizable bunker. There is a large pantry with a wide assortment of dry goods. The owners even left delightful collection of rifles, shotguns, sidearms and a shit-ton of ammo.

"Oh man," I say to Hoff. "I don't want to leave this place."

He locates a few big bags of sunflower seeds on one of the shelves in the bunker pantry and grabs all of them.

"Kind of a shame we are just here for the night," he agrees.

"Let's make the most of it then," I say.

"You bet your ass," he says as he heads for the stairs. "First, come give me a hand. I want to move those bodies outside before the kid sees them."

I follow him back out of the bunker, and we make our way to the living room. The patio doors open to a large deck, and together, we carry the previous owners outside and lay them on the ground.

"Doesn't make sense," Hoff says.

"What?" I say.

"Why'd they go through all this trouble just to check out when the shit hits the fan?" Hoff wonders.

It does seem strange but doesn't completely surprise me.

"Just because someone was a prepper doesn't mean they're mentally prepared for this kind of shit," I say. "That's a whole different ball game."

I head back inside, but Hoff lingers on the patio for a moment.

"Hey," Hoff calls me.

He pauses in the doorway and looks back at me.

"What?" I say.

"We just going to leave them out here?" he says. "Something will probably come eat them."

"That's not really our problem," I say. "Is it?"

"I guess," Hoff says. "Just kind of feels like we owe them a little more than this."

"They're dead," I say. "We don't owe them a thing."

Inside the house, country music blares on a stereo. I turn back and see Hoff still staring at the bodies.

"You want to spend your only night in this place digging graves, go right ahead," I tell him.

"I guess you're right," he says. "That hot tub is calling me anyway."

We head back inside and, in spite of everything that we've been through, everyone is already taking advantage of everything the ranch has to offer.

Stevie plays in the game room, blasting away at invaders from outer space. Steven flips on the television. There are no broadcasts, but he discovers a selection of movies to watch. Scout, Danielle, and Blake split a bottle of wine that Natalie brought up from the cellar. Stitch runs around marking the house plants until he locates the master bedroom and passes out in the middle of the king-sized bed.

The doctor finally locates a suitable pair of pants in one of the closets upstairs. He gets cleaned up and showers, too. He actually seems almost normal again, at least until you try talking to him.

Claire makes the best discovery.

There are actually fresh eggs, produce, and meat in the refrigerator and freezer.

"Steaks?" I ask when she opens the fridge.

She reaches down and grabs two frozen steaks from the freezer

"Ribeye or Porterhouse?" she asks.

"Both," I grin.

Even though I was pointing my rifle at her a few hours ago, it all seems forgotten now. That's just the nature of the world we live in now. Claire smiles at me as she takes out pots and pans and turns on the electric stove. I can tell this is something she enjoys doing.

"How come you never made dinner at the house?" I ask her.

"Anyone can heat up a can of beans," she explains. "But cooking real food is different. There is a science to it."

The aromas fill the house and the rest of us are salivating within minutes. We spend hours eating everything we can fit into our stomachs. Without question, this is the best night that any of us have had in a long time. At least until Blake decides to open his mouth again.

"Too bad Fletcher couldn't be here for this," he says.

The laughter dies. Everyone stops smiling.

Blake stares at his glass of wine, lost in thought.

"We'd have never got him to leave," Hoff says.

"You're probably right," Blake agrees.

"To Fletcher," Danielle says and raises her wine glass.

The rest of them follow her lead. I even raise my beer slightly and take a sip before I turn and leave the dining room when the conversation turns sentimental.

I head back down the hall and go into the den to check out the motorcycle. It's a pretty sweet Harley with an American flag painted over the gas tank and the fenders. Then I remember the map and I start to dig through the bookshelves and the drawers of the desk. I don't locate one there, so I check out the garage.

Six vehicles are parked inside beneath the humming halogen lights. There are a pair of high-end pickup trucks, one in red and one in black. There is also a green Hummer, an electric-powered economy car, a vintage Corvette, and a brand-new black Mustang with red stripes along the hood.

For a minute, I just stand in the doorway staring at the sight of all the cars and trucks. Then I remember the map. I open the door of one of the pickups and check the center console. I finally locate one in the glove compartment.

The sound of glass shattering on the floor startles me, and I jerk my head up.

Hoff stands by the door with his mouth hanging open. A shattered bottle sits in a puddle of beer on the floor.

"Oh my god," Hoff gasps.

"You scared the fuck out of me, Hoff," I say as I slam the door of the truck.

I walk toward him and can smell the alcohol from several feet away. The big guy has clearly been going at it pretty hard. He ignores me and wanders over to the Chevy parked near the other end of the garage.

"I can't believe my eyes," Hoff says as he places his hands on the hood of the car.

"Pretty nice," I say.

"Pretty nice?" Hoff says. "This baby is incredible!"

"I found a map," I tell him, but he doesn't seem to care.

"I had my doubts before," Hoff says. "But I know now that the big guy up there is watching over me."

"Are you crying?" I ask.

"No," he leans down and kisses the enamel.

He is definitely crying.

"I guess I'll leave you two alone," I say and then I head back inside the house.

CHAPTER
THIRTY-SIX

Morning comes around and I wake up to the sound of a rooster squawking in the yard and the scent of cooked bacon. For just a moment, I lie there with my eyes closed on the sofa and wonder if it was all a dream. Then I open my eyes and see the mounted deer heads on the wall, the family photos of the deceased owners in their hunting gear, and the expensive furniture and realize it is all very real.

I head to the kitchen and find everyone is already awake and sipping coffee in between bites of scrambled eggs, hash browns and fresh melon. It is rare for me to be the last one awake, but I must have been completely wiped out since I barely remember falling asleep on the couch last night.

"Coffee?" Blake asks me, holding out a steaming cup.

"No thanks," I say. "Don't drink the stuff."

Claire holds out a plate of food for me.

"I'll take some of that," I say. "Thanks."

I grab a seat next to Natalie and start shoveling food into my mouth. I'd really rather have my eggs sunny-side up, but I'm not about to start complaining about eating any of it. After weeks of stale chips, canned veggies, and the occasional jerky when I can find some, a meal like this is something I never thought I'd get again.

"We better get moving," Hoff says. "We probably should be on the road already."

No one gets up from the table. I can hardly blame them.

"I don't want to leave," Stevie complains.

Scout puts her arm around him and points to some of the food on the table to get him to eat more.

"Hoff," Scout says. "I think we're going to stay."

She looks over at Steven who nods in agreement.

"Scout," Hoff says. "Are you sure about this?"

"Yeah," she says.

"It's nice here," he says. "Real nice. But even if it seems like it is safe here, it is just a matter of time before someone else finds this place."

"If that happens, I'll be ready for it," Scout says.

"Is this because of what happened to Fletcher?" Hoff asks.

"No," Scout says. "That's not what it's about at all."

"Then come with us," he says. "We know where this place is. If we need to we can always come back here. But help us finish this."

She looks down at the empty plate with the scraps of food on it and thinks about it. I can't blame her or anyone else for wanting to stay. But this isn't a laboratory. Claire and the doctor won't be able to help anyone here. If we want to try and put an end to all of this, we have to keep going.

"Don't quit on me now, Scout," Hoff says. "Think about what kind of world you want for Stevie."

"Fine," Scout says standing up from the table abruptly. "Let's get moving then."

"But you said—" Steven says, but Scout interrupts him.

"That was before I realized that I'd only have you to talk to here," Scout says. "I think I'd rather go die in Colorado."

Steven gets up and follows her out of the room as everyone has a laugh at his expense. Scout is really something else. That gal has one hell of an attitude. You might not think it when you look at her, but she is as hard and tough and resilient as any Marine I've ever met.

We pack up the two trucks with as much food and ammunition as we can safely carry, and then Hoff pulls the Corvette out of the garage.

"You can't be serious," I say to him.

"This baby is coming with me," Hoff says. "The way I figure, the universe owes me for everything I been through. I'll take this as a down payment."

I know that driving a car like that around out here is only going to destroy the thing, but I don't have the heart to tell him that. It's just going to go to waste sitting in that garage anyway. The guy might as well have a little fun.

We pull down the driveway, and all of us can't help but look back at the beautiful mountaintop ranch and wish we could stay there. Most people would probably say we are crazy for leaving, but we might be the only ones able to help bring all this to an end.

We pass through the small mountain town of Questa. It's a beautiful place tucked between snow-covered mountains with dozens of dead wandering the street.

Even out here, way up in the mountains, the dead have taken over every small town. But in-between those towns are miles and miles of rugged terrain. There are stretches of wilderness along the road where the only things to be seen are huge meadows and towering peaks. The sight of them is so amazing. It makes me wonder how it was ever possible to navigate these lands before we had roads and automobiles. If we don't succeed, one day soon we might understand what those early settlers experienced.

Claire spreads the map out in her lap and tries to find the best route to Cheyenne Mountain.

We pass through the tiny town of Castillo, and then we pass a lop-sided wood sign that reads WELCOME TO COLORFUL COLORADO. I glance around at the bland grasses in the meadows surrounding us.

"Colorful, my ass," I say.

We continue along the same road for miles, passing by countless small farms and the occasional factory in the middle of nowhere. The mountains play games with my mind as I drive. They seem to take forever to get closer, then the road turns and you see another distant mountain ahead that seems to never get any closer. Finally, after an hour drive that seems three times that long, we come to the town of Fort Garland where the road we've been following comes to an end.

"Go right up ahead," Claire tells me.

I slow down at the stop sign. This place is a ghost town. The dead lie in the streets. Their bodies have been mutilated in horrific ways. Some of them aren't even dead. A few of them with their limbs chopped off slither around in the streets like slugs. A head stuck on top of the street sign stares at us and moves its jaws. I've seen a lot of shit since this started, but nothing like this.

Everything has been picked clean from the town. The stores are all empty. Cars methodically stripped down. Whoever did this took their time and made sure they got everything.

Then, in the rearview mirror, I notice the graffiti on the back wall of a gas station.

The grim reaper with a black cloak and a scythe stares at me and points a bony finger in my direction.

No one else says anything. I glance around the truck and see Claire looking at the map. Scout is thumb wrestling with Stevie, while Steven watches Scout. I am guessing they haven't noticed what I have seen in these towns. They just see another shitty destroyed town in a long line of shitty destroyed towns.

I could tell them, but I don't want to get them panicked for no reason. After all, we might never cross paths with these people, whoever they are.

I hope not, at least.

From what I have witnessed they are methodical, brutal, and they seem to enjoy what they are doing. They've bypassed small towns that had little or nothing to offer, but when they find a place with something of value, they take everything and leave plenty of carnage behind.

The narrow road curves around to the east through the grassy high plains. Deep green spruces and pines appear atop the hillsides across the meadows.

"Turn left here," Claire says.

At first, I don't even see the dirt road. It just looks like a driveway.

"Here?" I ask her. "Are you sure?"

"It's on the map," Claire says.

I make the left turn and steer the truck down the dusty gravel driveway.

"This doesn't seem right to me," I tell her.

"Look," she says and holds the map up.

I can't really see it, but I glance over and look at her expression. I can tell she is certain this is the right way, and that is enough for me.

The single-lane road winds between dense patches of birch and pine. Wedged between mountain peaks rest dilapidated cabins, some burned to the ground. Even the dead don't wander out here. The terrain is too treacherous. We should feel fairly safe out here, but I do not feel safe at all.

The sight of tire tracks in the damp dirt road make me uneasy. Someone must have passed through here recently. It could have been days. It could have been hours. There is no way to tell for sure.

I slow the truck down and watch anxiously around every bend.

"What's wrong?" Claire finally asks me.

"What?" I say.

"You look like you're worried about something," she says.

"It's nothing," I say.

I relax my grip on the wheel and lean back in the seat. I don't need to get them rattled. If it turns out to be nothing, it will just make the rest of the car ride unbearable.

The only problem is Claire isn't buying it.

"Chase," she says. "I know you."

I see an intersection ahead where the road ends.

"Right or left?" I ask her and gesture at the road.

She looks down at the map and tells me to take a left. I make the turn, my eyes staring at the tire tracks that still tread the road ahead.

"Well?" she asks me again.

Apparently my attempt to change the subject didn't work out.

"It's those tire tracks," I tell her. "We have been following them since we left the highway."

"So someone must have come down this way recently," she says. "What makes you think we need to be worried about them?"

"I have my reasons," I say. "Just keep your eyes open for anything out of the ordinary."

"In case you haven't noticed," Scout chimes in. "Everything looks out of the ordinary now."

CHAPTER THIRTY-SEVEN

The tracks in the dirt road lead us all the way back to a paved highway.

"Go left here," Claire tells me.

I stop the pickup before the intersection and shift it into park.

"What are you doing?" Claire asks me.

"Just hang on," I tell her as I open the door and get out of the truck.

I walk over and crouch down to inspect the tire marks in the mud. A door slams behind me and I look back to see Hoff climbing out of the car. He scans the road as he walks to meet me by the intersection.

"What's the hold up?" he asks me, and then he notices the tire tracks on the ground in front of me and his eyes dart around the road again.

"Been following these tracks for the last thirty Mikes," I say. "Can't tell which way they went from here."

"We don't got time for any rescue operations anyway," Hoff says.

"That's not why I stopped," I tell him.

Hoff adjusts the strap of his rifle and spits a shell into the dirt.

"Did you see the graffiti?" I ask him. "Back at Los Alamos."

Hoff thinks about it for a moment.

"You had to have seen it," I say.

"The Reaper?" Hoff says. "What about it?"

"The Reapers," I correct him. "I think it must be some kind of group. A gang. Whatever you want to call it. I saw something similar back in Fort Garland."

"Probably just some kids," Hoff says, but I can tell he is at least a little concerned.

"I don't think so," I say.

"Come on," he says and gestures for me to move back to the truck. "We're only a couple hours away, then we can forget about all this shit."

I follow him back and watch him get in the car before I glance back at the tracks. I really hope I am just being paranoid and overly cautious. After I get back behind the wheel and shift the truck in drive, I pull out onto the highway and resume scanning the landscape for any signs of danger.

"Don't take this the wrong way, Chase," Scout says. "But you're kind of starting to freak me out."

I glance up to the mirror and see her watching me from the backseat.

"You're not about to lose it or anything are you?" she asks.

"I'm fine," I say.

"I mean first you're pointing guns at people, now you're getting all paranoid," she continues.

For a moment, I wonder if she is right.

Am I just being paranoid?

Has the stress of everything started to get to me and distorted my perception?

"Just worry about yourself," I tell her.

"I am," she says.

I shift my position in the seat and notice in the mirror that she has the Glock in her hand. She isn't pointing it at me, but she is ready to use it if she feels like I am a threat.

Maybe I am a threat.

Maybe I'm not stable.

Maybe she isn't either.

These kind of things aren't so cut and dry anymore.

We've all been out here too long, and it has pushed us to our limits. It could be I am anxious now that we are so close to safety that something is bound happen.

When I was on deployment, Sarge told me that if I was planning on getting killed I should get it over with right away. No one wants to endure all those months in hell just to die so close to getting out. It seems like the same rule applies here and now.

I've come too far. I have to keep it together now.

I take a deep breath and try to relax. As we push north into the Rockies, I roll down the window and the cool mountain air calms my nerves a bit. At least until we reach the next small mountain town.

From this distance, I can tell by the number of buildings along the horizon that this community is only slightly larger than Fort Garland. The kind of place we could speed right through without much of a problem, but as we get closer I spot another ominous figure painted on the wall of a hardware store at the edge of town.

I shift my rifle slightly to make sure I can still get to it easily if I need to. Everything is more difficult with seven and a half fingers.

As we enter the town, I see the dead have been slaughtered here as well. I have to wonder if some of them were still alive when the Reapers rolled through here.

Hundreds of bodies line the streets. A handful of corpses still stumble around but most of them are badly maimed. Arms sliced off, legs bashed to hell, a couple of them even had their lower jaws brutally extracted from their faces.

There is a line between what normal people do to survive and what dangerous people do for kicks. The kind of people that tie a corpse to a stop sign and set it on fire are not just trying to survive.

"Who did this?" Claire wonders.

"The Reapers," I say.

"The what?" Scout says.

"Didn't you see that hardware store?" I say.

"The skeleton?" Steven says. "I saw it."

"There was one in Fort Garland, too," I say.

"And one in Los Alamos," Scout says.

"Still think I'm going crazy?" I ask her.

"Shit," Scout says as she scans the street.

"Turn right, here," Claire tells me as we reach the center of town.

"There's no telling how long ago this happened," Steven says. "Whoever did this is probably long gone."

I make the turn onto Main Street and head for the edge of town. The gas light flicks on as I steer around a cannibalized sedan in the road with a legless corpse tied to the grill.

"We might have another problem," I say.

"Gas?" Claire asks.

"How far away are we?" I ask her.

She scans the map again.

"Maybe a hundred miles," she says.

"We're not going to make it," I tell them. "We're going to have to find fuel somewhere."

"Something tells me that won't be easy around here," Scout says as she looks over at a gas station on the edge of town. "They even took the pumps."

"Had to take a lot of people to pull something like this off," Steven says.

We leave the town and find ourselves on a long stretch of highway through empty fields. I turn at another derelict highway and keep driving north as the fuel needle pushes below the red line and the warning light flashes on and off. Just as I think we are about to run out of gas in the middle of nowhere, we spot the steeple of a church above the treetops ahead.

I slow down to maneuver around a blind curve. A corpse shuffles into the road and the truck crashes into the thing before I even have time to react. I slam on the brakes and then I feel a jolt and hear a crunch as Hoff smashes the Corvette into the back of the truck. The corpse groans as it tumbles into the shallow ditch beside the road.

More corpses wander farther up the street. It is actually a relief to see the dead. That means that this place might not have been stripped clean yet. We may even find fuel.

"Is everyone okay?" I ask.

I look back and see Scout with her arm in front of Stevie to brace him. Then I hear Hoff curse as he slams the car door.

"Chase!" Hoff yells.

I get out of the truck and scan the road. A couple dozen corpses crowded around a church take notice of us and snarl and moan as they head our way.

"You fucking idiot!" Hoff screams as he looks at the crumpled hood of the Chevy.

"Hoff!" I yell to get his attention.

He looks over and notices the corpses and scrambles to grab his rifle out of the car.

I raise the Honey Badger and open fire on the dead. Scout leans out the window and fires as well. Within seconds, Blake, Danielle and Natalie are out in the street laying down fire, too.

That scrappy little mutt even hops out of the truck. He snarls and growls at the corpse that I struck and knocked into the ditch as it struggles to get upright again. It reaches out and the dog yelps and turns to run but the stiff gets hold of his tail. Stitch growls and snaps his teeth at the fingers of the thing.

"Stitch!" Stevie screams. He tries to fight off his dad when Steven restrains him from leaving the vehicle.

Hoff sees what is happening and jumps over the hood of the smashed Chevy and then I lose sight of him as I turn to focus my fire on the remaining corpses coming up the road.

I shoot a guy about my age with a beard and a ridiculous looking fur hat on his head. Then I center the rifle on a preacher with a face that was gnawed half off and fire off my last couple rounds hitting him in the shoulder and then the head. The last of the corpses falls to the pavement and then I lower the rifle.

I glance over and see Hoff holding Stitch. He raises the dog up and sets him in the back of the truck.

"Is he okay?" Stevie asks.

"Yeah," Hoff hisses. The big guy winces in obvious pain.

"What's wrong?" I ask Hoff as I swap a fresh magazine into the Honey Badger.

As soon as I ask him, I come to realize what must have happened.

Hoff lowers his head and looks down at his leg.

"How bad is it?" I ask him.

"It's always bad," Hoff says. He limps around the front of the pickup and I can see the blood spilling down over his right boot. "I'm about as fucked up as that Chevy now."

"Hoff! Jesus," Scout says when she sees him. She rushes to his side and he raises his arm to let her help him walk a few more feet to the back of the truck.

Danielle hurries over to help him but Hoff holds up a hand to stop her. I think Hoff already knows there is nothing anyone can really do to help him now.

Hoff leans back against the truck and pulls out a tourniquet from his bag.

"Let me help," I tell him. He hands me the tourniquet and I crouch down and slip it under his boot. I lift it up his leg, and tighten it above the bite. The thing really got him. With the amount of blood he has already lost, he won't last very long.

"Thanks, Corporal," Hoff says to me.

"I'm sorry, Hoff," I say. "I fucked up."

He holds up a hand to get me to stop talking.

"It's okay, kid," he says. "Some shit like this was bound to happen eventually."

"You should have just let that thing eat the fucking dog," I say.

Hoff manages a laugh. He reaches back and pets Stitch on the head. The dog tilts his head back and licks the palm of Hoff's hand and then moves to the edge of the truck and laps his tongue across the side of Hoff's face.

"Don't think I would do it any different if I could," Hoff sniffs.

The door to the church bursts open down the road and a body comes crawling out. At first, I think it's just another corpse as it tumbles down the stairs.

Blake starts walking towards the figure. The person raises an arm and calls for help. Scout, Danielle, and Natalie jog to catch up with Blake.

"Go on," Hoff says. "I'll be there in a minute."

"Stay here," I tell Claire and Steven as I walk down the road.

The man gets to his feet, grabs on to the railing on the side of the church steps and props himself up.

"We're here to help," I hear Blake say while cautiously approaching the stranger.

The man is shirtless, and I notice something metallic around his neck that glints in the sunlight.

Dog tags.

I quicken my pace. If he was armed forces I should be the one to talk to him. Before Danielle steps closer to him and blocks my view, I notice his clothes are covered in crusted mud and dry blood. He holds up his arm and pleads for water in a hoarse voice.

Blake grabs a bottle out of his pack and offers it to the man. He takes it and drinks eagerly as water spills out of the corners of his mouth. That's when I finally get a good look at his face.

"No fucking way," I say as I tighten my grip on the rifle. "I know him."

The man lowers the bottle and squints his eyes to look at me.

"His name is Jenson."

CHAPTER THIRTY-EIGHT

"Who?" Blake asks me.

I look at the face of the man again to be sure. It's been a couple of months since I've seen him. He no longer has a shaved head. His dark hair has grown out a few inches. The withered man is so thin that he can barely stand. His face is gaunt, and his lips are blistered, but it is definitely him.

Jenson.

You don't forget the face of a man that was responsible for the deaths of half of your platoon.

"I think you got me confused with somebody else, kid," Jenson lies.

I reach down and yank the dog tags off his chest and look at them just to be sure, then I hand them to Blake.

"This fucking piece of shit got half my team killed," I say.

"I didn't kill anyone," Jenson says.

I raise my rifle.

"Your team fucked up the mission," Jenson says. "That wasn't my fault at all."

"You son of a bitch," I curse him.

"Hold on, everyone," Blake says. "Let's all just take a breath and calm down."

He stares at me until I lower my rifle slightly.

"What's going on?" Hoff says.

I glance over my shoulder to see Claire helping him along as he hobbles over from the truck.

"Look, man," Jenson says to me. He pauses to clear his throat. "I'm sorry about your platoon."

"Sorry?" I scoff.

"Easy, Chase," Blake says.

"Don't tell me to take it easy," I warn him.

"Look at him," Blake says. "He's broken. He isn't going to hurt anyone right now."

I lower the rifle, turn around, and take a few steps away from them.

"I never meant for any of that to happen," Jenson pleads. "I was just trying to keep everyone at Holloman safe. We lost most of our men that night, too."

My head feels like it is ready to explode. I know Jenson is defenseless now. He is weak and desperate and killing him won't do anything to bring my brothers back. But I feel like if I turn around and look at him, I won't be able to stop myself from pulling the trigger.

"How did you get up here?" Hoff asks him.

"After his team led half a million fucking zombies to Holloman, we had to get the hell out of town," he says. "Tried to head up north, but of course that turned to shit real fast."

"What happened?" Blake asks.

"Reapers," Jenson says.

"You've seen them?" Hoff asks.

Jenson nods.

"Who are they?" Hoff asks him.

"You ever hear the story about that company in Nam that went into the jungle and never came out? Some people say they stayed there forever. Went insane. Bathed in the blood of the enemy. All that shit."

Hoff nods.

"Yeah," Jenson says. "They'd be like a pack of cub scouts next to the Reapers."

"They're military?" Hoff asks.

Jenson shakes his head.

"They're monsters," Jenson says.

"How'd you manage to survive?" Blake asks him.

"You all are going to help me, right?" Jenson asks.

Blake hesitates.

"I'll tell you everything," Jenson says. "Just don't leave me to die out here."

He sounds so pitiful as he begs us to save his life. Jenson seems like a completely different person than the asshole that caused so much chaos and death. Still, I can't bring myself to turn around and look at him.

"Yeah," Blake agrees. "We will take you with us."

"Where?" Jenson wants to know. "Because some places around here aren't safe."

"Cheyenne Mountain," Blake says.

"There's still people alive in there?" he asks.

"Yeah," Blake says. "We just talked to someone two days ago."

"No shit," says Jenson. "They never responded to our radio calls."

Probably because they didn't want fucking traitors in their goddamn bunker.

"So," Blake says. "How are you still alive?"

"We were in some little shithole Mexican town," he says. "Probably about sixty of us that made it out of Holloman. Reapers showed up in the middle of the night. Hundreds of them. Started dragging people out of the houses. I knew we were fucked. Hopped out a back window and crawled into a fucking sewage pipe. Just lay there all night listening to people screaming and howling while they killed every last one of them."

"That's awful," Danielle says.

"I ain't proud of it," Jenson says.

"No, I meant what they did to those people," Danielle says. "I can't blame you for hiding. You were just trying to survive."

"They killed all sixty of them?" Blake asks him.

"No," Jenson says. "I'd sent a team back to Alamogordo to look for supplies, but they fucking vanished."

Rhodes.

"Reapers probably got them, too," he says.

Or I did.

"But who knows," Jenson says. "Maybe they just decided to fuck us over and took off. I kind of hope that's what they did. Maybe they'd still be alive then."

I stand there with my back to him, and my eyes closed as I listen, but I can't tell if this is all some act, he is putting on to save his ass, or if he is right, and somewhere along the way it all got twisted up in my mind.

Maybe he was never the monster I made him out to be. Maybe it was me all along.

"All I know is none of it would have ever happened if that devil dog over there and his team had just done their fucking jobs," Jenson says. "It's all on them."

By the time he finishes his sentence, I've already turned around and raised the rifle.

I hesitate for a split second.

Maybe I should be the bigger man, the hero.

Show him mercy.

Fuck that.

I fire off a round and then another and another, and I keep going until Jenson falls backward and crashes to the ground.

Everyone just stands there and stares at Jenson for a long moment after I stop shooting. Then they turn their stunned stares at me. I can only imagine what they're thinking right now, but I don't even care. I lower my rifle and take a last look at Jenson lying on the ground.

Blake finally turns away from the scene and covers his face with his hand.

"We got all the intel he had," I say. "Let's get moving."

"Why?" Blake yells.

"Why what?" I say.

Blake raises his arms up and pushes back his messy hair. Then he flails his arms in frustration as he lowers them and approaches me. His eyes are wild, and he gets up in my face and points at Jenson lying on the ground.

"What the hell good did that do?" Blake says.

"He had that coming," I tell Blake. "Back the fuck off."

"You murdered him," Blake says.

"So, what if I did?" I say. I hold what remains of my hands out toward him. "You want to arrest me?"

What happens next surprises me.

Blake raises his rifle and points it at my face.

"Blake," Danielle says his name to stop him from getting involved, but Blake ignores her and keeps his eyes focused on me.

I doubt he has it in him to shoot me, but he doesn't seem to be in control of himself at the moment.

"You can shoot me if you want," I tell him. "Go ahead."

Blake adjusts his grip on the rifle, his finger rests on the trigger.

"It can't be like this," Blake says. "We can't just keep going around killing each other like this. It has to stop."

"This is how it is now," I tell him. "Same as it has always been."

Blake shakes his head slightly as he grits his teeth.

"If you kill me, it will just mean I'm right," I say. "So, go ahead. Pull that trigger."

I'm not sure if I want him to do it or not.

"Don't do it, Blake," Danielle says.

She walks by his side and places her hand on his shoulder, then pushes the barrel of the gun down.

"Come on," she whispers. Danielle pulls his arm and leads him back to the convoy. Blake hangs his head, and his legs seem unsteady as he walks.

If Danielle hadn't stepped in, I'm certain that I'd be dead right now. That is why Blake can hardly stand on his own. He knows I was right.

"The world is better off without him," I call after them.

I turn to see Hoff swaying slightly, so I help him walk back to the vehicles. I finally look around the town and spot some cars parked outside of the steakhouse fifty yards up the road.

"You still have that hose?" I ask Hoff.

"Yeah," he grunts. "In my bag."

I let go of him and he leans back against the wrecked Chevy. I open the door and climb across the seats.

"You might regret what just happened one day," he says.

"I had my reasons," I tell him.

"I understand why you did it," Hoff says. "I'm just telling you that you might feel different about it later. Be ready for that."

"Don't you worry about me," I say. "You got enough to worry about."

I locate the hose and pull it out of the bag and then extract myself from the car.

"At least I got to enjoy one last ride," Hoff grins.

"Hang in there, Hoff," I clap a hand on his shoulder. "I'm going to go get some fuel and we'll get you out of here."

I leave him and jog back up the road toward the parking lot of the steakhouse while I scan the surrounding woods for the dead. I glance down at Jenson lying on the ground, expecting to feel something, some sense of satisfaction or peace. I don't know what I was hoping for exactly, but I just don't feel anything at all.

I open the gas cap of an old sedan and slide the hose down into the fuel tank. Then I suck at the other end of the hose and gag on the fumes as I stick it into the gas can. As the fuel drains from the car into the container, I watch the rest of the group surrounding Hoff. Scout crouches down beside him and sobs into his shoulder; he reaches his hand up and squeezes her arm.

"Come on," I urge the slowly trickling gasoline, even though I know that it doesn't matter how long this takes.

Nothing will help Hoff now.

As soon as the can is full, I carry it back and pour half into each truck. It isn't that much gasoline, but it will get us to Cheyenne Mountain. After I toss the hose and gas can into the back of the pickup, I go over and help get Hoff up off the street.

"Come on, big guy," I say as I help him to his feet.

He is barely conscious. His legs are already doing little to help him stand. Scout gets on the other side of him to assist me.

"Let's get him in the back of the pickup," I tell her.

"No," Hoff mumbles. He lifts his head for a moment. "You both know I'm not going to make it."

"We're not leaving you," Scout says as she tries to pull Hoff toward the truck.

"Stop," Hoff coughs. He straightens up and manages to stand on his own feet again.

"Hoff," Scout pleads.

"It's okay," he says. "I'd rather go out on my own terms."

"No," Scout shakes her head. "I'm not comfortable with that."

She wraps her arms around him again.

"Get comfortable being uncomfortable," Hoff says to her. He wraps an arm around her back and holds her for a minute. She clenches the fabric of his shirt tightly as he gives her a kiss on the forehead.

When she finally releases him, Hoff manages to smile.

"Go on," he says. "Get that kid someplace safe."

Scout nods and turns to get back into the truck. I can tell she is trying to keep herself together, to be strong for Hoff.

I hold out my hand to say goodbye to Hoff and he takes it in his big paw but holds on to it for a long moment.

"It's all on you now," he tells me. "Don't fuck this up."

"I won't," I tell him.

"They'll make you a hero for this," Hoff reminds me.

"Whatever," I say. "It's not like I ever cared about that."

"I know," he says. "I'm just warning you."

He finally releases my hand.

"Get out of here," he says.

I climb into the truck, and we pull back out into the road. As we round the curve, I look back and see Hoff take out his sidearm before climbing into the Chevy. A few seconds after we leave town, we hear the crack of the gunshot through the thin mountain air.

CHAPTER
THIRTY-NINE

Claire directs me through the mountain roads as Scout stares out the window and lets the tears trickling from her black eyes stream down her swollen face.

"Are you okay, mom?" Stevie asks her.

"I'm fine," she tells him as she pulls him close.

"Just a bad day again?" he asks.

"Yeah," she says as she combs her fingers through his hair.

"It seems like every day is a bad day for us," his dad whines.

Scout gives him an irritated look.

I can only imagine how messed up this kid will be after everything that he has witnessed. My childhood was no picnic either, so I know that shit sticks with you for the rest of your life no matter how much you try to pretend it doesn't.

"Things will get better soon," Scout tells the kid.

"I don't think they will," Stevie says.

"Sure, they will," Scout says. "That's why we have been so busy. We're going to fix things so they can go back to how they used to be."

"Good. Because I miss the old days," Stevie says.

"It'll be like that again soon, Stevie," Scout tells him. "I promise."

Part of me thinks she shouldn't lie to the kid like that. She isn't doing him any favors by trying to protect him from reality. But the other part of me thinks, it's not really any of my business what she does.

If she wants to make stupid promises that will just give the kid a false sense of hope, then that is on her.

I just keep my eyes on the road and try to stay focused. Claire seems to even be a little wary of me after everything that just happened. The rest of them weren't there, but she knows what Jenson did. I don't understand how she can expect me to have done anything differently.

The sun begins to get low in the afternoon sky as we approach a series of large buildings set back across a field on the right side of the road. Hundreds of bodies decompose in the tall grass. A sign along the shoulder warns against stopping to pick up any hitchhikers. High fences topped with barbwire and towering light posts surround the perimeter. It must be a prison of some sort.

I flashback to the prison in Nevada.

All the men that we killed. We shot them down even though we knew they didn't pose a serious threat to us.

We could have just kept driving.

But we didn't.

This correctional facility is much larger. There are approximately twelve buildings, long brown structures, several stories tall and lined with countless tiny slits of glass. It probably housed thousands of criminals. As we pass by the front gate, the rotting body of an undead guard hangs from the flagpole. He shifts his legs and stretches his arms toward us as we pass by the entrance.

I read the gold lettering on the brick wall alongside the road. It confirms what I suspected. This is the infamous supermax federal prison facility outside of Florence, Colorado.

The Alcatraz of the Rockies.

It houses some of the most dangerous psychopaths and criminals.

At least, it used to.

Drug lords. Terrorists. Serial killers.

You name it.

By the look of the place, even the most secure prison in America did not manage to survive the apocalypse. I look down the frontage road to the facility as we pass, but from this distance, I can't see much, and I am not about to slow down to have a look around.

"We shouldn't have come this way," I say to Claire.

"It didn't say anything on the map," she says. "How was I supposed to know?"

I know it isn't her fault. If anyone is to blame, it is probably me. I knew about this place. I should have remembered it was up here, but it's not like I didn't have plenty of other things to be concerned about. All I can do now is try to get us out of this area as quickly as possible.

It doesn't take a genius to start putting things together.

The compromised prison facility.

The Reapers.

I scan the road ahead as we approach the town. It's a familiar scene. Mutilated corpses. Cannibalized vehicles. Graffiti scrawled across the buildings. Claire tells me to make a right turn and then we pass by the firehouse. The reaper is there. His skeletal hand reaches out to grab us. I push the gas down a bit to get through the area a little faster.

When I glance in the mirror to see if Blake is still following, I briefly glimpse another vehicle on the road behind us.

"Left here," says Claire.

I make a quick turn and can see the last few buildings along the edge of town. My eyes go back to the side mirror as I watch Blake making the turn. About ten seconds later, a black van rounds the corner.

That is when I notice the modifications. The van has been turned into an improvised fighting vehicle, fitted with armor. Murder holes have been created along the length of the chassis.

South of the border, drug lords have been making tanks like these long before the shit hit the fan. They call them narco tanks.

"Shit," I say. "We got a Victor on our six."

I forgot for a moment that I'm not still with my team. No one around me understands.

"What?" Scout says.

"Someone is following us," I say.

Blake flashes his lights at me, so I know that he has noticed the tail as well. Scout and Steven swivel in their seats to look behind us. Claire checks the mirror on her side of the truck.

The driver of the black vehicle starts to gain on us. I'm only doing sixty, so I press the pedal down to the floor once we reach a stretch of straight, open road to stay ahead of our pursuers.

"Think we can outrun them?" Scout asks.

"I don't know," I say. "We'll try."

The van continues to gain on us, even as I go over ninety miles an hour. I notice Blake falls a bit behind us. It doesn't surprise me. He seems like the kind of guy that would drive like a sissy.

"Come on, Blake," I say to no one in particular.

I notice the next town in the distance as the road widens to four lanes.

"The map," I remind Claire. "Stay focused."

She stops looking at the mirror and looks at the map again.

"Keep going straight," she says.

I switch lanes to drive around a corpse on the highway. Blake shadows the maneuver behind me. Then, I watch as the tank just plows into the corpse so hard that the rotting limbs of the thing fly across the road before the body vanishes beneath the vehicle.

The road narrows back to two lanes as we leave the small town and head back into a winding stretch of road through the mountains. I have no choice but to slow the truck down or lose control going around the curves.

As the van closes the distance on us, rifle barrels slip out through the murder holes. Blake swerves to keep the driver from pulling alongside him. These people must have done some work on the engine too because that van obviously has plenty of muscle under the hood.

I wait until Blake swerves into the opposite lane and then I slow down to drive beside Blake and prevent the van from flanking him.

"See if you can get a shot on the driver," I tell Scout.

She rolls down her window and reaches outside with the Glock in her hand and fires. The bullets just ping off the front of the truck. On the passenger side, a barrel emerges from the hole and sprays bullets all over the street. Several of them ping off the rear of the truck and one shatters the rear window.

"Take the wheel," I tell Claire.

She scoots over and puts her foot on the gas. Then she slides beneath me as I get into the passenger seat. I grab my rifle and prop it on the seat.

"Get down," I tell Scout and Steven.

They grab the kid and crouch behind the front seats, using their bodies to shield him. I try to look for some weak point in the vehicle behind us, but it is a moving fortress.

I shoot at the driver, and after a couple of tries, I manage to hit the window. The bullet just puts a small chink in the bulletproof glass. The passenger of the van fires the submachine gun blindly, and a hail of nine-millimeter bullets pepper our vehicles again. Claire ducks down in her seat beside me as bullets whiz through the interior of the pickup and hit the radio and the windshield.

"Do something, Chase!" she pleads with me.

I take aim at the truck again and focus my fire on the tires. There is maybe two inches of exposed rubber below the armor. It might be the only shot at stopping this thing. I fire and miss. Fire again, and again, and again and miss every time.

"Fuck," I curse.

It's an impossible shot, but I have to keep trying.

I steady the rifle and aim and squeeze the trigger. With all the movement of the truck, I know the shot is too low as soon as I fire. The bullet hits the concrete. But it ricochets off the street and punches the front tire. The front passenger side of the tank slumps down and the armor grinds against the concrete until it comes to a halt while we continue down the road. I stare at the van in disbelief for several seconds as it falls farther and farther behind us.

"You did it!" Claire says.

"Is everyone okay?" I ask.

Scout raises her head up and checks Stevie. Steven doesn't move. I look down and notice Scout panicking at the blood on the kid's clothes, but it isn't his blood. It all came from his father.

Scout pulls Stevie onto her lap. His father slumps down on the floor behind the seat and I can see the bullet wounds along his spine and the bloody hair on the back of his head.

Stevie sobs into Scout's shoulder. I'm not even sure he knows what happened to his dad. He is just terrified from the last few minutes. I lock eyes with Scout and shake my head to tell her that Steven is already gone. Scout clutches the boy to her tightly to keep him from turning around and looking.

"It's okay," she tells him. "It's okay."

She repeats it over and over again.

But no matter how much she wants the kid to believe it, that still doesn't make it true.

CHAPTER FORTY

After I swap seats with Claire again, we drive down the highway through quiet farmland in the shot-up pickup truck while the sun slowly sinks behind the mountains to the west. Even half an hour after we last saw the armored van, I continue checking the road behind us.

No one said a word in all that time. The only sound is Stevie crying softly in the backseat. Scout still clutches him, but the kid must know by now that something happened to his father.

The highway expands to four lanes again so we must be getting close to Colorado Springs. Claire scans the map and watches the roads that we pass. The dashboard emits a soft ding when the gas light comes on again.

Once we hit the west side of town, abandoned vehicles and corpses start to appear along the road. I have to reduce our speed enough to navigate the mess. There is no time for this. The sun is gone, and the sky is getting darker by the minute. A sense of urgency sets in, and I drive along the grass median to avoid the majority of the traffic.

"Left here," Claire points her finger across my face, and I turn into a residential district. The dead wander along the road, moaning and reaching for our vehicles. I drive a few blocks, and then Claire tells me to make a right. Then another left.

The sky turns deep indigo, and I have no choice but to flick on the headlights in order to see.

"How much farther?" I ask her.

"We're almost there," Claire says. "It's on this road."

We speed up the winding road lined with evergreens until we round a curve and see an abandoned guard post outside an office building. Several corpses wander in the parking lot amongst scores of cars covered in a layer of dust. It doesn't look like there is anything alive around here at all.

I pull around the parking lot and spot a round tunnel that leads inside the mountain. The door is closed, but this has to be it. I drive through the security fence and bring the truck skidding to a halt several feet from the door.

When I get out of the truck, I notice the security cameras and lights above the door. I wave my arms in the air and hope that someone inside is paying attention and can see me in the darkness.

Blake pulls the other vehicle to a stop beside us, and they climb out of the car. Stitch hops out and starts barking like an asshole at the corpses. I turn away from the door and take aim at the figures approaching the tunnel entrance.

I take down a couple of them but notice more and more of them emerging from the darkened streets and heading straight for us. Blake, Danielle, and Natalie begin shooting at the dead as well, but with so many of them coming at us, we might only be able to hold out a few more minutes.

Claire pounds on the steel door and screams for help, but no one inside will hear that. We will be lucky if they hear the gunshots at all. I'm about to give up and try to make a run for it to one of the buildings nearby when the floodlights flick on over our heads. The steel doors groan and slowly slide open.

As soon as the door is open a few feet, a security team emerges and rushes out.

"Get inside, get inside!" yells the point man as he takes up a shooting position. The team lays down heavy cover fire to hold off the dead as we rush inside; then they fall back behind the doors as they begin to close again.

A couple of corpses manage to get inside the tunnel before the guards drop them. One more gets halfway through the slow-moving panels as they come together and seal us inside. The thing hangs there, caught between the massive doors. The dead man snaps his teeth and waves an arm at us until one of the security force members walks over and fires a round into his head.

I look around the interior of the dimly lit tunnel as I try to catch my breath. I still can't believe we actually made it here. My eyes dart around at the guards, not sure what to expect. After everything we've been through, I am kind of anticipating that something is about to go terribly wrong.

"Hello," says someone behind me.

All of us turn around to find a man in a blazer, dress slacks, and a clean white shirt standing in front of a trio of black vehicles.

"Welcome to Cheyenne Mountain," he says with a smile. I recognize his voice. This is the man I spoke to on the phone.

"I'm Corporal—" I begin but he holds up a hand.

"I know," the man says. "We've been expecting you. If you'll all get in the vehicles, we'll get you inside."

We climb into the sport-utility vehicles and then the drivers take us down the long tunnel with pipes running across the length of the ceiling. After we drive through a chain link gate and get waved through a guard post, we come to a stop. We get out of the vehicles to see a white wall built into the rock. Government seals are painted on the wall and a plain blue awning over the doorway welcomes us to Cheyenne Mountain Complex.

The man in the white shirt leads us through the doors and down a hallway. We emerge back out in the tunnel and see a pair of large blast doors that sit open with a pair of military police standing guard.

After we walk through the blast doors, the guards and the security team follow us inside as the massive doors slowly swing closed.

The man in the white shirt stops by the entrance to the bunker and turns around to look at us.

"You all seem so nervous," he says.

"We've been through a lot," Blake says.

"Relax," the man tells us. "The nightmare is over. You've made it. You have nothing to fear anymore."

I glance around at the rest of the group. Scout clutches Stevie beside her. Stitch sniffs around on the floor and decides to lift his leg and piss on the wall. Danielle looks at Blake and then she reaches up and wraps her arms around his neck and hugs him.

We all want to believe we are safe. It's just not easy after everything we've been through.

"You must all be very tired," the man says. "We have some rooms ready for you. If you follow the guards, they will escort you there. If you're hungry there is plenty to eat in the cafeteria, which is right down that hallway on the right. In the morning, we will show you around and get you briefed on everything you need to know."

"Excuse me," Claire says. "Doctor Schoenheim should probably visit the medical center. His medication—"

"I'm well aware," the man says. "It's all been taken care of. His prescription is waiting in his quarters."

"Right this way," one of the guards says and we turn and follow him down a hallway.

The man in the white shirt reaches out to pat me on the shoulder as I walk by.

"Nice work getting them here safely, Corporal," he says. "You're a hell of a soldier."

I don't really know what to say, so I just give him a nod and follow the guards with the rest of the group. They lead us to a long hallway with a series of mahogany doors.

"We're a bit over capacity," the guard says. "You'll have to bunk up together."

Claire looks at me, but then she follows the doctor inside his room. I enter the room across the hall and Natalie follows me inside and closes the door.

The room is as plain as any of the barracks I'd been in during training. I set the Honey Badger down on the desk, collapse onto the twin bed, and just stare up at the halogen light on the ceiling.

Being here still just feels unreal. After more than two months of constant fear and tension, it is hard to shake the feeling that something awful is always lurking nearby.

Natalie opens up the locker and then closes it again. She sits down on the bed and stares at me on the other mattress across the room. I'm kind of afraid she'll start talking but she just sits there quietly for several minutes until she starts untying the laces of her boots. Natalie kicks them off and collapses on the bed. She quietly stares up at the ceiling, too.

"Chase," Natalie finally says.

I wait for several seconds before I answer. I really don't want to talk right now.

"Yeah?" I finally say.

"Can you shut off the lights?" she says. "I'm too damn tired to get up."

"I'll get them," I say.

I force myself to sit up and then I walk across the room and turn the lights off. I head back to the bed and kick my own boots off and lay down again. I close my eyes and let out a long, deep breath.

"Thanks, Chase," Natalie murmurs. She is already drifting off to sleep.

"No problem," I sigh.

"You're a good guy," she mumbles.

She starts to snore lightly a few seconds later.

"No," I say. "I'm not."

I stare up at the ceiling again. I try to close my eyes and not think about everything that has happened since I left Pickel Meadows, but even after I fall asleep my brain replays the nightmare over and over again.

CHAPTER
FORTY-ONE

The next morning, I wake up and look over to see Natalie standing next to the other bed. She doesn't realize I'm awake as she peels off her shirt and bra.

I can't help but look at her. Numerous scars mar the pale skin on her back. She bends down to pick up her shirt off the bed, and then she turns around and sees me awake and staring at her. Her hands bring the shirt up to cover her body and then she quickly slips it over her head and puts it on.

"Good morning," she says.

I sit up in the bed and swipe my hand over my face.

"Good morning," I say back to her.

"I'm going to go find some breakfast," she says. "I'm fucking starving."

"I'll come with you," I say. "Give me a sec."

She waits impatiently by the door while I pull my boots back on and struggle to tie the laces with my mangled hand. Then I follow her out into the hall, and we wander around the facility until we locate the cafeteria.

The two of us get a lot of strange looks. Everyone inside this facility wears clean clothes. They have trimmed hair and don't smell like shit. They have been here since the beginning. None of them have had to endure the type of things that have happened to us.

"Maybe we should have taken a shower first," I say.

"Fuck that," Natalie says. "I'm too hungry to care."

I can't help but smile. As much as I don't want to admit it to myself, this chick is growing on me.

After we eat, the man we met when we arrived comes and finds us in the cafeteria. He takes us to a conference room where two secret service agents in black suits are posted outside the door. We follow the man in the white shirt inside and see Scout, Blake, Claire, and Dr. Schoenheim sitting around a table. Stevie plays with Stitch in the corner by bouncing a tennis ball and watching as the dog tries to snag it out of the air.

The man in the white shirt leaves the room and we sit around for several minutes staring at each other. Maybe we should be happy that we're here. We should be celebrating or something. The truth is we all lost so much to get here, that it doesn't feel like we have any reasons left to be happy except that we're alive.

Maybe that should be enough. Maybe one day it will be.

A man in a navy suit opens the door and greets us as he comes in the room.

"Let me introduce myself," he says. "I'm—"

"Senator Bob McGrath," I say. "From Colorado. Pro temp of the Senate."

I never forget a face.

"Well, that's mostly correct," he says. "Now, I am the 47th President of the United States of America."

He looks around at our astonished faces.

"As you can imagine," he says. "A great deal has happened since Z-day. That is what many here have taken to calling it."

He proceeds to update us on what is happening around the country. We already know, it's not good. However, it is not as hopeless as I was afraid it would be.

There are still elements of the armed forces and the government that have managed to survive through the crisis. The remaining military assets are primarily submarines and a handful of aircraft carriers. Although the presidential bunker in Washington was compromised in the early days, several other top secret hardened sites around the country remain secure.

"We even have a few remaining doomsday cells that are still active," he says.

"Doomsday cells?" Blake asks.

"Yes," McGrath says. "I believe you were at one of their operations centers back in Chicago."

"The bunker," Blake says. "But it was empty when we got there."

"Unfortunately, many of them were compromised before they ever reached the operation centers," McGrath explains.

"Mr. President," Claire says. "We really appreciate everything, but Doctor Schoenheim and I would really like to get into the laboratory and get to work."

"I completely understand," McGrath says. He gestures to the man in the white shirt waiting in the hallway. "If you want to go with Agent Calloway, he'll show you to the lab. He was the one that made getting you here a top priority, so if you need anything else for your work, he will do his best to make it happen."

Claire and the Doctor get up from their seats and shake hands with the president before they follow Agent Calloway out of the room.

"Thank you all," says McGrath. "Our country owes all of you for everything you have gone through and the sacrifices you have made to give us hope. Please make yourselves at home here. The accommodations leave much to be desired, but it is my hope that we will one day soon begin to reclaim and rebuild our great nation."

We stand up from our seats and the new leader of whatever remains of our country stands by the door and shakes hands with us as we get ready to leave the room. He knows all our names. Apparently, he has been monitoring our situation all along, even if no one here was willing to risk their own asses to venture out there and help us.

After he crouches down to give Stevie a hug and pets Stitch on the head, he stands back up and looks me in the eye. I'm about to salute him, but instead he holds out his left hand to shake mine.

"Corporal," he says.

I hold out my hand and return the gesture.

"Mr. President," I say.

He hangs on to my hand for a long moment.

"I'm afraid I also have some bad news," he says. "It concerns your father."

I already know what he is going to say.

"Okay," I say.

"His helicopter went down during a rescue operation in Germany. He has been missing and is presumed dead."

The words sink in, but I don't feel anything. I look down at the floor and wait for him to continue. Then I realize that they don't know him like I do. I am certain the old bastard is still alive.

"I'm sorry," McGrath says.

"Thank you for letting me know," I say. "I appreciate it."

"Lastly, I wanted to say how much your journey has inspired everyone here," he says. "I'm going to be honored to present you with the Congressional Medal of Honor."

"Thank you, Mr. President," I say. "That is not necessary. I was just doing my job."

"I thought you might say that," McGrath says. "But it is not just about you. All of the people in here and around the world need a hero right now. They need to see that we are making progress. That we can win this fight. They need hope."

The thought makes me uncomfortable. I never wanted to be that guy. The one that was getting medals and being proclaimed a hero. It's not what I signed up for.

"I'm not—" I say but McGrath interrupts me.

"It doesn't matter," he tells me. "This is what America needs from you right now."

I don't know how to respond. It's not like I can say no to the President of the United States. So, I just reluctantly nod my head.

"Thank you, Mr. President," I say.

He releases my hand and I step between the secret service agents as I make my way back out into the hall. I find Natalie waiting for me just a few feet away.

"Medal of Honor, huh?" she smiles.

"Shut up," I shake my head.

"Come on," she says as she tilts her head toward the rest of the group. "We're going to have a look around."

She takes a few steps before she notices I'm not moving. I stare at all of them in the hallway. Blake shifts his weight impatiently as he holds Danielle's hand.

"You coming?" Natalie asks me.

"No thanks," I tell her. "I'm still just worn out. Going to head back to the room."

"Suit yourself," she says and then she follows the rest of the group down the hall.

I just don't feel like being around anyone right now. It's still hard to return to a world that feels so fucking normal and mundane. Maybe after a little more time to process everything it won't feel so strange to me.

When I get back to the barracks, I hit the rain locker and then notice that someone has been in the room. There are some clean clothes on the bed. Pressed dress blues hang in the locker. Probably for me to wear to the medal ceremony.

I close the locker door and sit down on the bed. I pick up a plastic package with underwear inside and pry open the wrapper. Then I pry open a package of undershirts. It is not easy to get stuff like this anymore. I wonder if they got it from outside, or if they have a bunch of this stuff in here. If I had had a look around, I guess I'd know. But there will be plenty of time for that.

I have all the time in the world now.

I get dressed and then I lay down on the bed and stare at the ceiling. I keep hearing Hoff's words over and over again in my mind.

"They will make you a hero for this when it's all over," he said to me.

I never gave it much thought, but somewhere inside I never actually expected to live long enough to get here.

But here I am.

CHAPTER FORTY-TWO

The next morning, I wake up and take the uniform from the closet and get dressed for the medal ceremony. I sit down on the bed and put some polish on the shoes.

"Wow," Natalie says. She blinks her eyes and then rubs them with her fingers. "Look at you."

That always was one benefit of the job. Women, whether they admit it or not, are always impressed by the uniform.

"Thanks," I say to her as I set the shoe back down on the seat of the chair beside the bed.

"Hard to believe I'm looking at the same guy," she says.

I pick up the white gloves off the bed and look at them for a few seconds.

"Not sure how to really make these work anymore," I say to her.

"Here," Natalie says and holds out her hand to get the glove.

I keep one glove and hand her the other. Then I slide my good hand into the fabric and watch as she tucks the fingers back inside the other glove.

"Try that," she says as she hands it back to me.

I put the glove on, and it sort of works, even though it feels a little ridiculous. It also sort of seems like I'm trying to hide it when the reality is I don't really give a damn. Not after everything I've been through.

"Thanks," I say to Natalie. "I better get going."

"I'm going to get dressed," she says. "I'll see you down there."

"You're going?" I ask.

"I was planning on it," she says. "Unless you don't want me to."

"No," I say. "I just didn't think you'd want to. But..."

She raises her eyebrows and tries not to smile at me stammering.

"I'd appreciate you being there," I finally manage to say.

"Okay," she says. "Get out of here and let me get dressed then."

"Right," I say and turn around. I head out into the hallway and close the door behind me.

"Real smooth, Chase," I mumble to myself as I walk down the hall.

I get to the room and take a deep breath before I open the door and walk inside. There is a podium with flags in front of rows of chairs. Four television cameras are set up on tripods around the room and there is a desk with a pair of guys in headphones messing with the mixing board and monitors.

They may only be broadcasting across the facility for now, but McGrath hopes to restore power and communications to reach more Americans in the near future.

I see Claire and Doctor Schoenheim sitting in the front row beside Blake and Danielle, so I walk over and thank them for coming.

"Big day for you," Claire says.

"I guess," I say. "I'm still not really sure how I feel about all this."

"Just relax," Blake says. "You lived through two months of hell. I think you can handle this."

"Thanks," I say. I might not be crazy about the guy, but he makes sense sometimes.

Several other Air Force officers in uniforms come into the room and take seats in the back rows. Then Natalie follows them in and sits down at the end of the front row.

"Where is Scout?" I ask them.

"She's coming," Danielle says. "Stevie wasn't exactly being cooperative about getting dressed this morning."

A few seconds later, I hear barking in the hall and the sound of Stevie laughing. The dog runs into the room with Stevie chasing after him.

"Quit running," Scout scolds the kid and paces quickly into the room behind him.

Stitch runs a few circles around the podium and Stevie giggles while he chases after him.

"Stitch," Blake calls for the dog. "Settle down, Stitch."

The dog pauses, panting, tongue hanging out of his mouth.

"Come here," says Blake.

The dog turns and runs the other way around the podium.

"Stupid dog," Blake complains as he gets out of his chair and captures the dog and pulls him by the collar as he returns to his seat.

Within a few minutes, the room fills up and then President McGrath is escorted in by the secret service agents. He comes up and shakes my hand. My heart is thumping away in my chest as I stand in front of the cameras rolling and the people in the chairs looking at me. I can feel the sweat forming beneath my shirt and around my neck. President McGrath seems to talk forever, but I hardly pay attention to any of it.

In the middle of his speech, Stitch darts up towards the podium and starts sniffing around the base of it. Blake tries to call him back, but the dog just ignores him and lifts his leg and pisses on the podium. The crowd tries to remain respectful, but there is a moment of subdued laughter throughout the room.

"Guess he thought he should have got the medal," the President grins, drawing more laughter from the crowd.

"Stitch, go!" I tell the dog when he stops peeing.

The dog chases his tail in a circle and barks at me.

"Get out of here," I point toward Blake who is trying to call him over as well.

The damn dog just chases his tail around again and looks at me and barks again.

Finally, Blake gets out of his seat and grabs Stitch by the collar and pulls him off stage.

McGrath pauses to allow the room to quiet down before he resumes speaking.

"The brave members of Nightmare Company fought side-by-side with members of Seal Team Four and the 375th Air Mobility Wing in a joint effort to make this day possible," McGrath says. "So, to honor them, let us take a moment to read the names of our fallen heroes and recognize their sacrifice."

He pauses and looks down at the list on the podium.

"Captain Calvin James Kellogg..." he begins. "First Lieutenant William Michael Reasoner..."

I stand there listening to the names being read. To everyone else in the room, it's just names, but to me I see every single one of their faces. I hear their voices.

"Sergeant Pedro Rodriguez," McGrath continues. "Corporal James Mackenzie."

It feels like they are all here in the room with me somehow, but not in a good way. It feels heavy, dark, and painful. My knees feel weak, but thanks to years of training, I remain perfectly still as I stand at attention.

"Lieutenant Charles Fletcher," McGrath says.

Scout cups her hand over her mouth as she is overcome with emotion. Danielle hands Scout a tissue. Blake sniffs and wipes the corner of his eye with his knuckle.

I take a deep breath and try to tune everything out. I don't want to be here anymore.

Finally, McGrath calls out the last name. Then he asks the ceremonial officer to bring up the medal and read the transcription. I turn around and wait for McGrath to put the medal around my neck and my eyes settle on the rest of the survivors in the front row. Except for the doctor and Stevie, all of them are a wreck after hearing the list of names being read.

Seeing their pain makes me realize that this medal means nothing.

I'm not the hero.

Not more than Hoff, or Fletcher, or Mac, or Sarge, or Will.

It feels like I'm suffocating here. My chest tightens up so much I can't even feel my heart beating anymore.

The transcription ends and the President raises the medal over my head. He lowers it down, so it rests on my chest and then fastens the latch in the back.

The crowd of people in the room stand up and applaud. It seems to go on forever.

I want to tell them to stop. This is all just bullshit.

They have no idea about all the things that I've done or the things I would have done if no one was around to stop me.

I don't deserve to be standing up here with a medal around my neck.

When I look around at their faces, I wonder how they can smile. I wonder how they can possibly clap for a person like me.

I feel the pain and anger and guilt boiling up inside me.

They must stop clapping.

Shut off the cameras.

Stop pretending that this means anything.

These people act like I'm some kind of fucking hero, but the reality is I am nothing.

I am just trying to breathe.

EPILOGUE

Crickets chirp as dusk approaches. Beside the road, frogs croak in the lake and cicadas buzz in the evergreens. I smack a mosquito that settles on my arm as we sit inside the black SUV.

I check the mirror to make sure the road is still clear. Can't be too careful.

Especially with the Reapers still around.

I know it's just a matter of time before we will have to deal with them again.

"It's getting late, Scout," I say. "We should start heading back."

"Give me a minute," she says. She lowers the binoculars from her eyes and squints and then raises them back up again.

"You see anything?" Natalie asks her.

"I see something," she says.

I look over to the dense shroud of spruce trees along the mountainside. It's too far away to see much from here, but there is definitely some kind of cabin tucked away between the trees.

"What do you see?" I ask Scout again.

"I don't know yet," she says. "Come on. Let's go take a look."

"It's late," I remind her.

"I know," she says. "We'll be quick."

We drive off the road through a grassy meadow and park next to the lake.

"Wait here," Scout says as she gets out of the truck.

I don't really like it when she says that, but that doesn't mean there is a damn thing I can do about it. I've learned by now to just accept it when she makes up her mind about something. Besides, I know she can handle herself out here. That gal is as tough as they come.

I had figured Scout would want to stay close to Stevie, so I didn't even bother asking her to come back out with us. But when I told her we'd be going she made me wait for her to leave. I still suspect she might be hoping that somehow Fletcher is still out here, but I know it's better not to bring it up.

As for me, I found it difficult to sit around in the bunker with nothing to do. When McGrath asked me to lead a team out to search for supplies and additional equipment for Claire and Doctor Schoenheim, I told him I would do it, but only on my own terms.

I didn't want a whole team that had no experience out here. It was too likely they would all just end up dead. I got more than enough blood on my hands already.

Not that I have any regrets.

I've learned to live with everything that happened.

Sometimes the hero people need is not the good guy. Sometimes it's the guy who is willing to do the killing to make sure they stay alive. I'm comfortable with that.

Hell, I even like the killing.

That might make some people afraid of me.

They should be.

Natalie pulls out one of the notebooks that belonged to Mac. I still can't bring myself to look at it and find out what it says in there, even though she says it is brilliant.

I pull out the worn-out copy of The Stand that Scout gave me. She said it might help even though I told her I don't like books very much. This one was actually okay, though. I'm on the last few pages. It is the only time I read a book where I felt like I already sort of lived through it.

Several minutes later, I look up to check on Scout and see her walking with two women and two children. They all look thin and frail, like they have hardly eaten in weeks. Out in this remote cabin in the woods they probably couldn't find much unless they were good at fishing.

We get out and help them all into the back of the vehicle. I look them all over real quick and then I start the engine so we can get home before sunset.

As I drive, I keep looking in the mirror. The women exchange glances but don't say anything.

"You want some water?" I ask them.

No one answers. They just sit quietly with their arms around the kids.

"They got names?" I ask Scout.

"I don't know," Scout says. "I couldn't get them to talk either."

They must have been through hell. I can only wonder how bad it was, though.

"I'm Chase," I tell them.

Blank stares in the backseat come back at me as the truck rumbles over the dirt road through the mountains.

I decide to give up on getting anything out of them. Some people are so rattled by what they have gone through they just sort of shut down. It takes time for them to believe that the nightmare is actually over.

We drive up to the gates and wait for the doors to open before we head down the tunnel to the entrance of the facility. We help the women and children out of the vehicle and lead them to the blast doors.

I don't know why but bringing people back has helped me feel better. Like maybe we will be able to put everything back the way it was someday, maybe things might even be less fucked up this time around.

Blake and Danielle wait by the entrance to greet us. Danielle keeps her arms wrapped around him as he gives me an annoyed look.

"How'd it go?" Blake asks.

"Not much luck on the supplies. Found four survivors today," I say. "They seem pretty rattled."

I turn around and gesture back at the group coming through the entrance behind us. One of the women pauses and stares at us. I think she might just be amazed at the facility until I turn back to look at Blake.

His face is pale, and his mouth hangs open as he stares at the woman.

"What is it?" Danielle asks.

Blake lets go of Danielle and takes a step toward the woman as he blinks his eyes.

"Amanda?" he says.

I have no idea how he could know this woman, but he seems to think he does.

"Blake," the woman whispers.

Then he moves past me and puts his arms around her and clutches her tightly as the massive blast doors close and lock all of us together inside the mountain.

ACKNOWLEDGMENTS

This book would not have been possible without the support of my family and especially my wife and editor. Thanks to Dominique Anders, the best creative coach in the biz, for being real and dropping the occasional truth bomb. Special thanks to my beta readers, Rosann Powell and Erin Braden for helping to make this story even better than I hoped. And many thanks to all of my readers that have been patient and supportive in waiting for this series to unfold. Because of all of you, there will be many more stories to come.

ABOUT THE AUTHOR

Jeremy Dyson is a fiction author who loves all things related to post-apocalyptic horror. He graduated from the University of Iowa where he studied English and dreamed of writing books one day. When he isn't writing he spends his time drinking beer, listening to metal, and gaming. He currently lives in Crystal Lake, Illinois with the love of his life, their two amazing daughters, and black goldendoodle named Duke. He is currently at work on another post-apocalyptic series.

amazon.com/Jeremy-Dyson/e/B01CZ41PIE/

facebook.com/jeremydysonauthor

instagram.com/jeremydyson

twitter.com/writerofthedead

♪

tiktok.com/jeremydysonauthor

For more information visit: **http://www.jeremydyson.com**

If you have enjoyed this book, please take a moment to **leave a review** to

show your support for the author.

ALSO BY JEREMY DYSON

ROTD Series

RISE OF THE DEAD

RETURN OF THE DEAD

RAGE OF THE DEAD

REFUGE OF THE DEAD

REMNANTS OF THE DEAD

Printed in Great Britain
by Amazon

55673103R00223